I0691835

THE REAPER'S KISS

A DEATHMARK NOVEL

ABIGAIL BAKER

This book is a work of fiction. Names, characters, places, and incidents are the product of the author's imagination or are used fictitiously. Any resemblance to actual events, locales, or persons, living or dead, is coincidental.

Copyright © 2015 by Abigail Baker. All rights reserved, including the right to reproduce, distribute, or transmit in any form or by any means. For information regarding subsidiary rights, please contact the Publisher.

Entangled Publishing, LLC
2614 South Timberline Road
Suite 109
Fort Collins, CO 80525
Visit our website at www.entangledpublishing.com.

Select Otherworld is an imprint of Entangled Publishing, LLC.

Edited by Tracy Montoya
Cover design by L.J. Anderson
Cover art from DepositPhotos

Manufactured in the United States of America

First Edition August 2015

For Grandma.
"Here's to you as good as you are,
And to me as bad as I am;
As good as you are and as bad as I am,
I'm as good as you are, as bad as I am."

Chapter One

"It is important to know that every single human being, from the moment of birth until the moment when we make the transition and end this physical existence, is in the presence of guides or guardian angels who will wait for us and help us in the transition from life to life after death."

—Elisabeth Kübler-Ross

12 APRIL, PRESENT DAY

I kill people with my tattoo machine.

The machine doesn't send out waves of lethal electricity or poisonous ink. Nothing sneaky like that. The moment a client requests a skull in any form, he or she will die within days.

That's what it takes—ask me for a skull, and you're on the fast track to your death.

My boss, Gerard Bastille, and I do not have a following

of devoted regulars from across the province like other tattooists. If it's not their time to die, people tend to instinctively stay away from us, with the exception of a few who are good at ignoring subconscious warnings. But the customers who come to *Salon de Tatouage* in our quaint little corner of Québec City never have a chance to continue building their skin art collection.

Obviously, Gerard and I are not run-of-the-mill tattoo artists. We are Scriveners from the world between life and the hereafter that we call Styx. Scriveners are harbingers of death, augurs of looming demise with tattoo machines. Our respective Deathmarks—Gerard's pinups and my skulls— help the Grim Reapers responsible for ferrying souls to the underworld zero in on elusive souls whose time has come, so they can satisfy their quota lists for the Head Grim Reaper.

If we were to get soft and reveal our identity to our human clients, or try to warn them off, we'd incur a lethal Level Eight Offense and face judgment by Head Grim Reaper Marin, the Big Bad King of Doom, who looks like an ordinary human with a penchant for black turtlenecks and fascism. He was in charge of the business of Death, but he ruled like a tyrant king. Any level of offense above five is guaranteed eternity in Erebus, the torturous and unforgiving Afterlife that humans prefer to call Hell. Ask any one of us and we'll tell you we'd prefer eternity in the paradise that is Elysia instead, our version of rainbows and sunshine in the afterlife.

I wasn't interested in committing even a minor infraction, since I have a preference for sunshine and rainbows and not misery and hell. With shoulder-length brunette dreadlocks and ripped denim jeans, I am a rebel of high fashion, not politics.

That day, like every day, I was flagging one more hu-man soul for a Reaper to take to the hereafter. I hadn't met this Reaper. I never meet any of them who benefit from my Deathmark. I simply leave my skull on a human so his as-signed Grim Reaper could find him in the sea of souls on Earth.

Moose the Noose, an American tourist from upstate New York, was today's Deathmark.

With a proclivity for bone-rattling motorcycles, unwar-ranted hostility, and inappropriate pillow talk, Moose was a cliché bucolic American, bloated around the midsection and surly from a lifetime of well drinks and bar fights. Or so I assumed. His smack on my ass and lusty, "Thanks for taking me on such short notice, sweetcheeks," was inspiring one of my best Deathmarks yet.

"Why a skull?" I said in my French-Canadian accent, an inflection that Moose referred to as "frog speak." But I have never eaten frog legs. I'm not French. I'm Canadian. Alas, teaching advanced astrophysics to a toddler would be more rewarding than explaining the difference between Canadi-ans and Frenchmen to this client.

"Skulls mean death. No one fucks with death," Moose grunted from his tanned neck the size of my thigh. Those lusty brown eyes were fixed on my cleavage, thinly veiled by the scooped collar of my black tank top.

"It's a good conversation starter, too." I feigned interest in his choice of artwork as I wiped ink and blood from the outline I'd just completed on his bicep. With my toe on the pedal, ready to bring life to my machine and imminent death to my client, I glanced at my salt-and-pepper-haired boss sitting in the rear corner of the shop.

From his perch behind his drawing table, the Scrivener's gray eyes were set on his artwork as his right hand danced over the paper. Gerard looked like any other fifty-something man with black-rimmed glasses. He had once been handsome, but after his years of smoking, his skin had lost what was left of his youth, and the tattoos that ornamented his legs and arms had faded into forgotten landscapes.

Gerard's demanding gaze rose to meet mine. "Mind your heat," he said, like he did every morning. And every morning his warning amounted to very little, because I was not particularly savvy at controlling my power. When giving a Deathmark, my hands grew hot like irons on a fire. It was an anomaly, and I was trying to learn to control it. In the meantime, to avoid burning my clients, I always wore opaque black latex gloves while working.

As for Gerard, well, he never became hot when giving a Deathmark. He never showed signs of anything. He was calm as Québec's arctic weather, his temperament in contrast to my shifty, fiery hands. I often wondered how we could possibly be of the same grim profession.

As I tried to *mind* my heat, already feeling the intensity as I filled in the skull's jaw, I spotted Moose rub his groin as he said, "Gotta take a piss."

The skull's chin on his bicep needed another pass of ebony ink. Its vacant eyes stared, awaiting a gray wash to add depth to its lethal gaze. As much as I wanted to finish this Deathmark and get on with my day, I gave a clipped sigh, killed the machine, and pointed to the door at the end of a hallway.

Moose lurched toward the restroom, leaving Gerard and

me sitting quietly in the shop. The only sound was the radio softly playing in the background. I was grateful that Gerard didn't start to lecture me on how to improve my skillset, but I would've taken his mentoring over having to listen to Head Reaper Marin's voice. His tenor monotone overrode AC/DC's "Hells Bells," which was playing on our radio. Whenever Marin had an announcement, all he had to do was get behind a camera and microphone, and any Stygian's radio, computer, phone, or television would broadcast his message. Humans didn't hear his ramblings, which was probably for the best since he was no Tom Brokaw or Jon Stewart.

"*Good afternoon, Stygians. I am disappointed to report that one of our own has betrayed us,*" said our overlord of death. Shivers ran up and down my spine. I feared Marin more for the violence he authorized than for his emotionless noon reports. Today, like every other day, he was speaking to us for one reason only—threats of eternal damnation. "*Last evening, Grim Reaper Violet Magby was sent to Erebus for failing to meet her soul quota for the fifth time this year, and for her possible involvement in a rebel cell in Buffalo, New York. With no soul payouts, Magby resorted to petty crimes and an illegal sugar addiction.*"

Gerard and I sighed together.

Another one of us down. Who would be tomorrow's tragedy? Who would Head Reaper Marin seek out next on his decades-long mission to crush Styx's morale for a fucking quota?

A flushing toilet and jingling bell hanging over the shop's door were enough for Gerard to flick the radio off, ending the Head Reaper's speech on not following the example of Violet Magby and the others.

"What can we do for you?" Gerard asked *Salon de Tatouage's* newest guest, as Moose shuffled back to my station.

His hairy bicep returned to my field of vision.

"I want a tattoo," said a girl with a thick French-Canadian accent. "My boyfriend's name wrapped around my arm."

Before beginning again on Moose's Deathmark, I observed the spiked green-haired girl in a heavy metal T-shirt itching to make a permanently bad decision. Although she appeared somewhat hardcore, I noticed a glint of uncertainty in her brown eyes. She hadn't asked for a skull or a pinup. She was in the clear. For now.

"There's a saying in the industry, kid—friends don't let friends get armband tattoos," Gerard said with harsh authority. He pointed at the appointment book we left out as a decoy. We didn't take appointments. Death doesn't need them. Besides, this soul didn't ask for one of our Deathmarks, and for that reason, she was off the list. "We are both booked out for the next four months. Go see Tattoo Universe across town. They take walk-ins."

I wasn't thrilled about Gerard perpetuating the misconception that tattoo artists are hard-ass pricks in order to chase away souls not yet ready for death. But this girl deserved to dump her boyfriend and find another Hot Topic toy, not a coffin and a tombstone.

The bell jangled again.

She was gone, thank Hades.

"You'd make more money if you tattooed punks like her, old man," Moose said to my boss, and then turned his lusty attention on me. "You'd make even more money if you made this pretty thing sprawl out naked over the counter instead of letting her tattoo. Should leave tattooing to the men."

"Gotta wonder why you're sitting in my chair then, Moose," I hissed through my teeth. "Why didn't you go to the old man here?"

Of course, the question was rhetorical. Moose didn't know why he'd asked me for a skull tattoo and not Gerard. He might very well conjure some reason, like letting me tattoo him gave him a chance to be inches from my boobs. *I* didn't even know why our customers chose me over Gerard, or vice versa. But in Moose's case, it meant death had finally called him, and he'd had a lucky near miss with his assigned Grim Reaper. Just to be sure he didn't get away again, the power embedded in my skull would identify him for that Reaper. The best consolation I would get from this session was that death would get the final jab at Moose. The snarky comment about my skills as a female artist was wasted air.

The empty eye sockets of the skull beseeched me to put the last touches on this Deathmark and begin the fatal countdown. With a smirk, I drove the needle deeper and with more ferocity than necessary. Moose failed to mask a "motherfucker" under his breath.

"Ollie," Gerard snarled, eyeballing my hands. "You're running hot. Take a break and cool down."

"I'm fine, boss." And I was.

"Remember what we've been talking about…for *months* now."

"Get yourself under control, kiddo," I mocked as I continued my work.

"Doesn't look like you're controlling anything."

"You know, maybe if you didn't hound me day in and day out, I would have more headspace to think about controlling my work instead of listening—oh, *shit*!" I jumped from my chair, threw my machine onto the metal table covered in inkwells, and darted behind Moose before he could swing around and spot me.

As the black latex gloves melted, they revealed my fire engine red hands. The sudden stink of burning rubber was nauseating. The sensation wasn't subtle. Considering that my raging, uncontrolled heat was a common occurrence nowadays, I should've noticed long before Gerard had had to point it out. In this case, irritation overrode reason.

Had Moose noticed, before his Grim Reaper could ferry him, he might have told somebody about the freak-show artist at the tattoo shop in Old Town.

"What the hell is with her?" Moose addressed Gerard because, evidently, I wasn't capable of speaking for myself.

"She doesn't like obnoxious clients. Best not to tick her off, or you'll wind up with your tattoo stretched from your chin-butt to your puckered asshole." Gerard raised a disapproving brow at me. "It's something Ollie needs to learn to *control*."

I darted into the back room after rolling my eyes at the elder Scrivener. My boss's timeworn lecture on discipline was inevitable. I needed to find my serenity first.

I flicked on the tap and ran my hands underneath. Cool water tempered the heat as I focused on the springtime mountainside tableau hung above the sink in the back of the shop. The idyllic landscape made my frustration recede, starting in my face, down my neck, chest, arms, legs, and pooling at my feet. Tranquility came as rapidly as anger. I was hot and cold. Manic possibly. Something Zoloft would never fix.

Quickly, my hands were back to pale white, cool and

benevolent.

The shop's bell rang again. *Salon de Tatouage* was on a quiet street off the bustling thoroughfare in Québec City. Two visits a day translated to a busy day. Maybe that teen-ager decided she wanted a different guy's name on her arm. But hopefully not a pinup or skull.

I waited silently in the back room for Gerard to send her away for good, or for Moose to make a pass and scare her off. Instead a heartbeat, faint and then growing louder, consumed the silence. This was not a regular, healthy cadence. It pounded faster and faster.

Bump. Bump. Bump. Bump.

The heartbeat reached fever pitch and then quickly decelerated.

Bump... Bump... Bump...

I burst through the beaded doorway of the back room, my own heart racing, to see a Grim Reaper standing at Moose's side, one hand clamped around Moose's left arm and the other pressed to his chest. This Reaper was an av-erage-looking man with light brown hair and a well built physique.

Death's employee was not carrying the stereotypical scythe or wearing a black robe. Not that Moose noticed the Reaper feigning concern. Even though Reapers look like everyday humans when they're not ferrying souls, the hu-mans who are passing into the Afterlife never realize the Reaper is there at the moment of the heart attack, the fiery car accident, the plane crash, or the random mugger who shoots them in the face over twenty bucks. But there's al-ways one waiting. Picking off seedy humans like Moose was their preferred job, the cherry on top of a grim sundae.

But here's the thing: a Deathmark always has to be finished to have the power to call a person's Reaper. But the one on Moose was only partway done.

This Reaper's eyes were gold, the warning that he was angry, horny, having a sugar craving, or ferrying a soul. In this case, it was the latter. Had a human seen him and understood what he was doing, he would've seemed callously unemotional, but he was focused on the task of transitioning the living to the Afterlife. The work was as important to him as the removal of a cancerous tumor was to a surgeon.

Moose's heartbeat slowed. His lips blanched and eyes locked into a familiar vacant stare. Gerard, who had obviously not seen an unfinished Deathmark with the ability to call the human's Reaper happen before, stared at me, broadcasting a stern, "I can't believe this shit is happening in my shop" look.

The surly American's heart stopped. Between Moose's dead lips appeared a silver coin. The Reaper plucked it from his victim, gave it a discriminating inspection, and then stuffed it in his pocket. Humans support our industry with their lives. Gives another meaning to blood money. Today that Reaper made enough to feed himself and his family for a week. And he'd have another week safely out from under Head Reaper Marin's watchful eye.

Job completed, the Reaper stepped away from Moose's body as it slumped and toppled to the floor with an undignified smack. The Reaper's yellow gaze faded into brown and met my shocked, wide eyes. His lips pulled into a smile full of perfect teeth.

"Thanks for making this an easy one, Scrivener," the Reaper said with a wink.

"Y-you're welcome," I stuttered.

He gave a nod, said "*Bonjour*," and exited our studio.

The little bell tolled another lost soul.

"*Calisse*!" I swore and threw my wadded paper towel across the room.

"I said mark that human gently!" Gerard roared.

"I did!" Well, obviously I didn't, but I wouldn't admit to that now. Or ever.

"That Deathmark called his Reaper before you'd finished the fucking tattoo, Ollie." Gerard stalked to my newly dead client, who sprawled indignantly on the white tile floor. He stared with confusion. "I've never had a client die in my shop."

"Do we call the police?" I said. "Or dispose of the body? We don't own a shovel. How much are shovels?"

"This is exactly why you need to keep your power under wraps. The Head Reaper is going to send his Watchmen in to keep an eye on every move you make now. That was just too weird for him not to notice." Gerard scored through my panic with a serious reason to worry. Watchmen were the Head Reaper's police force, who arrived in white utility vans and wrought havoc on anyone who showed signs of the smallest offense—or something odd that Marin could *label* an infraction. We did our best to avoid them at all costs. "You *don't* want him to notice you. You keep your head down, and you'll survive."

"Look, it's not like I'm showing off. I can't help it."

"That's the goddamn problem. You *have* to control it, Ollie, so the Watchmen don't come sniffing around here looking to cause trouble. You don't want them thinking you're some kind of fledgling Master Scrivener do you?"

I had not predicted this conversation would lead to the topic of the Purge—the genocide of Master Scriveners nearly seventy-five years ago, perpetrated by a rogue group of Stygians, rumored to have been led by Marin himself. But it was a damn fine reminder that burning through a human like I just did was a stupid mistake that could bring attention of the wrong sort. A mistake I'd never make again.

Unsure of what to say, but keenly aware of my worry, guilt, and remorse, I rushed to help Gerard lift Moose's body, but where we would put him wasn't immediately clear. Even so, we couldn't leave him on the floor—that seemed rude and unsanitary.

"The Watchmen won't care. I tattoo humans as I was taught and don't look back." Except now I was looking into the face of my not-so-dearly departed client. Usually, Deathmarks take weeks to call the Reapers, which meant we never witnessed this part of the process. "Maybe we shouldn't move him?"

"Why?" Gerard grunted when he lifted Moose's head and shoulders.

"Don't police ask questions if the body is moved?"

"Ah! That's what I should do. Call the police." Moose's head and shoulders plopped to the floor when Gerard went for the countertop. Before he grabbed the phone receiver, he looked over his shoulder, his foreboding expression pouring over me.

"It's time for your lunch break," he said, voice dry and pointed.

"Now? Are you kidding?" Struggling with Moose's right leg, I watched a dark emotion flood Gerard's face. Granted, we were in a nasty predicament, and it wasn't even noon yet, but he concerned me more than Moose's corpse. "Ger, I should be here when the police show—"

"I *said* it's time for your break. Go. And bring me a cup of coffee with double the sugar. After this mess, I'm gonna need it."

Chapter Two

"I am disappointed to report that one of our own, Violet Magby, was executed last night for failing to meet her soul quota for the fifth time this year and for her possible involvement in a rebel cell. With no Obol payouts, Magby resorted to petty crimes and illegal sugar addiction. She was found hiding in the Catskills. Violet is survived by her sister, Clover Magby of the Stygian Sector of Buffalo, New York."

—Head Reaper Marin, April 12th Newscast

Although there were plenty of places to grab a quality jolt of caffeine near *Salon de Tatouage*, the additional time away from the shop would give Gerard the space he needed to clean up my mess. Besides, my preferred coffee shop was a ten-minute cab ride away.

From Gerard's reaction, what had happened was unheard of. Had I meant to leave such an impression on my client—to doom Moose before the Deathmark was through—I would not have felt an ounce of concern now. I was not sad for his passing. This was the business of death. If I felt bad for every customer who sat in my chair and received a skull, I would be locked away inside a padded room by now.

No. I was worried for one reason only—Erebus, eternal suffering.

Fifteen minutes after witnessing Moose's heart putter to a stop, I disappeared inside Le Nektar Café where splendor is roasted, ground, and brewed to perfection. The coffee shop's heavy wood door swung shut behind me, stubbing out the crisp Québec air.

I inhaled and forced a smile as the images of Moose's untimely demise and my future inside the walls of damnation faded into the background. Le Nektar had a warm, nutty fragrance that made you think of croissants, a good book, and free time that is never ending. It was easy to forget the bad things there—like Grim Reapers and Deathmarks.

The usual customers hid behind assorted newspapers and laptop computers. The elderly couple still living their undying romance was tucked into a nook in the back lounge. Buried in a maroon-and-gold Université Laval sweatshirt was the always-present-yet-still-unnamed-student, typing away on her computer.

Le Nektar was my second home because I could politely watch humans engage in their daily routines at the leisurely pace of one sip of coffee at a time.

"Was wondering if you were ever coming by today, girl," called my one-and-only welcoming party, Eve Cassidy, from behind the cafe counter. Eve was the only human who bothered to converse with me in the café. I adored her for that.

"Consider this your reminder that my birthday party is Saturday. Mom is going to be there. I can't wait for you two to meet. She'll adore you," she said as I squeezed between tables, coats, and patrons.

"I wouldn't miss your birthday or a chance to meet your mom for anything." Now, as for getting Eve the perfect birthday gift, I had no clue. She pulled off a punk image with absolute perfection in black jeans, shirts that hung seductively off of one shoulder, ruby lipstick, and spiked pixie hair.

As blond hair fell across her eyes, a gift idea promptly came to mind. I'd get her a decorative hairband. Or a hat. Or hair gel. Her preoccupation with looking like a twenty-something punk was endearing, and I made sure to tell her that whenever the moment felt right. Eve called me her outdoorsy, freckled friend because of my dreads, ripped jeans, dirty brown hiking boots, and, of course, Irish freckles.

I did a sweep for any Reapers before I reached across the counter and gave Eve a hug. Had Watchmen—Grim Reapers with gold scythe badges, authority, and bad attitudes—caught me chatting with Eve, or any human, for pleasure not business, I could be sent to Erebus.

"Your hair is getting long." I pointed at the mop on Eve's head, trying hard to stop the mind train of terror from ripping me off course.

Think about coffee. Friends. Think about good things.

Eve brushed hair from her forehead and tucked it behind her ear. "I've been so busy getting ready for Mom's visit. I need to get it trimmed."

"It doesn't look bad. It's…*avant-garde*." I forced a smile as I slid my reusable mug in her direction. "I'll need a cup for Gerry, too."

"Sure thing," she said.

"Are you excited to see your mom in a few days? When was the last time you saw her?"

"Oh, it's been years. Strange how you don't talk to someone for so long, and then you reconnect as if no time has passed. Made me realize how much I missed her, girl." After plucking my empty metal coffee mug, Eve's hands moved with graceful speed as she prepared my usual order. No matter how simple pouring coffee into a cup and slapping whipped cream on top was, magic worked from those fingers.

"Well, you two will have a lifetime to make amends over her leaving your dad," I said.

"Yeah, we're lucky. Would have been a shame if we never got to reconcile because she passed away or something. Wasn't her fault that my dad was a high-functioning alcoholic. Glad I know that now. I never realized what had been going on with him—and them. I never gave her the chance to tell me—just walked away and didn't let her back into my life. And—I didn't tell you this part—but I just had this dream a couple of weeks ago that I went to visit her, and something started taking her away from me. I kept trying to grab her hand and pull her back, but I couldn't reach her. Made me realize that life is short." Eve paused to smile to herself and followed it with a grateful sigh. "You look a little *avant-garde* yourself. Everything okay in the tattoo world?"

Well, I could've said that I had inked such a badass skull on Moose the Noose today that he died before I finished my work, and that for the first time I bore witness to the power of my Deathmark and as a result I cannot quell the knot of raw, primal guilt growing ever tighter in my chest. But she didn't know who—or what—I really was. As an alternative, I muttered, "There are good days and bad days."

Eve slid my favorite metal coffee mug and a paper cup full to the brim for Gerard across the counter and gave a wink. "I slipped in a shot of whiskey. That should make your day a little better."

I put the mug to my lips and inhaled the sweetness of whipped cream, caffeine, and barrel-aged spirit. "When is your mom flying in from Vancouver?"

"I'll pick her up Saturday morning." Our eye contact broke when she turned her focus on her black-lacquered fingernails. "She asked me what I want for my birthday."

I lowered my drink to the counter. "What did you tell her?"

Those green, dark eyes of hers, much like my own, twinkled with happiness. "I want a tattoo from my favorite hippie artist. I—"

"Excuse me, don't mean to interrupt you two, but I believe the lady dropped this back there on the street," said a man from behind me in a sweet-as-pie Southern accent that had enough brown sugar and bourbon to tease a girl's sensibilities.

Considering this was Québec City, a good thousand or so miles north of the American South, his drawl was intriguing, and it was evident from the assortment of cat-like female eyes peering over their laptop computers that I wasn't the only one who noticed.

"What do you mean you want a tattoo...from *me*?" I said, trying to hold off the man to get Eve, who was as agog over him as her customers, to answer. If she asked for my Deathmark, I would lose her in a way that was unfathomable. But for the moment, I had lost her to Southern Charm behind me.

"Um…" was her thoughtful reply. Then she bit her bottom lip.

I turned to see what had left her speechless. My gaze rose to meet a man with chestnut hair and a five o'clock shadow. He wore blue flannel under a soiled down coat and looked as if he'd crawled back from the high country after an arduous winter in unforgiving Canadian weather—the type of man who needed a woman's touch to soothe the lingering brutality of his job.

The fluttering in my chest that had begun at the lilt of his drawl exploded into a heart-squeezing throb. I was victim of my starry-eyed fantasy. Had I been any more socially eccentric, I would've been president of one of those lumberjack fan clubs where girls get hot and bothered over red flannel, axes, and beards. I usually observed such men from afar, but right now, I was standing before this fangirl's dream, and I was, to be honest, a little tongue-tied.

Until I saw what he was holding.

My pink, glittery cell phone looked odd in this man's massive, tanned hand. He might as well have been holding a baby doll in a lacy dress with "Olivia" sewn into the fabric. In moments like this, I hated that Mama pushed her ridiculous hand-me-downs on me.

"Thu—thanks," I said. "I didn't realize I dropped it."

Beguiling sapphire eyes glinted when the southerner smiled. "City people are a lot faster than I remember. Had to chase you four blocks to return it."

I wanted to take the phone back. Really did. But I was afraid to, as if this man was the proud new owner of the pink shame, and I'd break his heart if I took it from him. So, I stared at his hand…I mean, the phone, and mumbled something like, "You didn't have to trouble yourself."

"You're a sweet thing. I couldn't let you run off without your phone, darlin'. Besides it gave me a chance to introduce myself and ask your name."

I spied a sparkle of Grim Reaper gold in his eyes.

My heart thumped inside my ribcage, quickening its pace, but not because I was still dumbstruck with lust. Now, I was terrified. What if he was an undercover Watchman hoping to arrest me?

Did this one follow me from the shop after what happened to Moose? Is he undercover for the Head Reaper, here to make trouble?

Channeling Eve's articulateness, I sputtered "Thanks," snatched my phone from his hand, and whirled back to see Eve wearing a proud, tigress's smile. I didn't need her egging me on with The Pylon of Sexy Death behind me.

"Wow, Ollie. Here you were going on about how there are no good men left in the world, and Lumbersexual shows up to prove you wrong," Eve said.

The playfulness in Eve's words reminded me that she had declared it her job to find me a good man to go to bed with. A boyfriend was the last thing I needed in my life these days. "I've gotta get back to work."

"Might I accompany you then?" the Reaper said.

"That's a great idea." Eve's grin was impish. "It's a long walk. You'll have plenty of time to get to know each other."

"No, thanks," I said. "I like the time to myself."

"Don't let her scare you off, sir. She's shy around handsome men. I'll see you later today, Ollie. Don't do anything I wouldn't." Too soon, Eve was off taking another customer's order, abandoning me with this Reaper.

"Walk away from the human, darlin'. There are Watchmen nearby," Flannel Death whispered, so close to my ear that the skin on my neck prickled.

His warning registered as I threw an elbow in his side to get him to back away.

He wasn't lying.

In their uniforms of black suits and gold scythe pins—ones that made them look like FBI super-agents to humans—were a male and female Watchman peering through Le Nektar's front window at me. Although they weren't demanding I join them outside so they could strong-arm me into confessing to some minor infraction, they watched intently.

I wanted to say good-bye to Eve and ask one more time what kind of tattoo she wanted for her birthday, but I kept my lips sealed as I made for the exit. With my new friend the Grim Reaper nudging my back, I slipped through the door of Le Nektar, coffees in hand and my head full of mounting worry for Eve. The familiar, cold squall swept around us. I shivered under my parka and glanced up at the sky. Where humans saw scattered clouds with sun peeking through, Stygians saw millions of ashen, moaning souls. No sun. No stars. Nothing but bone-chilling murkiness. And that's all we ever saw.

The Watchmen closed in on our left, tearing my attention away from the soul-cloudy sky and frosty nip.

"Stop right there, you two," called the male.

"We're in a rush. Can you make it quick?" said the Southern man, whose drawl had transformed into a flawlessly articulated French-Canadian accent. He didn't stop to chat, nor did he stop herding me away from the Watchmen.

"We're looking for a person of interest," the female announced, following our retreat.

"Sorry, can't help you now. Late to work." He grabbed my elbow and pulled me into a quickened gait. His flesh was cold against my warm hand. The feeling of his hand on my elbow was oddly welcomed. Panic made me grip him tighter, and the man's unexpected alliance with me grew into an instant friendship, at least until we were out of sight of the Watchmen.

"*Bonne journée,*" he shouted over his shoulder.

"You're a Québecker?" I whispered as we trotted hastily toward our escape.

"Kentuckian, but I've been here long enough to mimic the locals. Don't want my accent stirring up trouble."

"By Head Reaper Marin's law, you two must show us your identification," one Watchman bellowed.

"Let me handle this," the southerner said, squeezing my elbow and letting go before he faced our pursuers.

My anxiety rocketed into full alarm. I was certain this confrontation would come to blows or mean an arrest or both, so I was staggered to find my ally facing off with the male Watchman. The female pushed in between them as the pair engaged in a discreet conversation that I couldn't interpret from ten feet away.

The southerner's broad shoulders remained squared when he stuffed his hands in his jeans pockets with a cool but annoyed casualness. And that was it. The female gave me a once over and pulled her coworker back from my ally. They slinked toward Le Nektar, turned on their heels, and made off to harass another Stygian a block away.

"H-How did you do that?" I asked when the southerner

faced me, smiling in a way that had me curious what it was about me that was worth smiling about. To avoid his eyes—and those dimples—I looked down at his black boots. Duct tape encircled the toes, looking just like my ten-year-old pair of L.L. Bean hikers.

He was *perfect* for me.

"Let me buy you a drink tonight, and I will explain everything," he said.

I could've accepted his offer because, there would be no reason to say no to such a brave soul. But Papa had always told me, if it feels too good, it probably is. Papa was what I call a jolly pessimist, and I was smart to remember his lessons. He would give me a two-day earful if he knew I was chumming it up with this god of flannel without a proper introduction.

Moreover, what had happened to Moose at the shop was concerning. I was running straight back into a mess that would put me under the spotlight of Marin and his allies. This Southern Reaper could be trouble. While, sure, he was handsome and my type, I could not risk making yet another mistake today.

"You're kind, but no thanks," I said and began the twenty-minute walk back to the shop.

One step behind, blowing past people to keep pace with me, the southerner said, "I really mean no harm. Please, I'm new to town and would like to get to know the locals."

I didn't notice that I had come to a stop until I was face-to-chest with him. I spat out the first excuse fresh in mind, "Welcome to Québec City. I don't date men without tattoos."

He looked at me no different than a moose staring down

the barrel of a twelve-gauge—incredulous and vaguely challenged. "Does that mean you want to see the dolphin on my left butt cheek? I assure you, it's remarkable." His hands went for his ZZ Top belt buckle.

"Hades, no! I do not want to see your dolphin." Well… maybe. Yeah, definitely.

His long fingers fell away from his buckle. "Right then, I'll save the porpoise for later."

"I'm sure you'll find some other friendly soul to show your porpoise to." With Papa's words of wisdom in my head, I was back to speed walking. The southerner followed on my heels.

And why wouldn't he? My day was brimful of one Reaper encounter after another. At the rate I was going, Head Reaper Marin would soon pop out from behind a tree with black balloons and an ice cream cake. If Gerard couldn't hold off the Watchmen, what would I walk back into? My arrest? A trial right there in the middle of *Salon de Tatouage*?

No one would believe me when I said I had not meant to be so aggressive with Moose. My heat—my power—was unwieldy. I was still learning my skills, trying to hone them into perfection. It wasn't my fault!

"I'm sorry," the southerner said, wrenching me from inner turmoil. "I'm a little rusty at courtship these days. I hope you don't mind my…oh."

A shot of terror ran from my toenails to my bulging eyeballs when I caught him staring at my hands.

Not again. Please.

I found my fingers were pink like rare meat, and that meant big, red-hot trouble. Lamenting what I had done had brought on fear and anger, and that always led to my hands overheating. When I was a teenager, I'd burned through my foster mom's entire silverware set. Adolescent Scrivener hormones do that, I guess.

Rising panic had me scanning for a water fountain or ice cream truck to cool the forthcoming inferno. Most importantly—I needed to get the hell away from this Reaper.

His big blue eyes softened, and he slowly backed away. Even though he gave me space, the blistering heat in my hands intensified. A familiar spine-prickling sensation, like bugs crawling under my flesh, fanned out from my fingertips.

The lumberjack shrugged. "I don't mean to upset you. I'm sorry."

"Please, I need to—"

"But I think you should know that—"

"—get back to work—"

"—your coffees are smoking."

"What?"

He pointed at my drinks.

Charged ozone attacked my nose an instant before the metal mug and Gerard's cup dissolved in my hands. Coffee and bourbon splashed over the sidewalk.

I don't know why I blew on my hands, like that would cool them down and salvage my melted cups of joe and my ego, but I did it with vigor. The color of my once pink and ink-free skin was now ruby red, exactly as it had been when I jumped away from ill-fated Moose that morning.

I hated the sight of it even more than the way it felt. Even more so, I loathed how the few Reapers and normal Scriveners who had seen this happen stared at me like I was a freak that should be locked away in an inflammable asylum for unstable pyromaniacs.

"By Hades, you are gorgeous," Lumberjack uttered, his cool blue eyes locked on the fire red skin of my hands and wrists. "Are you too hot to touch?"

"Don't." I jerked back when he reached for my fingertips. If he knew I struggled daily to control my power, he wouldn't have called my hands gorgeous or tried to touch me. Only today did I learn what would happen if I got this hot while tattooing a human. I didn't need to learn what would happen to a fellow Stygian.

Would I mark them like I had marked Moose? Would I burn through their souls, too? Gerard didn't know how to help, and neither did Mama and Papa. Everything about my goddamn abnormality was a pioneering misadventure.

"Leave me alone. Please."

He watched my hands slide inside my jacket pockets. The singe of disintegrating cotton was unmistakable. With it, my self-respect frittered away.

"I'm sorry, darlin'. Let me buy you another coffee for the trouble. I'll even throw in a donut or two."

My stomach rumbled and my heart trembled in spite of my shame. Diamonds or fancy meals meant little to someone like me. But... "Coffee?"

"And a donut." He smiled warmly.

Grim Reapers loved their sugar cane. Candy, cakes, even sugar packets. The substance gave them a blissful high that often distracted them from their task of ferrying souls. Marin's reason for banning sugar was a practical one. Sugar made Reapers lethargic drunks. Lushes would not compromise the balance of humanity if Marin had any say in it. This threat didn't stop them from consuming every gram of sugar they could get their hands on, however.

Sugar never had any such affect on me. My drug was coffee—something this handsome Reaper was smart to notice.

"I can't carry my coffee if I am hot." I started to pull my hands from my pockets but stopped myself.

"I have an idea," he said. "Give me your hands."

"No!" Was he nuts?

"Trust me."

How I found it in me to trust him was not clear, but I slowly pulled my fingers from my jacket pockets and dropped them to my sides. As I did, he collected a bundle of fresh white snow from the sidewalk. Though no Stygian had dared to touch my skin in this state, and rightfully so, he covered my hands with the snow.

Steam rose from our connection. The snow melted, cooling the heat within seconds. Once all that remained was dripping water, I gradually untangled my fingers from his. Together, we dried our skin on our jackets. There was no particular way to break from such a connection without making awkward but flirty faces at each other.

"I've never done that before," he said. "Glad it worked."

"Me, too."

"Now you can hold your coffee."

I giggled.

Fuck! I *giggled*?

"Thanks," I said and then began a lazy stroll back to work in Old Town. There was good reason for this forced calmness. Acting casual seemed like the sexy-confident thing to do. But I would have preferred to stay far away from the tattoo shop for the remainder of the day. Since I couldn't, delaying my return was my only means of controlling a situation that had spiraled down the toilet bowl of shitty luck.

"So what brings you to Québec, uh…?" I gave the universal "I don't know your name" look as I waited for him to formally introduce himself.

"The name is Brent Hume, hailing from Beattyville, Kentucky, ma'am." He slid his hands inside his jacket pockets. "I'm in Québec because I'm looking for work."

"Ferrying?"

"Nah. I need a paycheck so I can eat."

"You don't get Obol payouts from each soul you ferry?" Whenever Reapers removed a soul from a human body and sent it to the Afterlife, a coin—an Obol like the one plucked from Moose's lips—appeared. Obols weren't much money after they transformed into local currency, just enough to cover food and incidentals, but something is better than nothing.

"I was banned from receiving Obols. Don't ask," Brent said before I could. "It's a story I'll dredge up another day. Do you have any job leads?"

Gerard occasionally hired Reapers to clean the shop, but for some inexplicable reason, inviting this hunk to work where I tattooed Deathmarks seemed no different than putting a hungry lion inside a cage filled with bleeding zebras. Or maybe deep down I knew he'd be too distracting, pushing a mop around me as I worked.

Brent didn't seem like he was in such dire straits that he was starving anyway. However, he did wear a worn jacket, jeans ripped at the knees, and those hiking boots taped at the toes.

"Chez Ashton serves cheap grub," I said. "Great poutine. My treat."

"No, darlin'. I'll never take a penny from you." Judging by

his strained grin, he didn't enjoy the hodgepodge of French fries, cheese curds, and gravy called poutine quite like I did. Too easily, I visualized a hungry Brent Hume eating alone in Chez Ashton, and it tugged at my sympathy. I had a talent for finding melancholy in everything, even this rugged Reaper dining by himself.

Papa had teased me for it, and Mama had said it was humanity, Hades' gift to me that Mama swore no other Stygians were privileged to have. I still had yet to understand why this was a gift, as I wept over sad television commercials as I shoveled pints of Ben and Jerry's down my throat.

"I haven't spoken with a Scrivener in ages," he said rather abruptly.

I was suddenly nervous and craving Chunky Monkey. "How do you know I'm a Scrivener?"

"Lucky guess. But don't worry, I won't tell anyone." He reminded me why we were walking to another coffee shop. My fucking, red-hot, trouble-making, death-dealing hands.

"Well, Brent Hume, I'm not just a Scrivener," I said with a bite. "I'm an artist. One of my favorite pastimes is sitting in Le Nektar and drawing pictures of the visitors. I have a dream of opening an art studio and selling my charcoal drawings."

As we crossed the street, Brent's hand splayed over my lower back to guide me toward the sidewalk. I jumped onto the curb, dodging a puddle of gray slush. He sloshed right through it, kicking water without a care for the mess he was creating.

I buried my cooled hands into my threadbare pockets as I thought about Le Nektar and its best barista, Eve.

Hell would have me by the throat if I had to come up

with a plan to keep her from coming to the tattoo shop, where she might feel compelled to request my Deathmark. Surely I wasn't the only Scrivener in history faced with such a dilemma. Unlike Reapers, this job made it difficult *not* to connect with humans. Scriveners spent hours inscribing death into people's skin, and that inevitably led to conversation.

Sometimes we grew fond of our doomed clients. And then we grew a conscience and, well, we don't want to tattoo them any longer. That was what I had been toying with since Eve mentioned the birthday wish she'd told her mother, but listening to me rationalizing my thoughts wasn't the kind of conversation Brent the Kentuckian Grim Reaper sought, was it?

To change the subject, I mentioned the first thought that came to mind that didn't have to do with Eve. "I'm intrigued. Do you really have a dolphin tattooed on your butt?"

He looked off to the left, seeming to ponder a question that had a simple yes or no answer, and then set his blue eyes back to me. "I don't have a porpoise on my ass."

"That's probably for the best."

"I'd let you put one there if it strikes your fancy." He winked.

Brent did have a very nice backside, the kind asking for a slap and a bite. I supposed a dolphin was benevolent enough. Although tattooing another Stygian—no matter the reason—was a Level Ten Offense, punishable by death and eternity in Erebus. No buttock—not even one as round and fine as Brent's—was worth the offense.

"After we grab a round of coffee, it's probably best if we go our separate ways," I said, as I forced my mind away from his backside and what it would look like with a dolphin there. Or my bite marks.

Disappointment washed over his face, an emotion I recognized in many faces these days. "We didn't get off on the right foot. After your shift today, why don't we start over with a beer and honest conversation?"

My initial instinct was to scream "no" and take off running in the opposite direction. But why was I so afraid to get to know this Reaper, who had seen my hands grow hot and didn't seem freaked out about it in the slightest? What was wrong with letting my guard down for one day? After all, maybe spending some time with this sexy out-of-towner would be enough to eradicate the incident with Moose from my memory.

So, I went with my second, less guarded instinct and said, "Beer and conversation sounds harmless."

Chapter Three

"We are border patrol officers, not wayward gods, but humble servants to our human masters."

—HermesHarbinger.com, Rebel Blog

When I turned the corner onto Rue Charlevoix, I quickly back stepped and sought refuge inside the doorway of a used bookstore I had grown to love during my years in Québec City. Outside of the tattoo shop was an ambulance, its backdoors wide open as two paramedics loaded a gurney covered in Moose's dead body into the vehicle. The ambulance was not what sent me into alarm. The white, windowless minivan did.

Watchmen drove those minivans.

Clutching a drink in each hand, I was reminded of Brent's audacity with the Watchmen outside of Le Nektar, and his kindness in tempering my heat *and* buying me two cups of coffee—one for me and one for Gerard. After reluctantly agreeing, before parting ways, to meet him after work, I hustled back to the tattoo shop. Only now did I wish that I had encouraged him to join me on the return trip for one reason—Brent had a way with handling Watchmen.

As I sank into the protection of the doorway, I reminded myself that showing fear would give the Watchmen a reason to think I had done something wrong. Truth was, I *hadn't* done anything wrong. I simply let my abilities get the best of me. But with Master Scriveners on Marin's list of troublemakers, showing signs of anything out of the ordinary—even though I wasn't a Master—was problematic.

Breathe, I thought to myself, honoring Gerard and Mama's advice. Breathing with intention tempered my heat. It always had, but I seemed to forget this whenever fear or anger gripped me.

"Face your fear, Ollie, and keep breathing," I quietly rallied. Of course, that voiced confidence did little to force me from the safety of the doorway. It took another ten minutes before I inched my way out and around the corner to peek at the red and black awning of *Salon de Tatuoage*. This time the ambulance was gone. The white van was not.

"Brought you coffee," I said to Gerard who sat behind his drawing table staring at me when I came in, with his eyes full of concern. He was trying to get me to notice the person standing in the back corner of the shop, but I had spotted the dark blond male when I walked in the door.

"*Bonjour,*" I said as I set Gerard's coffee down on his drawing table, addressing the stranger. "You are?"

"I'm Chad," the blond man said. He smiled in a way that was forced and marginally wicked. When his eyes flashed not gold but red, I was acutely aware of why Gerard remained quiet. Chad was not a Watchman, but an Eidolon Reaper. Eidolons ranked high above Watchmen and lowly Reapers and Scriveners like Gerard and me. They were Grim Reapers for Grim Reapers and Scriveners—that was their one and only job. The only two Stygians above the Eidolons were the Deliveryman of Styx's Deathlists and Head Reaper Marin.

There was no clever or discreet way to slink out of the shop's door. I couldn't announce that I suddenly felt feverish and needed to rush home. I had to stick to my dwindling confidence. What I had done to Moose had been an accident. There were no signs of anything strange or rebellious. Nothing.

"I'm sorry, Gerard didn't tell me we would have a guest, so I didn't bring you coffee," I said to Chad, trying to kill with kindness. "I can run back out if you like."

"That won't be necessary, Ollie. You have a client," Gerard said and gestured with his eyes to the corner behind me.

Frustration hardened into dread when I turned to face my newest customer. And when I laid eyes on her for the second time that day, my heart swelled and pounded inside my ribcage.

"Hey, sweetie." Eve waved. "Did you get lost on the way to the shop?"

"I, um, spilled my coffee and grabbed another. Eve, why are you here?" My voice broke.

"I didn't get a chance to tell you before you left with the sexy foreigner that I would come by today for a tattoo. I'd love to have it done and healed before the party this weekend so Mom sees it in all its glory. She will love it. Her first birthday gift to me in years." Eve's face, with its charming innocence, would have made me smile on any other day.

I was profoundly aware of Chad the Eidolon just feet away. He had the power to take Gerard and me out with minimal effort. Eidolons had that kind of sway, something they earned after decades of moving from the ranks of average Grim Reapers to third in command after Marin. Chad was here for one reason only—to observe and to catch me in the act of breaking the rules.

Gerard peered over the rims of his glasses. His eyes were full of urgency. He wanted to talk, to tell me something dire, but wouldn't with the Eidolon hovering nearby.

"So you finally decided to get tattooed, Eve?" I tried to speak evenly as the tension grew and grew. Eve was unaware of what was happening between three of Death's employees. For her own good—and mine—I needed to remain oblivious.

"Figured now is no better time." Eve's face glowed with anticipation. Her attention swept to Chad who lingered in the corner, watching, waiting. Warmly, she grinned at him. He returned the expression with eerie precision, much like a serial killer to his victim.

I passed my tongue across my dry lips and glanced at Chad. He had the same look I had seen from tortured Stygians who had avoided Erebus by going to prison. They wore a tormented but cruel expression, itching to impart their suffering on others. What left my skin in goosebumps was Gerard's obvious apprehension. Something happened between them while I was away. And it was ugly.

"What about Victorian rosemaling for a tattoo?" I asked my client, knowing full well that I could not do such a thing. "I've been wanting to do a piece like that. It'd look beautiful on your arm."

"Oh, that sounds nice." Eve's cheeks squished her green

eyes with a grin. "But I want a Day of the Dead skull on my bicep. Mom's favorite. And since you're known for your skulls…"

My world started spinning off its axis.

Whenever a skull crossed my path—around Halloween or embroidered on a woman's purse or on a man's T-shirt—I pushed the images into the recesses of my brain, where I hoped they'd fade away forever. Eve's comment jogged my memory of her pristinely accomplished Day of the Dead makeup this past October, which I would gladly forget all over again.

And another thing—I never talked about my work, about skulls in particular.

"Where did you hear about my skull work?" I asked through my teeth.

"He came into Le Nektar bragging about your killer skull work." Eve gestured to Chad. "Said his friend got one done by you earlier today. What's his name?"

Chad the Eidolon revealed a set of yellow teeth with his sneer. He made no effort to disguise what was happening. I had been set up, and he was the mastermind. "Moose," he said. "People like Moose come here to get one of her special skulls. Ain't that right, Scrivie?"

"Scrivie?" Eve snickered. "What is a Scrivie?"

"What those in the know call tattooists, my dear," Chad said.

I gave Gerard a look, hoping that perhaps he'd know what to do. He hung his head, visibly outranked. Then my heart broke.

I pressed the stencil against Eve's goose-pimpled flesh. My hands were warm, edging toward hot as I felt Chad's eyes cut through me. Three times now, I had to rush into the backroom and cool my hands under the faucet. I was positive that I would have to revisit the sink several more times to quench my heat, as well as to breathe. But my lungs were barely capable of taking a full breath. To cover up any semblance of grief, I pulled Eve over to sit in the tattoo chair and sank into my own swivel stool. As I peeled the stencil off, noting how senseless it was to put it on in the first place because I didn't need one for a Deathmark, the view of Chad sitting with his arms crossed, his attention locked on me like a hawk's on dinner, was nightmarish.

The room with its fluorescent lights gently spun. Gerard, who was observing his own artwork, was washed out behind a barrage of the same anguish that had been eating at me since returning to the studio. This wasn't how it was supposed to happen. The Eidolon had set me up. I was convinced that if he hadn't manipulated Eve, she wouldn't be here now. But she was here, and there was nothing I could do to stop what happened next.

I tried nonetheless.

"I can't." The truth was better than any lie. "I'm not feeling right."

"You're fine," said Chad. "Wouldn't want to get Gerard in trouble, would ya? Big Boss doesn't like quitters."

I bit my tongue. The situation was plain—I could refuse to do Eve's Deathmark, and the Eidolon would likely send Gerard and me off to Erebus without a trial, or I could do as I was told and save our hides and condemn Eve's. I looked to Eve, hoping she would suggest a different tattoo or that I stop altogether. Perhaps she had picked up on my agitation and didn't think I should continue. Her face was blank with tension, eyes glassy, and the muscles in her arm tight. She couldn't speak because, like most clients getting first tattoos, she was too nervous to use her faculties.

Gerard offered sympathetic support from across the shop. He knew what this meant. And somehow I knew that this situation was not unfamiliar to him.

I gave Chad another glance. Chad watched on, acting as Marin's eyes.

"Will it hurt?" Eve asked, when I revved the tattoo machine.

Eyes squeezed shut, I pressed my sweating forehead to the brick building, not caring if I was noticed by the two men smoking outside the front of the shop. A breeze kissed my hot cheeks as the two praised the pin-up girl Gerard had done on the one's back piece earlier in the day. The cold temporarily chilled my guilt but didn't ease the nausea.

Nothing would, after what I had done.

A hand cupped my shoulder, and I slapped it away.

"Don't be hard on yourself," Gerard whispered.

I dragged my fingertips down the brick, burning ten deep notches into the wall.

"You did a good job. You kept yourself under control. That's all he wanted—to catch you firing up so he could send you to Marin. You could've been the next Violet Magby, Ollie."

Somehow I had managed to keep my head together

throughout Eve's tattoo. Now the words that had been on my mind since I came in to find her and Chad in the tattoo parlor burst out of me. "Fuck Violet Magby and Erebus! I should've done more to stop it."

"You couldn't have stopped it with him there. You protected yourself. And me."

"It's just…if Chad hadn't been there, I wouldn't have had to put a Deathmark on her. I could've avoided it somehow."

Gerard never showed affection, but he pulled me into a hug I wasn't willing to ask for but needed in the worst way. This was the first moment since arriving at the tattoo shop that I felt safe enough to cry.

"Eve wouldn't have come to you for a skull if it wasn't her time," he said.

"I was set up. Chad persuaded her to get a Deathmark."

"No," he argued. "Do not allow yourself to believe that."

"I have to. It's too coincidental."

"Good souls die. We're Stygians. Death is our trade. We pull humans from this world. We do it because that's what keeps things balanced. We're not bad guys. It's her time. Accept it." His words were not new lessons, but they stung far worse than ever before. Eve was an important anchor in my life, alleviating the yearning for companionship, and she would be gone before her time.

Because of me.

Chapter Four

"Dear Mr. and Mrs. Balanchine: It is with regret that I must expel your foster daughter, Olivia. Avers cannot afford to replace every desk and textbook she sets fire to. I suggest she be examined for impulse control disorder and possibly spontaneous combustion."

—Henry Atkinson, Principal of Avers Middle School, New Orleans, Louisiana

Pub Saint-Alexandre was a dark and cozy watering hole with mahogany wood and barrel-backed stools, and a beer list long enough to momentarily take my mind off of what I had done to Eve. Beer and conversation—that was what Brent Hume had promised, and I desperately needed both.

When Brent poured the fourth stamp-sized packet of sugar into his Belgian ale, I pointed to the petty crime between us and said, "That much sugar consumption is a Level One Offense."

He scanned for any spies inside Pub Saint-Alexandre who might snatch his sugar stash.

"Don't worry. I'm no snitch," I said to ease his worry.

He poured the rest of the sugar into his drink. "I don't need to draw unnecessary attention."

"You on the run?"

"I've got a target on my back if I cause trouble again." He produced his tattered Stygian ID from his inside coat pocket—the customary offering of peace among Stygians—and slapped it down on the table with little reverence. Kind of an I'll-show-you-mine-if-you-show-me-yours type of agreement between new allies.

At least, that's what Mama and Papa once said.

Our axiom—*The Sun Shall Never Shine on Styx*—was embossed on the ID's cover. The saying is a reminder that while our human clientele bask in sunshine, getting vitamin D and a golden tan, enjoying the cosmos's greatest pleasures, all Stygians see in the sky are gray wisps of moaning human souls racing toward their Afterlife.

Our existence between life and death is forever in shadow. No big happy ball of light for us.

I reached for the document. "May I?" Manners, manners.

"By all means." He sipped his sugar-beer, and I peeked inside the ID folder.

Red stickers stacked upon red stickers covered every inch of his ID. Brent's had three times as many as my own. The stickers indicated we had done something illegal, though they didn't detail the crime or its level. And he had done enough to get eternity in Erebus. That might've explained his off-kilter personality and sense of style.

My eye snagged on a red mark with a black dot. Any

other day, I would have shot out of my chair. Thank Hades beer makes me as lazy as sugar makes Reapers.

"*You've* got a rebel's sticker?" I whispered, eyes darting back and forth.

Brent Hume was a dissident? A bona fide fuck-the-big-man guy? He must have tried to overthrow Head Reaper Marin, or possibly another Eidolon, to have earned such a mark. Or maybe, just maybe, Brent was part of a rebel cell that had been captured. Whatever he had done was treason-ous, and a far greater crime than befriending humans or get-ting too hot and burning through a cup of coffee or Moose's life. That red and black sticker of Brent's meant he was a threat to Head Reaper. A serious threat.

"How did you get a sticker without going to Erebus?" I asked.

He plucked the ID from my hand and stuffed it back in his pocket.

"It's just that I thought Marin sent every rebel to Erebus for—"

"I'm not easy to banish. Enough about me. Tell me about yourself, Scrivener Dormier." He eyed me like I was a favorite cut of meat that he was too broke to order. "Where were you born? How long have you been tattooing? Why do you look like you've been crying all day?"

I focused on my beer bottle when my eyes started to well again with tears. "Just tired."

Defying me with a cool stare over the rim of his glass, he chugged his syrupy drink and said nothing to further conversation. His discretion was appreciated. Even though it would be foolish to air my personal struggles to this new acquaintance—rebel sticker or no—the real reason I fell quiet was that I couldn't bear to speak about what had happened.

If only Eve would make it to her reunion with her mother on Saturday at her birthday celebration. Maybe if I could gift her that time, I might be able to forgive myself.

"Since you're a rebel, you wouldn't happen to know who is running the Hermes Harbinger site, would you?" Some might call my question bold. I'd call it a chance to turn the conversation away from my swollen eyes and the reason for them.

Besides, Brent was the only Stygian I knew with a red and black sticker who wasn't in Erebus. Surely not every rebel—however many there were—was responsible for contributing to or running the Hermes Harbinger blog, but it couldn't hurt to probe. After all, the blog was growing in popularity. Multiple inflammatory posts speaking out against Head Reaper Marin went up hourly. Someone like Brent could easily be contributing to the seditious speech.

I waited another beat of silence, but the Reaper was stone-cold calm and silent.

"Of course you wouldn't tell me even if you knew," I added. "That'd break rebel code or whatever they call it, right?"

He sipped his drink. "There are better ways to speak out against Marin than a blog. An anonymous blogger is barely the start of the rebellion we need. The Head Reaper has Stygians scared witless that we'll get charged and executed for farting under the bed covers. And you're a Scrivener who exhibits signs of Masterhood. Who gives a shit about people complaining on the Internet? We should talk about the important stuff, like fixing Styx."

I stared, eyes wide, suddenly ill at ease from his speech.

"What makes you think I am showing signs of becoming a Master?"

He broke into a playful smile and said, "Your hands melted your metal coffee mug this morning. Average Scriveners don't do that. Masters do. Or they do before they know how to control it."

"Well, I'm not a Master," I said, hoping to end this silly conversation. Given that the only signs I showed—according to him, anyway—were my overheating hands, I decided to ignore the problem for now. "Bet you were that Reaper who ran for student council president and rallied for safer monkey bars on the playground as a kid."

"There's nothing wrong with standing up for what I believe in."

"Is it worth eternal damnation?"

He shrugged like the rebel his Stygian ID said he was. "Some causes are worth the punishment. Some *people* are, too."

Prickles of desire, like hot shower water on a cold morning, moved across my skin as his eyes, dark blue pools of interest, bored into me.

"Tell me more about yourself," he said, aware of my interest in *his* interest.

"Well..." After crossing and then re-crossing my legs, I gulped some beer to refuel my buzz. "I was born in Québec, but lived in New Orleans until I was ten when I was kicked out of grade five. When I turned fifteen, Marin mandated that we move to Québec so I could start my apprenticeship with Gerard."

"Why would a sweet thing like you get kicked out of

school?"

"I burned through my desk in math class. The principal said I was a pyromaniac. I think I'm more of an arts girl than a sciences girl." He laughed with me but said nothing more, which meant he was waiting for the rest of the story. Great. "Anyway, Mama and Papa, my foster parents, pulled me out of school and told me what I really was and what I was destined to do. My life went from normal to paranormal before my first kiss. It sucks to know what normal is and have it taken away."

There. He wanted it? He got it.

I rolled the bottle between the palms of my hands, remembering how livid I had been with Styx for pilfering my innocence. Why couldn't Marin and his cronies have forgotten about me? Let some of us Scriveners go under the radar instead of putting us to work.

"You're something special." Brent jarred me from my recriminations.

"Special is not how I see myself."

"But you are. Before the Purge, some of my greatest allies were Scriveners. Only one was a Master."

Before the Purge, huh?

Brent Hume was growing more and more intriguing as this conversation unfolded. I knew little of the Purge because no one cared to talk about it. Some things were better left forgotten, I supposed. What I did know was that nearly a hundred years ago, a group of Eidolons destroyed all of the Master Scriveners, and by destroyed, I mean killed and then sent to Erebus. Master Scriveners were powerful enough in their own right, nearly more so than Head Reaper Marin. They could Deathmark Stygians, and rumor had it that any

Stygian with a Deathmark would die, even the Head Reaper. It wasn't a stretch to assume Marin had ordered his legions of Eidolons like Chad to execute Master Scriveners, considering his predilection for running Styx like a merciless, power-loving overlord. But who had balls big enough to call him out? Not me.

Meemaw lived to be a hundred-and-two, and we celebrated her last birthday as if it were the Canadian Centennial. Although Brent didn't appear a day over thirty-five, if what he was saying was true, he had to be over a hundred. This revelation might've explained his success with the Watchmen back at Le Nektar—age trumps a lot of things with Stygians. But still.

Aware he was one of those cool-cat enigmas who shared information on a need-to-know basis, just as I imagined true insurgents were, I cleared my throat and leaned over the little round table, practically tipping our drinks. "Since you were *alive* when it happened, do you know why Marin supported the Scrivener Purge?"

He took a swig of his ale, thick enough to chew. "The reason Marin offed so many Scriveners was to protect his own ass. If there are free agent Master Scriveners and Eidolons afoot, he is vulnerable to being overthrown."

"What do you mean? The Eidolons helped him with the Purge."

Brent raised an eyebrow. "Not all Eidolons were involved in the Purge. Just a select few who bow incessantly to Marin's will."

"Well, in my mind, they are all responsible," I grumbled, feeling that my prejudice was entirely warranted.

"Olivia," Brent said with tension, "not all Eidolons want

to bring down Scriveners. A Master Scrivener and an Eidolon can dethrone Marin. And believe me, there are Eidolons out there who would love to have one half of that honor."

Eidolons and Scriveners dethroning Marin together?

I had never heard this before. Not one hint. Nope.

Inside, I wanted to scream from this shocking and rather delightful idea. Outside, I shrugged as if I already knew all this obvious information, thankyouverymuch. "Of course that's how Marin can be removed. I've known that for years. I'm not prejudiced against *all* Eidolons, you know."

"That's a relief."

"Yep." I took a massive gulp of beer.

"Yep." He followed my lead and drank his sugar beer, too. Afterward, we sat in silence, staring at various items in the bar, humans, anything that wasn't each other. Somewhere I read that there is always a lull in conversation every ten minutes. This was one of those moments, coupled with a hefty slice of awkwardness.

"Anyway," Brent went on when the silence became too much for us, "Stygians prefer not to face truth, no matter how heinous. It's easier to chug our sugar beer and pretend like the Purge never happened."

True. We weren't that different from the humans we served. Without humans, we wouldn't exist, so it stood to reason we would adopt human behaviors. Groupthink. Political Corruption. Murders. Wars.

Nice, happy things.

I slouched with the sophistication of a trucker. "Marin bitches on and on about the balance of life, yet he eliminated the Stygians who can help him achieve balance. It's wrong."

"Makes you want to stand up for what is right, doesn't

it? You could stop giving Deathmarks and see what happens to his precious balance," said the rebel.

Rebellions were dangerous. I grew up in foster care with the Balanchines due to the results of a failed rebellion. Right after I was born, my parents, both Scriveners, were sent to Erebus because they fought for justice. I would not become another story for the ages. I would keep to myself, keep my head down, and watch the rebellion from afar. That's how I would survive.

"I'm not about to tell the Big Guy that I won't work." Although with Eve's long-term future cut short, it would be an excellent time to give Marin my middle finger salutation and resignation. In another life, maybe.

"Hear me out," Brent went on, ignoring my disinterest in revolution. "The human population has almost tripled since the Purge. He's scared someone will call him out on it, so he rules with an iron fist." His heavy brow shaded his deep blue eyes. "He needs your kind now more than ever, Dormier."

I snorted, nixing any spell my French-Canadian charm might have had over him.

"If you and your kind were to stop working, souls wouldn't cross over, and Earth would erupt in anarchy. Scriveners hold a lot of power; you have to see it for what it is."

I couldn't figure Brent out. Sort of like if Prince Charming saw Cinderella in sweats, pimply-faced, and covered in ice cream stains, and he still took her to the ball. What did he see in me that screamed "rebel"?

"Did you chase me down this morning because you want to start a rebellion?" I said, half joking, half serious.

"I chased you because you dropped your phone. That you're a potential dissident Master Scrivener makes you the full package."

"You're trying to flatter your way into my bed," I said, after the kind of silence that makes your skin want to crawl off your bones and make for the nearest exit.

"You make flattery sound like it's a bad thing."

"Goal!" roared the hockey fans in the pub, distracting me from the dark pools of untamed intent in Brent's eyes. I spotted a small television perched on the bar top, encircled by humans.

"*Good evening, Stygians,*" a familiar voice crooned, heard only by Brent and me. Our low-frequency station, which humans couldn't perceive, replaced the clash of hockey players dashing for the puck with a picture of Head Reaper Marin on the TV screen.

His pale skin was a perfect complement for his textbook strong features and bald head, but left him looking washed out in his black turtleneck. It was his obsidian eyes, devoid of irises, that disturbed me, as if he could see through the television and into my soul.

"*I'm disappointed to report that a hospital fire in Phoenix, Arizona, did not reap Styx its due share of souls today,*" Marin intoned. "*Human emergency personnel retained all lives. I do not like reminding you that our job is to deliver souls to the Afterlife. Slipups like this will not be taken kindly.*"

I worked the top layer of varnish on the table with my nails. Marin wasn't directly chiding me, but I couldn't help but feel his threat score through the noise to latch onto my conscious and eat it raw.

"*In other news,*" he continued, "*my Watchmen have reported that the rebel blog, HermesHarbinger.com is being run by a turncoat in the northeast of North America, possibly*

the Province of Québec. They are tracking down the exact
location as I speak. I ask that you be on guard for anyone
technologically savvy, as they—"

Brent turned back to me, annoyance cut into his brow.
"Overheard someone saying the Montreal Canadiens are
playing the Predators. Must be the game we're missing."

I already knew. I had religiously watched the NHL as
soon as I had rigged my home television to pick up on anything between 54 and 806 megahertz—the human stations.
I called the clever electronic box the Interceptor. Most Stygian radios and televisions only picked up Marin's messages.

I couldn't say what level of Offense hotwiring a television
into my homemade Interceptor was, but it surely wasn't
execution-worthy. Marin might've had me living in fear, but
he would not separate this Québecker from her hockey.

Suppose Brent and I had more in common than I had
thought: we both needed our fixes of sweaty men on ice
skates body-checking each other over a six-ounce piece of
rubber. Of course, I was certain he didn't find it quite as de-
liciously sexy.

If he did, we'd have a lot more to talk about.

"Betcha the Canadiens will win," I taunted.

"I'll tolerate a win so long as I don't have to listen to
Marin's bullshit."

"*Très bien, Monsieur Hume.*"

His sly smile seemed to enjoy the sauciness of my French
inflections. "Does that mean I get to go home with you tonight?" Those blue eyes twinkled gold.

I ran my fingertip along the curve of his beer glass. "Not
a chance."

Chapter Five

"Our alliance can elicit change. Our deliverance will come with only a whisper into the void."

— *HermesHarbinger.com, 10:25 am ET Thursday, 13 April.*

"Sorry I'm late," I said to Gerard after I set my coffee and backpack on my workstation. "Didn't sleep well after what happened yesterday."

"With Moose?"

"Eve." *Mostly* Eve.

"Heard on the news this morning that another Stygian was sent to Erebus," Gerard droned, bored, when ordinarily the mention of another Stygian down would inspire regret. "Seems like there's one every day."

"We should start a pool," I said, cynically. "By Christmas more than half of Styx will be in Erebus."

From my side of the studio, I watched Gerard leaning back, studying his artwork. My lifelong mentor and boss was the only other Scrivener I had met, and he offered minimal information about himself when I pried. Whatever secrets he kept, he locked them behind an iron wall—one that even I couldn't burn through.

He'd been born shortly after the Scrivener Purge, and he was careful to wear that as a badge of pride for the entirety of his life. All I knew was that his Deathmarks were pinup models. Betty Paige, Jayne Mansfield, Betty Boop—lethal beauties to some ill-fated souls.

With a tired but tense sigh, I sat down at my drawing table and fished my toolbox out of my backpack. The black plastic box glistened in the shop's lights. A flick of the latches and the lid popped open. Packed safely against a bedding of silver foam was the rotary tattoo machine I had built specifically for my skullwork. Today I didn't like the way it looked at me, a reminder of what damage we had done together.

As I went about laying my tools out in a precise order—from left to right went the gun, needle, eye loupe—I pictured the sugar skull I left on Eve's bicep yesterday. When would it take her life? Did she have hours or weeks left?

Eve, Eve, Eve.

Her fate—and what part I played in her demise—would haunt me.

I would die with it burned into my conscience.

Once everything was aligned and awaiting sterilization, I pulled my brunette dreads into a chignon and then took the first sip of the coffee of the day.

"Got any Deathmarks on the books?" I asked my boss.

"None that I know of." His tone was bright.

"My last client is getting her first…and last tattoo," I said. "I think she's a model."

Gerard's soft gaze rose from his drawing. "A Playboy model?"

"If she is, she probably doesn't dig the old silent type who has 'Hard Cock' inked across his knuckles." I raised the eye loupe toward the light to check the needle for contamination.

Gerard observed the obscene words on his tattooed knuckles. "You never know, Ollie. Some women might call me dark and mysterious."

The bell over the shop's door jangled and in strutted Chad the Eidolon in yesterday's attire, hair tousled and sporting a five o'clock shadow. He gave me a loathsome wink, nodded to Gerard, and quietly sat in the back corner, where he had spent yesterday afternoon.

"Everything should've been cleared up with headquarters," Gerard said to Chad. "Why are you back?"

Chad's brownish-yellow teeth almost glistened when he smirked. "My job is to find suspicious activity."

I wanted to say there was nothing for him to see, but I knew better. What happened to Moose was not a common occurrence. Chad the Eidolon had been sent by Marin to force me to slip up and then—*Bam!*—I would be the next to be made an example of to any Scriveners and Reapers who dared to challenge his rigid authority.

My inner grumbling about Head Reaper Marin's reign of terror was cut off by a whirl of cool air that rustled Gerard's artwork and almost knocked my coffee over. Behind the counter stood a man in a black canvas jacket pulled tight over a muscular frame. From Eve's iPhone pictures, I knew exactly who this blond was.

"Remy." I rocketed out of my chair, confused at seeing Eve's latest boyfriend in person for the first time without Eve by his side. Had he come to tell me Eve was already gone?

"Ollie." His voice was remarkably soft compared to his mass.

The weight of Chad's hard gaze briefly withdrew my attention from Eve's beau. Once I connected with the Eidolon, the anxiety slinking upwards from my toes intensified.

"How is Eve?" Introductions were not as important as

a status update.

"That's why I'm here actually." Remy tucked his hands into his pockets.

Nervous tension spread across my chest. "Is she okay?"

"Her tattoo is infected. She asked me to come by and see if you have more of that ointment you gave her."

Remy's words echoed in my vacant head.

Infected tattoo.

Fresh wounds like tattoos could easily get infected, for a myriad of reasons. I had a good idea, though, that this infection was not bacterial, but supernatural. Death was already closing in on her, and likely before she'd have her chance to reconnect with her estranged mother.

"Of course." My voice wavered. I pawed under the counter for the box filled with tins of ointment meant to help in the healing process. The box crashed to the floor, spilling the containers, before I realized that my hands were covered in sweat. Gerard and I jokingly called the herbal ointment Death Goo because the treatment mattered not, when death would come in weeks or even days.

Death Goo.

I covered the pewter lotus pendant I wore with one hand as I released an anxious grunt.

"Ollie, you need some help." Gerard was at my side. Having worked with him since I was a teenager, I knew his words held a deeper understanding of my grief.

I dove to the floor and hurriedly shoved the tins back in the box.

Gerard handed Remy the ointment. "That should heal her tattoo."

Gerard rolled his chair alongside me as I drove the needle of the tattoo machine along the last few passes of the young model's back. As was customary, he was playing the attentive mentor, but there was an ulterior motive. Chad was outside taking a rare cigarette break.

"Don't forget, he's waiting for you to show signs of Master work," Gerard whispered just over the buzz of my tattoo machine, so as to keep my client from hearing.

There was that word again—Master. Gerard had never actually said that before. Seemed ill fitting. Or maybe I just wasn't willing to accept it. Whichever it was, Chad the Eidolon wouldn't see anything worthwhile unless it was the sole of my shoe coming at his face.

But there was a very real truth to consider. The Purge. Master Scriveners. And if I was one of them, what would that mean for me?

Erebus?

The tattoo machine nearly slipped from my fingertips. I removed my foot from the pedal, killing the power. My client couldn't see the look of terror in my eyes. Gerard did, though.

"Do *everything* you can to look average," Gerard said when the door swung open and a cloud of tobacco smoke burned my nostrils. Gerard grudgingly rolled back across the shop to his station, giving Chad a sidelong glance.

"You know, Dominique," I said to my client as I tried to shake off Gerard's warning, "if I ever get ink, I'd definitely get a skull like this one."

"*Merci,* Olivia." That was the best she could muster over the pain. Poor thing.

Like Gerard, I gave Chad a look that would've turned the cheeriest person cold. The Eidolon didn't appear to care, however. There was not much I could do to provoke him. I promised myself that I would not let him see anything worth reporting to the Head Reaper and, more importantly, I would not let him see my uncontrollable skills.

For the remainder of my shift at *Salon de Tatuoage*, I did what I had always done, keeping my power reined in. The effort was not met without a challenge. Just seeing Chad sitting in the corner, watching every move I made, charged my rage, which in turn made my hands hotter than usual. I kept myself under control as Gerard had advised, by frequently running my hands under cold water, breathing with intention, and reminding myself to stay calm.

Trouble was, I wouldn't be able to do it forever.

By closing hour, I was exhausted, far more than any other night. Yawning led to heavy eyes. Fatigue swept over me, begging me to curl up just about anywhere for a nap.

I slipped quietly into the crisp night, tightening the scarf around my neck. The commute was one mile. Not far, not close. By eleven, there were few people out and about. Bars and clubs did not populate our neck of Québec City. I never feared my nighttime walks home, and they were a chance to ruminate over a day's work.

But something about this commute did not feel normal.

There were eyes on me.

Eidolon eyes, if my intuition was trustworthy.

Gerard had told me Chad would wait for me to show signs of blossoming skills and then he'd pounce.

A glance over my shoulder showed no one there. Still, I slowed my pace and checked the windows of the shops that I passed, looking for anyone who might be following. Papa and Mama had taught me to be street smart. For a Stygian, the rules of nighttime safety were different. A human couldn't do much damage to someone like me. Another Stygian, especially an Eidolon, could.

Then again—I looked at my hands—maybe I could do some damage, too.

"Scrivie," whistled an unwelcomingly familiar voice.

Tucking my hands, which were cold as ice, into my jacket pockets, I turned and faced the yellow teeth and sneer of my pursuer. And as anyone would upon seeing such a grim face, I startled.

"You were holding back today," Chad said.

"I'm off duty. You don't need to follow me home," I said with confidence.

"A Stygian is never off duty." His cigarette breath, something even the crisp air could not diffuse, offended my senses.

"Scriveners work shifts, and *my* shift is over." The words came out of my mouth, but I was sure they weren't mine. Speaking back to an Eidolon—who as a group were third in command of all Stygians—was not the wisest of responses. An obedient "yes, monsieur" would've been far more diplomatic. Yet even when I knew what I should do, my mouth flapped on anyway. "Why don't *you* keep working and let me go home in peace?"

It was stupid of me.

Very, very stupid.

Chad's eyes bled into angry rubies, the uniquely demonic stare of an Eidolon. This show of dominance and rage did not thwart me, and it occurred only in passing that the reason I was not afraid was fairly simple—I was numb. Eve, my best friend, wore my Deathmark. Her finite time was quickly ticking away. Whatever Chad could do to me was not as menacing as what my own mind was doing.

I broke from our standoff, glided around him on the walkway, and made for my apartment. As I rushed away from him, he sniggered as if to say he had let me off easy tonight, but I'd pay for my insubordination eventually.

Chapter Six

"Come, come, Godfather Death. Not too soon but not too late. Come, come, Godfather Death, Drown all evil in the river of hate."

—Styx Nursery Rhyme, circa 1922

Dudley, my thirty-pound black and white mutt that I rescued from the snow-covered streets of Québec City nearly five years ago, dove into his midnight dinner as if it was the greatest thing he had ever experienced. I was certain that couldn't be true, after the delight he showed when he peed on his favorite mailbox in front of my apartment building five minutes ago. Then again, dogs seemed to think everything was great—food, toys, a good pat on the head.

As for me, there was too much on my mind to even enjoy Dudley's happiness.

Shame. Regret. Frustration. Suspicion.

The consolation was that I wasn't on guard inside the

safety of my home. I didn't have to worry about Chad watching over my shoulder, waiting to trip me up. Not a worry of either of Marin or Chad destroying my soul. I had done nothing wrong, at least nothing criminal.

The tradeoff didn't bring relief.

On my perch on my kitchen counter, I kept my head buried in *Reaper Monthly* as I waited for Dudley to finish his meal. Staring back from the glossy magazine was Head Reaper Marin in his usual black attire. He stood in front of three Reapers charged with a Level Ten Offense for allowing a suicide bomber and his victims to survive an attack last month. The humans lived when Death had ordered them to die.

The Reapers' heads were hidden under black bags as a way to stamp out their individuality, to make them cattle in a slaughterhouse before they were sent to Erebus to endure an eternity of torture. Reaping meant revenue, and someone had to pay. If it wasn't a human's soul, it was a Stygian's.

My demise could end up in the next *Reaper Monthly* if I wasn't careful.

Dudley took the last bite of his kibble and quickly began nosing the metal bowl across the linoleum floor for remnants of flavor he might have missed. The squeak of metal against plastic was unpleasant, but I would not stop him from getting the most out of his dinner. Hades knew I had taken enough from others today.

As the screeching intensified—because Dudley left nothing for scavengers, including himself—a dark mass moved behind him. I sat up, rail straight.

My apartment was playing optical illusions on me. Home sweet home was one of the disregarded buildings in a forgotten part of Québec, with nauseating floral wallpaper from the 1920's, yellowed water stains in the ceilings, creaky floors, and a constant chill even in July. Shadows were par for the course.

Dudley whined.

I tossed *Reaper Monthly* aside. It landed cover up, pages crumpled against the countertop. I leaped off the counter. When my feet landed with a soft thud on the peeling linoleum, I saw the dark mass again. Movement. A hazy outline of a person making for my bedroom.

I burst inside the room and flicked on the light, but there was nothing in the bedroom, not a rat or a bug or a ghost. My overactive mind loved to play tricks on my sensibilities. An odd noise was definitely a burglar. A mysterious shadow was a ghost. Straddling the worlds of the living and the dead made it difficult to dismiss mysteries as benign.

Dudley stopped at my side. His black nose twitched as he sniffed the air. A spine of raised fur ran down the length of his shoulders and back. He, too, sensed something peculiar.

"You saw it, too, didn't you, Duds?"

My furry companion's awareness was the validation I needed to put the chain lock on my front door, turn on every light in my apartment, and bury myself under my bed covers. Daybreak couldn't come soon enough.

A tug on my foot woke me from a dream about the Montreal Canadiens skating through the streets of Québec, away from a hockey team of giant Band-Aids. Dudley had a habit of this. After tiring of sharing a pillow, he'd dig at the end of

my bed, pulling and shoving my feet into the perfect nest.
I returned his fussing with a gentle kick, but didn't feel his
body.

I peeked over the comforter at the foot of the bed. Dudley wasn't there. In fact, he wasn't anywhere nearby. Horror
dripped down my shoulders when I realized that the lights,
which I had left on, were off, and the ambient light from
the street lamps pouring through the windows spread a pale
glow across the bedroom.

"Duds?" I whispered.

My dog never left the bed, especially not on those cold
Québec mornings. He'd stay buried underneath the blankets
until he was forced to face the day. That he was gone in the
wee hours of the night left me riddled with tremors.

I slid quietly out of bed. My feet barely registered the
icy wood floor.

"Dudley?"

I peered around my bedroom door, where I had a direct
line of sight to the front entrance to my apartment. My heart
slid into my stomach. The chain lock had been undone, and
the door hung ajar.

"Dudley!"

Someone—or something—*had* been in my apartment
after all.

But who? And for how long?

With only the desperate need to scoop Dudley safely
into my arms, I ran through my apartment door and into the
dark hallway dotted with dim sconces and other apartment
doors. The tile floor that led to a flight of stairs felt a million
miles long, one that would take hours to clear.

"Dudley!" I screamed, on the off chance he was hiding

in a dark corner, or a neighbor had found him roaming the apartment building in the middle of the night.

The horror at the invasion of my apartment and fear for Dudley peaked the second I reached the top of the stairway. Staring up at me from the landing, like he was preparing to drag me into the bowels of hell, was Chad. The Eidolon's blood-red eyes froze me between shock and a full scream.

A chill washed over me when, silent, he climbed the stairs between us in the time it took me to blink. It wasn't winter cold, but a weight of despair and resentment and murderous intent that held me paralyzed. My breaths were clouds of visible panic inside this arctic horror.

"You killed Eve, Scrivie," he said in a guttural bass. "Her blood is on your hands." With each word he grew louder, rattling everything—the walls, sconces, doors. The old, dusty paintings jumped with each spiteful syllable.

I threw my hands over my ears and backed toward my apartment.

"You are a terrible creature, you are." Chad followed my measured retreat. "You killed your *friend*. That deserves some kind of hell, doesn't it?"

"Fuck you!" I was scared, but I was also cornered. "You set me up. If only I could put a Deathmark on you, you piece of shit."

In an instant, he and his cigarette-breath hovered inches away from me, but behind him, outlining his form, was a black-as-night miasma creeping across the walls and ceiling like the fingers of a beast. I had never seen anything like it—not in my worst nightmares. Every molecule in my body trembled at its gravity. The *thing* behind Chad was an Eidolon, or at least it had to be, because Scriveners didn't have the power to transform into black masses of energy. Eidolons did. And this one was far more powerful than any ordinary death dealer.

That's a goddamn Eidolon, too. Just like Chad.

At that revelation I found enough air for a full-bodied scream, one that shredded my vocal cords as terror poured out of my lungs.

Unlike Chad, this Eidolon was death in rare form, and its mass swathed the hallways from floor to ceiling. A pair of eyes bright as rubies cut through the blackness. Its magnetism dragged Chad toward it.

One stomp of its shadowy foot shook the whole apartment building. I grabbed onto the doorknob of my next door neighbor, the only thing that kept me upright.

The hallway quaked again. A sconce toppled from the wall and hung from a thin brown wire. Picture frames fell to the floor, cracking the glass.

I dared to look at the Eidolon behind Chad, wondering if he was here for me, possibly to take me to see Head Reaper Marin, possibly because they were working together. A skeletal face emerged from the darkness. Its massive jaw unhinged and dropped like a snake swallowing its kill as a chorus of blood-curdling screams rattled me from the inside out. My eardrums throbbed.

I threw my hands over my ears and watched on in horror as the Eidolon took on Chad, and not me. Chad fought back, transforming into his own version of a monstrous blackness, but he did not compare. Whatever challenged him outweighed his influence, despite his best effort. I could not help but think this other Eidolon was there to knock Chad out of the way, set on taking me to Head Reaper himself.

As I had done before, and without thinking, I ran for my apartment, slammed the door shut behind me, put on the chain lock, and shoved my entertainment unit in front of the door. These things wouldn't stop Eidolons from entering my home, but the layers of obstacles gave me an illusion of protection.

Rigid, I stood in front of the barricade listening to the sound of two Eidolons settling their scores in the hallway, and I wondered how no one else heard the ruckus. Or were my neighbors too scared, or too smart, to emerge from their apartments?

Heart racing, I waited. And then I remembered Dudley. I waited a moment longer. Just as suddenly as the bedlam erupted, it was over. The room fell into silence. From under the couch came a soft whimper and the thin white tail of my black and white mutt.

"If I explain it again, will you let me in?" Noted rebel, Brent Hume, the Kentucky Eidolon Reaper, asked from outside my locked living room window. He sat scrunched on the fire escape wearing the same blue flannel and taped boots ensemble as the day before.

Eidolons were responsible for eliminating the Master Scriveners with Marin's full endorsement. Brent had told me that *some* Eidolons did not agree with Marin's destruction. Was Brent one of them? Or was he duping me?

This locked window would not keep me safe from him if he wanted to cause trouble, but it felt more reasonable to lock it than to leave my future completely to fate.

Dudley peeked around the lip of the couch at me. He didn't want another visitor tonight. Neither did I, but Brent was determined to have a heart-to-heart about what happened in the hallway only minutes earlier.

"Ollie, please, it's cold out here," Brent nudged.

"You're an Eidolon. You could be up to no good, like Chad."

There was a distinctive, tired grumble and then, "But I'm not. Chad was following us when we went out for drinks the other night. Since I've known the Eidolon for decades, I knew he was up to something, so I followed him to your apartment tonight because there's only one reason he is stalking you."

"What for?"

"Getting you to exhibit more signs of Masterhood," he said as if I was an idiot for not considering this. When I glowered, he raised his hands and said, "Sorry. It's just very cold out here. It looks very warm in there."

"I keep it a balmy seventy-two degrees." I was a compassionate Stygian. Despite witnessing Brent's obvious discomfort with Québec's frigidity, this was not one of my empathetic moments. "How can I be sure you aren't here to finish what Chad started? You two could be working for the same goal for all I know."

"I get that." He sighed and raked his fingers through his hair. "Is there something I can do to assure you I'm not out to harm you?"

I gave minimal thought to my answer before I said, "Go away."

"I will once I know Chad is no longer a problem."

"I don't need you to protect me."

"There's nothing wrong with help from your friends." He was playing to something I knew too well. I preferred doing everything on my own—tying my shoes when I was seven or learning to bake cookies when I was ten or starting my work in the business of Death when I was sixteen. Now I was facing the greatest challenge—keeping myself from being a target for Head Reaper Marin and his cronies.

Perhaps I did need help, but was Brent the Rebel the *right* help?

"I won't hurt you. *Ever*," Brent stressed. "Please, let me in. I'll stay long enough to warm up and then I'll keep watch outside in case Chad returns."

"Better you stay outside."

"Look, Ollie, if I was set on bringing you down, I would've done it already, and I could easily do it now. Please trust me," he said with a slight of cockiness that, oddly, didn't aggravate my sensibilities, something that Chad, the *other* Eidolon, never failed to do.

Brent had a point, however. For good measure, and without making an announcement, I jumped to my feet and ran to my bedroom closet to retrieve Miss Piggy— the Mossberg shotgun that Papa had given to me as a birthday gift three years earlier. Brent's blue eyes widened when he saw me reappear with the weapon. Loading a couple of buckshots into the barrel did not invite friendly conversation, but I couldn't let the Eidolon sit outside in the sub-zero temperatures. Even though nothing felt like the "right thing to do," I took a long, deliberate breath and opened the window wide enough to let Brent slide gracefully into my apartment.

After rubbing his hands together for warmth, he gave me and Miss Piggy a soft, concerned smile. I didn't know what to give back. A high-five? A hug? A cap in the knee?

The most logical thing to do was sit down and pretend everything was normal, so I planted myself on the couch with Dudley hiding underneath my feet, the gun on my lap, and Brent standing across from me, a powerful Grim Reaper with a predilection for pummeling bully Stygians in the late hours of the night.

"This is Miss Piggy," I said, addressing the metal and gunpowder elephant in the room.

"Charming." He never took his attention off the weapon.

"This won't kill Stygians, but it will hurt bad enough and long enough that I can escape."

Eyebrows raised, he nodded. He understood.

"Sit." I pointed at the chair behind him. Not one to argue with a Scrivener holding a loaded shotgun named after a Muppet, he slipped out of his jacket, set it aside, and did as I said. Once he settled into his chair, I regarded him with a smile—not a happy, welcome-home sort of smile but one that addressed two very important things about our budding friendship—he was *still* a rebel and he was an Eidolon, powerful enough to ferry someone like me to very bad places.

"Did they teach you that screaming shadow technique in Worst Nightmares 101?" I asked after minutes of silent, racing thoughts.

With the sleeves of his flannel cuffed around his elbows, he crossed his arms, flexing every muscle. My toes curled inside my socks at such unassuming machismo.

"It's more of a graduate level course. Worst Nightmares 666," he said, dryly.

"When we went out the other day, were you gonna tell me you're an Eidolon?"

"I was until you spoke so negatively about them."

"You killed the Master Scriveners and then sent their souls to suffer in Erebus," I growled, fingering the trigger of the shotgun.

"*They* killed the Master Scriveners. I never touched one and never will. My loyalty has always stayed with the rebellion, not Marin and his mindless followers."

I scrunched my brow as I tried to discern Brent's emotions. "So you don't like Chad?"

"No. He has got his head so far up Marin's ass that it's difficult to see where one stops and the other begins."

The visual of a Chad-Marin hybrid should've been scary. But it wasn't.

"So was Chad involved in the Purge?"

"He and others, yes."

"Where do you come in?" I remained vigilant as the conversation unraveled.

"That red and black sticker on my ID came from my attempt to stop several Eidolons, Chad included, from taking out Master Scrivener Flemington years ago. I didn't succeed. Her soul was sent to Erebus after she was killed, and I was sent to prison."

So many Scriveners had been sent to Erebus that their names blended into a collection of words and nothing more. However, Scrivener Flemington was familiar if only because her Deathmark had fascinated me since I was a child. Hers was a sun and moon, day and night.

"Why didn't Marin do away with you when you tried to help Flemington?" I asked.

"I'm more useful to him alive. He thinks he can convince me to join him. Hope springs eternal." Brent's cunning grin, one that seemed to say a hundred things about him in just the slightest shift in his lips, forced me to tighten my grip on the shotgun. As much as I would've preferred to overlook it, this Eidolon made my center tremble from across the room. Power and composure mixed with perfect charm—it was impossible to resist, no matter that I was still quivering from seeing his Grim-Reaper-on-steroids alter ego.

"So you're here because you want something. What is it?" I wasn't born yesterday. He was here for one thing and because he had already helped me, I was, in a sense, indebted to him.

His eyes narrowed. "They know you are on the fast track to Masterhood. They don't want Master Scriveners. You are a threat. They will eliminate that threat as soon as they can."

The shotgun felt like an icicle in my hands.

"You interested in earning the rebel's red and black sticker?" he asked.

I pulled Miss Piggy closer to my body, preparing for something, though I wasn't sure what. "Why would I want that?"

"To make Styx a better place. To make things *right* and as they should be." Brent's voice never rose in pitch or tone, but his conviction was tangible, hovering over every syllable, over every word.

"What about saving a human I care about?" I said. "My friend, Eve—"

"The barista."

"Yes. If we make Styx a better place, we can help her."

Brent leaned forward and put his elbows on his knees. "What do you mean?"

I didn't immediately answer because trust was a valuable

commodity these days. I wasn't sure that I trusted Brent—or anyone—but my aching conscience begged for relief. I would find a way to help her, and it was possible the source was sitting across from me.

"I had to give Eve a Deathmark yesterday," I confessed. "It's infected, from what her boyfriend said. If my Death-mark works anything like it has been lately, she'll be dead in hours. A day, maybe. She won't get to see her mother on her birthday. I should not have done it, but Chad was there. He made sure I went through with it. I want to help her… to delay her death so she can get her affairs in order. It's the least I can do."

Brent rubbed his chin. The gesture made me aware of his stubble and that it was a fine look for him. Noticing his attractiveness during a conversation about Eve made me feel even worse.

"Eve asked for a Deathmark. It's her time," he said. "If we worked together, we could make sure that Styx is work-ing fairly, not like it is now. We could do it in honor of Eve, though."

My mood quickly turned sour. His reply wasn't what I wanted to hear. Had he told me he'd help me secure Eve time to say good-bye to her mother and this world, I would have been more inclined to give his request some thought. Rebellions were idealistic. Giving someone a second chance was a noble *and* practical act.

I sniggered. "Would we be Batman and Robin running around Gotham saving the day if we do this? Would we get to drive the Batmobile and jump off buildings, too?"

He looked at me as if I'd sprouted offensive, coin-sized warts on my face. "I'm serious. I cannot do any of it without your help."

I returned a perplexed, hard stare.

"Ollie, a Master Scrivener and an Eidolon can take out the Head Reaper. This is why I need you—we can do it, but only together." His summary sounded more like he was dictating directions for putting together furniture.

But his request was twenty-four hours too late. Yesterday he and I could have taken Head Reaper Marin out, and today Eve wouldn't be wearing my Deathmark. I had one response to his brazen and treasonous proposition. After setting Miss Piggy on my lap, I held out both my fists at Brent. He looked perplexed, so I said, "Choose one."

He picked my right hand. I turned it upright and opened my fist. He stared for a moment, looking at my flattened palm. "There's nothing there."

"Exactly," I said with cheer. "That's how many fucks I give about your rebellion, Eidolon Hume."

He blinked incredulously. I could see "Is she for real?" running in a hamster wheel inside his head. And then, he unfolded his arms and rose to his full, gargantuan height. The visual should have frightened me into hiding in a closet, but it didn't. He wouldn't draw me into his one-Eidolon rebellion.

"I see," he said in a forced calm, jugular vein popping from his muscular neck. "You're too scared to stand up for what's right. I don't blame you. Fear is how he gets us."

"I'm not scared. We simply don't have the same goals in mind." My hands were back on the stock and trigger of Miss Piggy as I stood up across from him.

For a while we stared at each other in silence, because neither of us had anything more to say. Dudley was still underneath the couch, nails scraping the wood floor as he tried to get comfortable.

"Thanks for your help with Chad tonight," I said with as much gratitude as I could muster. "I'd appreciate it if you'd leave. I can—"

"Ollie, please, I think we're getting off on the wrong—"

"—take care of myself from here on out." I disliked knowing Brent would spend the remainder of the night out in the cold, assuming he had nowhere else to go. But he wasn't my friend if he spent every interaction trying to lure me into a rebellion.

His shoulders drooped when he turned to the window. "I'm sorry that I've offended you."

With that, he left, and my vise grip on Miss Piggy eased.

Chapter Seven

*"Give me the waters of Lethe that numb the heart, if they
exist, I will still not have the power to forget you."*

— Ovid, The Poems of Exile: Tristia and the Black Sea
Letters

14 APRIL

Dudley whimpered to remind me that he had not gone on
his morning walk or had his breakfast—two of his reasons
for living. I looked over to see his lazily swinging tail. It
wasn't his usual good morning wag, but it still held happiness. And hope.

The digits on my smartphone read nine o'clock. A night
of perusing HermesHarbinger.com had left me with time to
brood since Brent had left my apartment. Eve's time had
been diminishing as I idled, feeling sorry for myself.

Dudley trotted into the kitchen and glanced at the stove.

Every morning I gave him blueberry pancakes in addition to his kibble. The dog liked his pastries.

I slowly stood, my spine cracking thanks to the shot springs in my hand-me-down couch, when the sound of keys in the door turned my focus from breakfast and the injustice of back troubles at twenty-six, to the possibility of a full invasion. Travelling ten feet in a panic, I jumped onto the television stand that was still braced against the door.

Through the peephole, I saw a familiar lavender eye looking back at me.

"Open the door." My foster mother Lorelei Balanchine's voice carried through the apartment with a cutting ping. The sound fired shivers through me like it had when I was a teenager hiding in my bedroom and rereading the raunchier parts of her romance novel collection—an indulgence I wouldn't normally admit to.

"Hold on, Mama."

After I'd shoved the television stand back to its place and slid back the chain lock, both of my foster parents barged in with well-rehearsed purpose. I stumbled to the side, a hand to my tender back, and sighed.

"You knew we were comin' over. How are we supposed to get in if the door is locked?" Mama ranted as she brushed past me, carrying a plate of cookies. She was an emerald blur to my tired eyes. Her familiar green maxi dress accentuated her full-bodied curves. Waist-length black braids were wrapped in a color-matched headdress. Plastic limes dangled from her ears. The monochromatic green washed the warmth out of her nutmeg skin.

I wasn't thrilled to update them on the last harrowing few days, but if I avoided it, Mama would know. She was a

Grim Reaper who could sniff out dishonesty with the skill of a bloodhound. "I set the lock because one of Marin's guys was at the shop, and he followed me home last night."

Papa squared his massive shoulders. "What do you mean?"

"His name is Chad. He's an Eidolon. Marin sent him to keep an eye on me and, well, he did. I think he might've broke into my apartment, but I can't be sure."

"You should've called. I would've come over, baby girl," Papa said, with spite for Chad in his bass voice. His iron arms pulled me into a hug and popped the knot out of my spine. I was melted butter as I sank into his embrace.

Papa's hugs were worth getting lost in and not just for their chiropractic assistance. Even now, my cheek pressed to the soft cotton of his shirt, I felt as safe as I had when I was a little girl. Maybe I should've called him after Chad's creepy visit.

The knot in my back started to tighten all over again.

"Thanks, Papa, but everything is fine now," I said, pulling back from his arms to look into his dark brown eyes. Today Papa had shaved, displaying the glow in his dark chocolate skin. I always preferred him without a beard because I could see his smile better.

"You know my feelings on Eidolons and Watchmen," he hissed. "They are all a bunch of self-serving sons-of-bitches. One sure as hell shouldn't be following you home. What's this Chad's last name? I'll have words with him." He deposited his jacket on the kitchen counter as we converged on the plate of chocolate chip cookies that Mama set between us.

"Papa, it's not a big deal." *Liar.*

"Like hell it isn't. Best you be on your guard until I can

get my hands on this—"

"Stone, baby," Mama addressed him with firm warmth. "Let's not get worked up right now. Our girl is fine, and we have fresh cookies for breakfast." Mama was not dismissive, even though it would seem so to an outsider. While anyone would be fearful of Papa for his sheer mass alone, Mama was the overlooked threat. Behind that plate of gooey chocolate chip love was a Reaper who would not back down from a badger, an armed robber, or the Head of Death himself. Plots for Chad's downfall were already twinkling in her smiling violet eyes. "Your Papa baked these cookies with me this morning. Let's celebrate his first step into the kitchen with a bite."

"*You* helped?" I cocked a brow. Papa's bowling team would love to see a picture of that: Papa in a pink, frilly apron rolling out cookie dough. Come to think of it, *I* would love to see a picture of that.

"This lady from Québec Bookanistas said that learning together would revive our marriage." Mama's smile made her freckled cheeks bunch up. I had always liked that Mama and I both had freckles despite the fact that our skin was different colors—mine pale and cool; hers dark and warm. When I was little, I imagined she'd sprinkled her freckles over my cheeks when she'd give me kisses goodnight. I still liked to think that.

"I guess after so many years you'd need a little romantic rekindling. What are you reading in Québec Bookanistas these days? Any suggestions?" I said.

She put on that sassy smile I learned to copy at a very young age. "We're reading Regency romances. Such lovely literature."

"Don't be fooled, girl. Your mama skims for the steamy parts."

So did I.

The doorbell rang. It had been so long since I heard it I didn't recognize it.

"What's that sound?" Papa didn't either. But then, he and Mama found the use of a doorbell odd because they preferred to barge into a room, not use pleasantries like doorbells.

"Probably the wrong apartment."

The bell rang again.

"Be right back." I pulled away from the counter.

As always, I used the peephole to assess the threat. No Eidolons. There was nothing but the hated 1920's pink and gold floral wallpaper. What I would've given to have a strong chat with the interior decorator who'd gotten her hands on the wrong roll of bad taste and went bonkers covering every square inch of the common areas of the apartment building.

The bell rang again, and I jumped.

I opened the door a smidgen and faced one cerulean eye. My heart pattered. I expected him to come back in a few weeks, not hours. That he came back now made him really desperate to lead that rebellion, or just excellent boyfriend material. I wasn't ready to decide which, since I still didn't know what he actually was. Insurgent, Eidolon, hero…

He has food?

Brent the Rebel Eidolon held a bag of Chez Ashton and a to-go cup of coffee from Le Nektar. Without delay I reached for the treats. He jerked them away. His smile turned wicked, and I wanted to slap it and kiss it and then slap it some more. I was not proud of that dilemma.

"Why are you here?" I stared down the treats in his hands.

"To talk."

How sweet. His timing was awful. Brent with Mama and Papa? Erebus would be Elysia in comparison.

"No thanks." I tried shutting the door because it was my only defense, but Brent jammed his tape-booted toe through it to stop me. He was as smart as he was stubborn.

"I want to make things right, Ollie."

Come to think of it, I should have set the chain lock *after* Mama and Papa arrived.

"I spent some time thinking after you kicked me out… into the frigid cold night. All alone in the world."

I glared. His playfulness was wasted on me.

"Ahem. I was wrong. I don't expect you to become a rebel with me overnight," he said hastily as I crushed his toe harder with his every word. "But sometimes we have to take risks. I think we might be able to help Eve, at least give her some extra time, as you asked."

My world stopped spinning for a moment. "What?"

"We can help her, but it's a Level… Hell, I don't know what level of offense it would be. Probably off the charts."

"What in the world does that mean?"

"Means it's serious enough to talk about *inside* your apartment with the door locked and voices hush-hushed. Possibly in bed, under the sheets, naked while I make it up to you. I at least owe you that."

Too fucking tempting.

His smile spoke volumes. I glanced around the door at Mama and Papa who were hovering over the cookies. They weren't eating or talking, which meant they were trying to listen.

I could already see Brent's squashed face if Papa got his hands on him. Four years ago, Papa had discovered that a Reaper I had been dating for a month was promoted to Watchman. I had to break off the relationship after Papa put the guy through a stained glass window. Papa didn't like authority, so if he thought for a moment that I was interested in an Eidolon—for an honorable and rebellious cause or not—it wouldn't matter if Brent outranked him. Papa would take it as a personal challenge.

"Come back later," I conceded. "And bring those treats."

"I thought we could discuss it over breakfast." He waved the Chez Ashton bag and coffee.

"Not now. I've got company."

"Who?"

I chewed my bottom lip and threw out, "A man. We've been…busy."

Only the slightest lift of his right brow gave away his suspicion. "Slap me silly, you moved on fast. Mind if I shake the hand of this Romeo? I'd like to know who I lost out to and he better not be Chad."

"Moving on would mean we had something to begin with, Hume."

"Just because you didn't let me in your panties doesn't mean you didn't want me there. I see how you look at me."

"How does your ego fit into that head of yours?"

"I wear relaxed-fit jeans." He curled his fingers over the edge of the door and tried to glance around it. There was no time for me to explain that my foster father would string him up by his toes if he had the chance.

"I'll give you a pound of sugar if you leave right now." I put a hand on his chest and noticed his hard muscles, something I shouldn't notice in a Grim Reaper for Stygians. He could destroy me. And yet he hadn't. That fact made me feel like he'd reached into my chest, grabbed my heart, and gave it a sensual squeeze.

"We have business to discuss," he said. "Tell your booty call to leave."

"He's not a booty call, he's… You…*you* leave." I drew my hands back. They were turning pink, warm, and prepared for a battle. But that also meant I couldn't touch the door. The brace of my foot was the only thing protecting everyone from an unplanned gathering.

His grin suddenly turned excruciatingly mischievous. "Howdy there."

Patchouli wafted over my shoulder. Nervous chills zipped through me.

"Ollie, who is your friend?" asked Mama.

Shoulders rigid, I turned around to find Mama's violet eyes as broad as dinner plates. But it was Papa who caused my head to spin.

When he was off, he was the sweetest, kindest Reaper imaginable. When he was flipped on, he was the incensed grizzly bear uprooting pine trees to make a very specific—vicious—point.

And judging by the flare of his nostrils, Papa had flipped on.

To be fair, his aggression came with the territory. Papa took it upon himself to use intimidation to protect me. But it only worked if my would-be suitors knew Mr. Stone Balanchine personally. Brent did not.

"What's this about? That Chad?" Papa asked in a wrath-auguring bass. When I assessed them both, Papa was a hair shorter than Brent but wider by far in musculature. His size alone was usually enough to send others scattering.

Size evidently didn't matter to an Eidolon.

"No, Papa, he's not Chad. He's a friend who stopped by to say hello," I said. "He was just leaving."

"What's your name, sugar?" Mama pulled Brent inside, completely unfazed by her husband's fury. Mama lived to antagonize Papa, evidenced by her boundless collection of Beanie Babies, which layered every square inch of their apartment. This was probably why Papa liked to visit my place. No piles of stuffed animals to wade through.

"Reaper Brent Hume, ma'am," he said, smiling from ear-to-ear. "Now, I may not be a brilliant man, but you must be Olivia's momma."

"My, you're a southern gent. How nice." Mama put her hand to her chest. "The name's Lorelei Balanchine, Grim Reaper. Pleased to make your acquaintance."

I rolled my eyes—*again*. So did Papa. Brent's sparkling blue gaze could have charmed the knickers off a nun, but did he really have to take Mama's hand and kiss it?

"Miss Lorelei. That's a lovely name indeed."

"Mm. Ollie, why didn't you invite this devil in sooner?" For the first time in my life, I could have sworn I actually saw a swoon in the wild.

"Yeah, Ollie, why?" Papa asked.

I backed into—and almost crushed—Brent, our breakfast, and that sweet, sweet caffeinated nectar. "I was trying to get him to come back another time."

Papa's face danced a jig between murder and torture. "You didn't try hard enough. You should've given the choke-slam or the brain-buster. Those moves will get rid of troublemakers. Your last three boyfriends were up to no good. Do I have to remind you of Alexander and Jacob and—"

"Please stop." There was no masking my embarrassment at that point.

I could never tell when Papa was reddened from anger, but whenever the vein in his forehead popped—like it did just then—I knew he was pissed off beyond compromise.

"Mr. Balanchine," Brent interjected, then handed off the squashed bag and sweating coffee and stepped around me. He crossed his arms over his chest, flexing those muscles to make it crystal clear to Papa that he wanted a brand new asshole. "I don't have any ill intentions toward your daughter."

"See there. He has no ill intentions." Mama's plastic lime earrings swung violently as she sought to calm Papa. "I taught our daughter to find a decent man. One of these days she'll get it right. Now Ollie," she turned to me with a strained smile, ignoring Papa's seething stare, "Stone and I are going to leave so you two sweethearts can do whatever it is you were going to do."

"No, no. We're not dating." However, if we were, I'd at least have the glow from a recent orgasm to make this conversation bearable. "I barely know him."

"You don't have to disguise how you feel. We understand."

"Mama, there's nothing to understand. Brent came by because we… um…we're gonna save a client I marked from death."

The conversation fell silent.

Dead silent.

The only sounds were the traffic below my apartment and my upstairs neighbor using his rowing machine.

"What did you say?" Papa's dark skin glistened in angry sweat.

I wasn't sure what to do. Run? Hide? Kool-Aid Man my way out of the apartment building? I looked between Brent, Mama, Papa, and then back to Brent, who was staring like I had punched his elderly mother in the throat. I shouldn't have spoken, I knew.

Desperate measures were in order.

My grand resolution to this problem was coming in three, two…

"Mr. Balanchine," Brent said, "What Ollie *meant* to say is that since I'm an Eidolon, I can help her fix a problem with an elusive Deathmark before Marin catches on. No big deal."

"My ears must've heard that wrong, son. You're a *what*?" Papa growled.

"An Eidolon."

Papa's paws clamped around Brent's throat.

"Here." I tossed Brent a Ziploc bag stuffed with ice.

His mouth finally stopped bleeding after twenty minutes, a surprisingly long time for a Stygian. Usually our wounds healed within minutes, so long as they weren't too deep. Thank Hades for that. My accident-prone childhood would've been predominantly hospital visits if I weren't Stygian.

I plopped down on the couch next to him. "You shouldn't have told him you're an Eidolon. He doesn't trust Eidolons after the Purge."

Not that I needed Papa telling me why Brent was six million reasons wrong for me to get entangled with, because I knew. Still, he was my type in every which way. Well, except for being a rebel. I could have done without that, thank you very much.

"I had to say something." Brent pressed the bag of ice to his gradually healing lip. "We're talking about challenging the fundamentals of Death by interrupting Eve's death. If we get caught because your parents narc on us, we'll be serving shit sandwiches to criminals down in Erebus."

"Excuse me?" I bristled.

He appeared confused, one eyebrow elevated.

"There are a lot of Stygians in Erebus for bullshit charges. They aren't criminals. Like my birth parents for one."

"Didn't mean to be insensitive. You know what I meant." He tossed the bag of ice onto the coffee table. It landed with a clunk next to a collection of *True Blood* DVDs.

"What's this plan then?" I asked after a temper-cooling breath.

"There's a place in Québec that holds Deathlists for Reapers, called the Registry Vault. I worked there as the Deliveryman before I was kicked off the job."

The Deliveryman was the second in command next to Head Reaper Marin, the big honcho. Brent Hume had been one degree away from the seat of power that many would fight to acquire. The notion was surreal and disturbing. "*You* were the Deliveryman?"

He nodded, completely nonchalant.

"Are you fucking kidding me?" I barked.

Brent released a long exhale. "I'm not fucking kidding anyone."

I couldn't count how many times I had tried to catch the mystery Stygian who delivered Mama and Papa's Deathlists when I was a child. He or she was an enigma, like Santa Claus to human children. How does he get to every house in the world on Christmas Eve? How does he fit through chimneys?

"I don't get it. You're a rebel. Rebels don't work *that* closely for Marin."

"I joined the rebellion after Marin kicked me off the Deliveryman job."

"What did you do to get fired?" I was not afraid to pry.

"Stole Deathlists."

"Why?"

"Deathlists tell Reapers who they are supposed to ferry. I wanted to know who was on my list." It seemed a logical explanation but there certainly was more to it.

"Let me guess. You found out you had to ferry your beloved, right?" I said with a shit-eating grin.

He looked away and refused to say anything in response. Of course, his silent reaction was enough to fill my face with heat.

"Sorry," I whispered. "That was insensitive."

"Consider us even."

Brent wanting to save someone he loved from himself explained a lot. Or maybe not enough. I was unsure. Nonetheless, he had experience in pilfering information, something important to helping Eve.

"You know, access to their Deathlists would make it easier for Reapers to get their assignments," I said, trying to avoid further awkward conversation.

"Sure, but entire lists aren't supposed to go public. If one got into the wrong hands, it would be bad news for humans."

He didn't need to explain further. I was already envisioning a Reaper ticking off his human assignments like he was blazing through a hundred-mile long grocery list to avoid a Level Five or higher Offense. That was another reason why Scriveners were so vital to Styx—they kept Reapers from ferrying too many souls at the wrong time.

Except this time I was trying to prevent a soul from getting ferried at the right time.

"We have to find the Reaper responsible for Eve," Brent said.

"Then what?"

"We keep him from ferrying Eve until she gets her business in order."

"You are willing to risk Erebus to give her some extra time?"

"There's a caveat." The muscles in his forearms rippled with tension. I enjoyed the effect of his nerves on his body, but I had a bad feeling about what he was about to say. "I'll help Eve if *you* help me."

I stared at him. I couldn't stop myself. I should've seen this coming.

"I will do whatever I can to make Eve's last days good ones, but only if you agree to my plans," he said.

Then I laughed. And I hooted until my sides started to tighten.

"Ollie, it's not funny."

Perhaps he needed me to stop, as if my amusement mocked him in some way. What he failed to notice was that while, sure, his suggestion was idiotic, my laughter stemmed from a feeling deep inside of me that was not ridicule, or even fear of his proposition. In fact, I liked the idea, and that scared the shit out of me.

"No," I said.

"Are you sure?"

"Nope."

"You're confusing me."

I wiped tears of amusement from my eyes. "I know."

"Are you okay with this?"

"You're blackmailing me."

"That's a tough word. I'd like to call it exchanging favors."

Nothing in life is free. Brent would risk his neck to help me with my trouble and, in return, I would risk mine to help with his. This proposal would be an easy one if it were as simple as borrowing someone's car in return for doing their laundry. You know, ordinary things.

Brent was talking about bending the rules of Death, ones I had abided by for my entire life. In exchange he wanted to challenge the big guy. Erebus was a very real notion for us if we failed.

And yet. Eve. I couldn't let my part in her fate go. I couldn't ignore the gut-eating remorse. One human should not have had such an effect on me, but she did, and it was too late to let it all fall by the wayside. I cared for her. For that, I owed her.

After clearing my eyes of tears and forcing a smile that Brent undoubtedly saw through, I said with a quiver in my voice, "Seems like a ridiculous plan, going into the Registry Vault."

"I didn't say it was a perfect plan. We can give Eve a chance at something that few humans ever get— the time to say good-bye. That's the best gift we can give her." He had been serious when he said he had a plan. It hadn't been some ploy to get into my bed, which, right then, might've been more appealing. And this plot was, without a doubt, treasonous.

"I don't know," I said when I realized he was awaiting my response. "What if we convinced Eve to get the Deathmark removed? I know of a place. It's called Bad Decisions Tattoo Removal, a couple blocks from here."

"It's a Deathmark. It's not going away because someone puts a laser to it."

I had been tracing filigree on my thighs. My fingertips were warm, so I had to have been doing it for a while. I shook out my hands. "Where is this Registry Vault?"

"Under the city, inside Cape Diamond. It's where Marin does his broadcasting and official work. Calls it Lethe."

"*That's* where Marin is hiding?" I about jumped to my feet but stopped when Brent's face whitened. I continued in a serene but pressing voice. "Brent, the rebels would die to know Marin's hideout. Imagine if they could voice their complaints directly to him instead of posting to some blog or shouting at protests. They'd go straight to the—"

"I thought you didn't want to get involved in a rebellion?"

"I don't," I sniped. "I was speaking of the rebels, not me."

He might've rolled his eyes. I couldn't be sure. "There will come a day when Lethe will be exposed, but not now. Styx isn't ready yet. Neither are you." His biting conviction put an end to my case. "Promise you won't tell anyone about it, not even Ms. Lorelei and Mr. Stone. This is serious. I have to know you will keep mum."

He could depend on me, sure, but how could I keep Lethe secret from my parents? All they had ever wanted was to voice their frustrations to Marin. Knowing where to find him would give them that chance.

"You are serious, aren't you?" I muttered.

"That's why I need you to keep this between us. Mouth shut."

"So we really are gonna be like Batman and Robin," I said.

He raked his fingers through his hair. Chestnut threads fell over his forehead. As I had done so many times with my own hair, I brushed his back from his eyes. Brent looked at me as if I was his long-lost love touching him for the first time. His expression faded quickly when I retracted my hand.

"In Lethe, I'll find the name of Eve's Reaper," he explained. "Then I'll keep whoever it is at bay, at least until Chad and the Watchmen start to notice something is up. You don't have to be involved. I'll go into Lethe alone. Your hands will stay clean."

"No. I want to do this with you. I'll go into Lethe with you." My voice was stern, and though Brent seemed to want to argue further about my involvement, he didn't. Perhaps he knew better.

The room felt like it was closing in around us. Level Ten meant a healthy eternity in Erebus. Sighing, I slouched into the couch cushions. Brent watched every move I made.

"When do we do this?" I asked.

"Tonight."

Perhaps running headlong into danger was better than thinking about it for too long.

"Promise to keep quiet about Lethe." Brent's eyes had turned bright yellow. "There's a reason Marin keeps Lethe secret. Reapers would flock there to bargain for less work on their Lists. Marin won't hear their requests. Death despises bartering."

As I understood it, Death doesn't barter at all. Dead was dead. There was no middle ground. That slice of truth made me uneasy over what we were about to do.

Chapter Eight

*"If we knew from where Death comes,
could we thwart his approach."*

– HermesHarbinger.com, 10:50 pm ET February 27th

"We can't fit in there," I griped when Brent lifted the manhole cover in front of a sleepy apartment building in Old Town. I scanned left and right. No Watchmen were lurking that I could tell. "Can't we go another way?"

"I told you already. We have to go through a drainpipe behind the Château. We can't use the front door like polite folk."

Brent had told me there was an official entrance into Lethe in Québec City's most famous hotel. Le Château Frontenac sat atop Cape Diamond, looming over the Saint Lawrence River like a red brick fortress. When I had asked him why Québec City had been chosen as the entry point for all of humanity into the Afterlife, Brent had answered that Marin was a big fan of Canadian weather, hockey, and maple syrup.

From his pithy description after I had pushed further—because his joke was neither funny nor helpful—I had deduced that the world-renowned hotel sitting atop Cape Diamond was a brick-and-mortar façade to keep humans from spying too deeply into the inner workings of Styx's hidden lair. Québec City, built on top of a three hundred foot escarpment, was the perfect place for Marin to hide out underground and yet move easily in and out of Lethe as he wished. No one would ever suspect Canada to be the gateway to the Underworld. Too nice.

Disappointing really. Since I was a little girl, I had seen the Château as an enchanted castle of a lucky princess. It was magical, but mysterious.

I now wished I didn't know that underneath it the top Grim Reaper was up to things he couldn't share with humans or his lowly Stygians.

Guess that explained why Québec City was the only fortified city in North America—it had something very important to hide.

"Isn't there a safer way to get down there?" I peered into the rabbit hole.

"This is as safe as it's gonna get. If you're not okay, then stay here."

I gave him a hard stare. I barely saw Brent's face in his all-black ninja outfit, save for a sliver of his steely gaze.

"You go first," he said. "I'll be right behind you...er, above you."

"I'll go second. Rather be on top."

"I'll remember that for the bedroom." His voice dripped

with suggestions of things we had no business pursuing here in the middle of Old Town. "You're not strong enough to pull the drain lid back."

"But if we do that we might have trouble getting out if they come after us."

"We're not coming back this way."

"How are we getting out?" I asked.

"There's a tributary from Lethe that empties into the Saint Lawrence. We'll swim out."

I wouldn't faint. I wouldn't be *that* woman. "Brent, swimming isn't my thing."

He almost dropped the manhole cover to catch me if I collapsed. Oddly, I preferred the idea of him wrapping his arms around me and carrying me home instead of whatever hell we were about to enter into… Just as long as Papa and Mama didn't make a surprise visit, of course.

"I'm a fine swimmer. I'll help you," he soothed.

This was bad. A narrow tunnel? An exit we would have to swim out of? Why had I insisted on going with him? I should have left the expert to his job. I should have told him this was stupid. "That's why we have these goggles?" was the best I came up with.

He patted his pocket where he had stuffed a Ziploc bag, triple-checking that it was there. "We have to keep the name of Eve's Reaper in this bag. Wouldn't do us any good if it got wet and the ink bled."

"We can't recall one stinking name?"

I think he grinned, but I couldn't see his mouth, only the squint of his eyes. "We're going into Lethe."

"So?"

"You don't know your Stygian history, do you?"

"You've never been given a purple nurple have you?" I hissed.

"Ollie, Lethe is the Realm of Forgetfulness. We won't remember anything that happens in there after we leave. Sort of like Las Vegas. What happens in Lethe stays in Lethe…in a manner of speaking."

"Won't we forget everything about our lives?" I should've asked this sooner.

"No, only what happens *in* Lethe." He smirked as I struggled to articulate a smartass comeback. "Relax, kitten. Forgetting what happens isn't nearly as bad as the free fall we'll take to get out of Lethe."

"F-free fall?" Suddenly all I wanted to do was grab his hand and run like mad back to my apartment. There are levels of bad choices. Riding cowgirl on a sexy Eidolon was a less severe choice over free falling out of the underground lair of the king of death.

My thoughts went right back to Eve's face as I worked the skull into her arm. She had spent the entire sitting holding back tears so she wouldn't appear weak, or ungrateful for her birthday gift.

Fear of heights, or of dying with my head up Brent's ass if he slipped on the ladder, would not matter if I didn't try to do what I knew was right. So, I pulled the goggles over my eyes, casting my vision into shades of gray.

I would do it.

For Eve's chance to say good-bye with dignity to her mother.

I climbed onto the metal ladder that led into the vertical tunnel, and descended into a darkness heavy with the stink of mold. The rungs were icy. My heart thumped. My hands shook so badly I was forced to grip the rungs tighter. If I could have felt my legs, I was sure they, too, were quivering. But somehow, some way, I climbed down.

"How much further?" I whispered after a couple minutes of steady descent.

"Twenty feet."

"Then what?"

"I don't remember." His chuckle echoed.

"Son of a bitch." My heartbeat counted the seconds until my feet hit the floor.

Brent was right. Twenty feet.

Thank Hades and all his ladies.

I stepped off the ladder and looked around, my headlamp swinging back and forth. I was in a tunnel carved out of bedrock. Wide enough for one body, it went in only one direction. The stone was smooth and shiny.

Water dripped between crevices, trickling into a rivulet in the center of the tunnel. I knew who would be going first through this mine of stone—me—because I was not about to follow with my head up Brent's Moonpie.

"That wasn't too bad, was it?" He wedged himself next to me. Had we been lovers, the closeness would have been tantalizing, but ringing in the back of my head was Papa's warning. Papa had been right about all the other Reapers I had dated. I couldn't help but wonder if he was right about Brent, too. But the other question that I had been asking myself was, what if Brent *wasn't* like the others?

"We're halfway there," Brent said.

"Let's go then." I figured I had roughly ten minutes left before I self-destructed.

He clapped a hand on my shoulder. "Not that way."

I looked behind him, where there was nothing but a wall of bedrock. "What other way are we—"

His eyes bled into the piercing rubies I remembered from my apartment. That would've been okay had I not watched his body give way to his demonic shadow. The sight of his darkness punctuated by blood red specks drained the breath from me. And too soon icy fingers enveloped me in a bear hug. I stared down an Eidolon, and he was not as playful as his humanoid counterpart.

"What are you doing?"

"What you can't," his dark alter-ego rumbled. "Trust me."

When a gelatinous weight pressed against me, I tensed. He lifted me up. Pain like a fever saturated my bones. My teeth chattered so violently they risked cracking when I exploded into convulsions.

This was not how I imagined my first bodily encounter with a sexy lumberjack would be. Who would?

Nevertheless, Brent had said to trust him. I did. I had to. Whatever he was doing, I had no expectation of fighting him off. I was his whether I trusted him or not. So, I burrowed within myself, thinking of tranquility, of Dudley fetching his favorite tennis ball in the park across from my apartment.

Breath returned as fast as it had left. Wintriness evaporated, and I was warm again. I opened my eyes to see that the man, not the apparition, knelt at my side.

"Welcome to Lethe. Try the veal," Brent said.

We were in the tunnel. Behind me there was a wall of rock like the one that had been behind Brent. The tunnel ahead of us looked exactly the same, except that...

"We're facing a different direction. What did you do?"

"It's an Eidolon trick. Half-death. I possessed you so I could ferry you through the rock." He flicked on his head-lamp and pulled a small leather booklet from his pocket, re-moved it carefully from a plastic sleeve, and flipped through the pages until he came upon a hand drawn map. "Not ex-actly how I wanted to get inside your g-string, but I'll take it."

If he knew the g-string had green polka dots, I would have to kill him.

"That's *all* we needed to do to get into Lethe?"

"Sure, because ferrying you through thirty feet of solid bedrock is really not that complicated. Try it some time."

I resisted when he pushed me forward. "Couldn't hu-mans drill through it?"

"They've tried."

"What happened?"

"Sudden mine collapse. No survivors. Catch my drift?"

I caught it. And I shuddered.

"What's that?" I pointed to the booklet.

He was quick to slap it shut, put it back inside the plastic, and tuck it in his pocket. "It's a map of Lethe that I drew up ages ago. Now let's get moving." He scooted aside and swept a hand out toward the passageway. "Crawl until you reach the third metal grill."

I rolled onto my hands and knees without a lick of grace then twisted to face the tunnel. With Brent's face and head-lamp right up my girly bits, I crawled. Oddly, Brent's proxim-ity I could handle.

Heights and water? Not so much.

I slowed to gaze down the narrow shaft after clearing several feet. There was no light except for my headlamp sweeping back and forth. How far would we crawl? Would we creep into a trap?

For the second time, Brent rammed my derriere with his headlamp. This wouldn't have been an issue if he didn't have the forward momentum of a buffalo.

"I assumed the first time was an accident. Now, you're getting personal, Hume."

"*You're* too slow."

Had I been on wheels strapped to a jet pack I couldn't have crawled faster. I kicked, catching his shoulder with my boot heel. "Back off."

"Go faster."

"I can't."

There was silence and then a strained, "I hate this part."

I came to a full stop, inviting his headlamp to ram my backside again. It did.

"Is there something I should know about?"

"I don't like enclosed spaces," he quietly confessed.

Hold the phone. The Eidolon is claustrophobic?

He palmed my buttocks. "Go, before I flip out."

I feared heights. Brent feared enclosed spaces. We should have disclosed our list of phobias before we crawled into a three-by-three tunnel to hell. But after several more minutes of knee and elbow scurrying, I spotted slivers of pale light through a ventilation grill.

I flattened onto my belly and used my elbows to drag myself to the grill. A whiff of that familiar aroma of death—sickly-sweet with a hint of musk—crept through metal slats.

Below us there was a hallway like any hotel hallway. Damask wallpaper and carpet scrolled with green and rose tulips adorned the walls and floor respectively. *This* was

Lethe?

A black shape popped into view and ruined any thoughts of taking a vacation here. I recoiled and collided with Brent. My buttocks crashed into his triumvirate of man bits. What a lovely way to introduce our privates.

Someway the Eidolon had maneuvered himself above me without me feeling him and gazed down through the grate. I wasn't sure what intrigued me more—Brent's skills or the spirit below, wandering aimlessly through a hallway inside the underground portal to the Afterlife. At least Brent was alive.

"Is it a human soul?" I said, not bothering to ask why Brent covered me like a Reaper-blanket. Later. Later I would ask…if I remembered.

"Yeah, human," he whispered into my ear. "They spend time in Lethe, forgetting their lives, until they're fully crossed over."

The ghost stopped in its directionless route and looked toward us. Brent yanked me back. Our limbs entangled into an erogenous jumble. Had I let him put me over the back of the couch and dishonor me however he wanted, would it have been anything like this?

I waited until the ghost carried on then asked, with Brent's better bits pressed to mine, "How long do they stay here?"

He gave a shift of his hips, a gratuitous but very nice gesture, and he said, "For as long as it takes for them to forget. Be quiet. The Vaults are two more vents ahead."

I thought to ask what the next vent would reveal. I saved my words, and I climbed out from our leg-and-arm pretzel to stealthily scuttle toward the next grate. After several minutes I came to our second destination. I paused, took a breath, and looked.

I wished I hadn't.

The lost soul looking to erase his or her memory was as sweet as running into Mickey Mouse in a haunted house. The creature I now stared down on was far less cuddly-cute. It gave a resonant growl that vibrated the air duct.

Grasping his collar, I put my lips against Brent's ear, not caring how he interpreted it. "W-What the hell is it?"

"A sentinel. Don't stop." He nudged me forward. "They smell fear."

The sentinel had an elongated face with fangs protruding from its jaws. But the body was a skeleton of an overgrown dog. Ribbons of fur clung to its bones. The monster glowed with an unknown light source, and I didn't plan to hang around to it figure out. It released another growl. I shuffled onward, ignoring how my knees protested. Brent was closer to my backside than before.

Our escape took far too long, as I imagined that sentinel climbing into the air duct after us. Then a whiff of stale paper wafted through the third vent—our destination. The Registry Vault was beneath us. I looked through, praying to Hades I wouldn't spy a hairy dog skeleton there.

Droplets of water trickled from the grate. The view didn't indicate the room's size, but I saw walls packed full of wooden cases with words on the front of each drawer. And no monster.

I put my hands on the opposite side of the grill and crawled over it, careful not to touch the metal or make a sound.

"It looks like a giant card catalogue," I said.

Lines of soft light washed over what I could see of Brent's face. "Sort of is."

The Head Reaper and his closest confidants didn't bother converting their paper files to electronic ones.

"This place looks exactly as it did in 1910," he said.

"Reapers don't tend to redecorate."

"Guess not. The cases were falling apart when I was here. Such a pain to—"

"What now?" I wasn't interested in listening to Old Man Hume reminisce.

"See those wood cabinets?" He pointed to several lined up along a wall. They looked as rotted and timeworn as Greek antiquities. "Gotta find Eve's name in the catalog. Then we cross-reference it with the Reaper's list to be sure we got the right one."

That sounded peachy. But I had no intention of moving.

He curled his fingers around the grill, pulled it free, and handed it to me. Like an upside-down gopher in black goggles, he lowered his head, checked the scene, then snapped back. "You first."

I handed the grill back. "When hell freezes over. *You* first."

Grumbling, he dumped it and proceeded to unfurl inside the tunnel, which for a six-foot-five giant was no small feat. He wasn't elegant, especially not after getting his right knee wedged on the lip of the ventilation hole. *This* was why he didn't like small spaces.

I stifled laughter as he slipped headfirst through the hole and did some kind of acrobatic twist. He hit the flagstone floor with both feet, crouched like the ninja he resembled. That performance quieted my amusement with admiration.

He might have been apprehensive above in the cramped tunnel, but now he was on the alert as he scanned the room he'd once known. With a wriggle of his finger, he said it was my turn to do a nimble twirl from the ceiling.

I lowered my feet until I felt something squishy. A glimpse down. My boot squashed his cheek.

Good, he had me.

I pulled my torso out of the vent as best I could as his hands caught my calves. They slid up my thighs, stopping short of my hips. He was helping, but somehow his touch felt sensuous when it should have been all business. I lowered tentatively into his grasp until I was stretched out with my hands on the rim of the ventilation hole.

"Let go," he whispered.

Boy, I wanted to, until I looked down another four feet. I was about to give a protest, maybe a slur of dirty words, when he gave a tug. I was going down whether I wanted to or not. My hands slipped as his arms coiled around my waist. Brent had proven he had some slick moves, so it wasn't any shock when his arms slackened, and I found myself feeling every muscle and bulge as I rode down the length of his body.

The fact he had half-deathed me through a secret entrance and we were in the middle of the underground vaults of the hostile Head Reaper home base had no effect on the fact that every time we touched, there was more to it than breaking and entering. Too bad I wouldn't remember any of it.

When my feet planted on the floor, my knees buckled. He caught me before I crumpled.

Lit by oil lamps tacked on the walls, the domed room

was lined with carvings of skulls in the polished stone. Skulls were fitting. We *were* in a library crammed with stacks upon stacks of Deathlists.

However, why the room wasn't packed with Watchmen was beyond me. I didn't pause to ask. All we needed was Eve's Reaper and to make our way to that damn free fall of an exit.

Brent put his mouth to my ear, his breath hot against my flesh. "Remember the plan. Stand guard."

Right. Standing guard I could do while rubbing the Eidolon-induced goose bumps from my arms. I looked back and forth, then turned to him and nodded. There wasn't much I could do if a Watchman or those ghost-white sentinels came to have a chat.

Ten of the longest minutes of my life crept by. The raised hairs on my arms tingled. Every possible danger raced through my mind. Would we get caught? Would I trip and knock down the entire Vault of Reaper lists? Was there a ladies' room nearby?

Someone tapped my shoulder. I jumped a foot in the air and then breathed in relief when I saw the tall man in black with my boot print on his cheek.

"Eve's guy is in section B." Above the card catalogues, twice as tall as Brent, hung wood signs with letters burned into them. Section B was halfway across the room, underneath a skull chandelier. How swanky.

His hand gripped mine as he dragged me toward a wall of cases. We passed through one row, then another. Brent's headlamp flashed across the square drawers marked with surnames. *Bainbridge. Baines.* He slowed. *Bains. Bainter.* He dove for a low drawer. *Baird.* The index cards clicked when he yanked the drawer open. Dust attacked my nose. I scratched it to keep from sneezing. I would not get caught because of an allergy.

Brent's fingers danced over the cards with lightning speed, so I did another sweep of our surroundings. Something about the stillness didn't feel right. I looked down as he ripped out a certificate, scribbled two words on our notecard, stuffed the paper inside the Ziploc bag, and slipped it underneath his shirt.

"Who is her Reaper?" I asked.

"Nicholas Baird."

He replaced the certificate. The drawer slammed shut with a kick of his foot. He straightened, returning to his towering height. I whirled toward the ventilation hole but he cupped my wrist. Every hard muscle of his pressed against my backside when he pulled me close.

"Not that way."

We made a hard left at the end of the cases and down two more rows, further into the middle of the room. I looked up to the wooden sign above us. Section H. Lovely. I should've assumed Brent would want to peek at his list, too.

Had I slightly more guts, I might have asked him to find my Reaper.

When we reached the drawer for *Hume*, he zipped through the cards, plucked his Deathlist, slipped the whole certificate into the Ziploc baggie, and tucked it back under his shirt with well-rehearsed precision.

"You said not to take the whole List," I said. "Jot the names down."

"No time."

"They'll come after you if—"

He put a finger to my lips. I stilled. There were determined footsteps off in the distance. The red dots of his eyes behind his goggles broadened. We had no need to verbally exchange words. Brent bolted upright. We took off through the labyrinth of bookcases.

"Over there," shouted a foreboding voice that surely belonged to a five-by-five brick house of a Watchman.

My heart was between my throat and eyes. Just as I was about to break from Brent's grip and head back to the ventilation exit, we came upon another grating in the floor. The faint sound of rushing water beckoned. *This* was our way out?

Brent grabbed the lattice and yanked. "Shit."

"What?"

"It's welded shut. Used to be loose." His brow creased from his straining.

"Then half-death us through it." I was okay with the idea. No problem. I'd even let him see my panties. Hell, he could sniff them if he got us out of here.

"Can only do it to get into Lethe. Getting out is different." He bared his teeth and pulled again.

"You're not trying hard enough."

He glared up from under his rumpled brow. "I could lift a backhoe with this grip."

"They're by the drain," shouted a Watchman.

Now was not the time to panic, but I never lived by anybody's schedule. I shoved Brent aside and dove for the grate. Maybe all it needed was a fresh set of hands to haul the steel blockade free. I put in my best effort.

Brent sat back on his heels. "Told you."

"Don't sit there. Help."

The advancing footsteps grew louder.

"You and your polka dot g-string seem to have it handled."

"You motherfucker. You *looked*?" But at least they were my cute panties.

"I'd be an idiot not to," he snickered.

"I'm going to—" Smoke called my attention to my hands, melting the obstruction. A breath later, the barrier was gone, dripping glutinous metal down into another void.

"I've got them," shouted a Watchman at the end of the aisle.

"Go. Go." Brent practically threw me down the hole.

Astonished because I hadn't considered using my heat to my own advantage, and aggravated I didn't have time to delight in the discovery because the brick house was practically on top of us, I dropped into the darkness, not knowing where I was going or if this was the free fall or if it was still to come.

At the bottom, I found myself inside another tunnel with two feet of moving water tugging at my legs. A deafening roar gave away a waterfall. Dread superseded the urge to get away. I looked, intent on climbing back up the ladder, when Brent cleared the last rung. Flashlight beams swung over us.

As my fingers found their way around the ladder's rungs, Brent pulled on me. I collapsed into blubbery defeat, screaming and going limp in his arms to foil his effort to get me into the water. He pulled me close so I couldn't fill my lungs for another shriek before we were no longer standing in the waters flowing through Lethe, but plummeting with them over the precipice of an underground waterfall.

Chapter Nine

"The hypothalamus is one of the most important parts of the brain, involved in many kinds of motivation, among other functions. The hypothalamus controls the "Four F's": fighting, fleeing, feeding, and mating."

—Marvin Dunnette

Not a single word passed between us, from the moment we smacked through the water's surface on the Saint Lawrence River, to when we stumbled, dripping wet, into my apartment. There was nothing to discuss because, as Brent had promised, we could not remember anything after reaching the bottom of the manhole beneath the Château. Besides, stopping to debate whatever we thought had happened, soaked as we were, was not possible. Québec. Winter. Enough said.

However, we must've gone through Lethe. The last I remembered was fixing to scoot through a tunnel before Brent turned into his wraithlike self. Nothing, not the pounding of our feet on the pavement from the sprint to my apartment had loosened the remainder of the experience. Nothing but an abyss remained. How eerie that I had gone through the portal to the Afterlife and couldn't recall anything about it.

After cranking the heat in my apartment and flicking on the lights, and most certainly after I gave Dudley a warm greeting, I looked at my co-conspirator. His mask and goggles were gone, he was shivering, and, for some reason, he had a size-seven muddy boot print on his cheek.

"What ha-happened?" I asked through chattering teeth.

"Not sure, but it was a ride."

We convened around a piping hot radiator in my living room. The temptation to sit on it and warm my buns was there, but I resisted. What was impossible to resist was standing side by side with Brent without touching. And the more we sought warmth, the closer we became. Too soon we were all but hugging in effort to regain our body heat.

Had he suggested removing our clothes, I would not have partaken. I would have liked to know what the rebel Brent Hume was like in the bedroom, but not right before Lethe, in Lethe, or after Lethe, and certainly not standing over a radiator, shivering ourselves silly.

My clicking teeth slowed as the radiator, and Brent's body heat, melted a layer of ice on my clothing. "Did you… you get the Reaper's name?"

He pulled down the collar of his shirt to expose a white notecard inside a plastic bag. A name was scribbled on it, but from what I could see the writing had bled. Brent noticed a second after me.

"Mother fucker," he groused. "The ink got wet."

"Of course it did." It was too much energy to roll my eyes. For now, I needed heat. Lots and lots of heat.

He held the baggie up to the overhead light. "I see a name. Baird."

"Is that a last name or first? Is it a male or female? Who is it?" My shivering worsened my panic, which in turn worsened my shivering. "We did this all for nothing, didn't we? Didn't we?"

"Good Hades, calm down, Scrivener." He turned from me when I tried to get a peek at the name through the soggy baggie. Not one to take such an obvious cue to give him space, I went for it, using my own shivering to launch into the air. Quick as he was, he underestimated my determination. The baggie was in my hands before my feet touched the floor. Being short and swift was a fine offense against tall and slow.

"Hey!" he barked.

"It says Baird. It's a last name." I ducked when he reached around my shoulders, thwarting his effort to retrieve the baggie. "But I can't read the first name. No knowing if it is a guy or gal."

"Give it back." Brent refused to continue reaching for the prize, as if little ol' Olivia outplaying him was an affront to his ego.

"I don't know a Baird," I said.

"Neither do I. This means I can't just look the Reaper up and distract him or her like I had planned."

"So I was right?" I dropped my arms to my sides as we faced each other, Brent looking as bewildered and broken as I felt.

"Seems so."

I sighed to keep from breaking into tears. My shoulders and head felt heavy. The couch seemed a great place to throw myself down and let my emotions pour out. I would've found out, if Brent didn't rush at me and grab the baggie. There was only a small glimpse of his wicked smile before we found ourselves entangled, both vying for the prize. A moment after, I found out what it would be like to collapse onto the couch, only with the Eidolon, too, falling over top of me. The springs of the beast cringed from our weight.

Thoughts of Eve and the name Baird flitted away in exchange for one very real thing hovering above me.

I grew tense but hopeful when his eyes turned to my lips. I knew what that meant. Every woman did. However selfish and grossly out of place it was, I was okay with one kiss, more curious than frightened to discover what it was like to kiss an Eidolon who could drain my life. Perhaps my motivation was to ridicule Fate by kissing the lips of Death himself. Or maybe I was cold, tired, and downright horny.

"Brent, we should not—"

His mouth covered mine. I lost myself for a moment, forgetting how to kiss back. Even if I'd wanted it, I hadn't expected him to follow through so brazenly.

But when his tongue grazed my closed teeth, that sphere of bliss in my center dropped down between my legs. My body begged me to give in, to let him have his way.

I dug my fingernails into his back. He growled and the sound vibrated my chest. I smiled a smile he couldn't see before returning his kiss with twice the vigor. Our teeth scraped as I enjoyed his sweet spice. I had to feel every movement of his jaw and lips and tongue with my own.

He overpowered me. Not by strength, but with a carnality that had me begging him not to stop, like I could enfold myself within his kiss forever. Pawing at his back, I pressed my breasts against him, inviting him to feel the rest of me if he wanted.

But he jerked away, and I snapped my eyes open.

"What?" Sensuality drained through my toes.

"I can't," he said, and quickly backed away.

Everything upsetting and wicked—like Eve and her Reaper—that I left behind just a second ago returned like a flood. Full as I felt with renewed grief, I still deflated when Brent stood to his full height. In one hand was the baggie with the card "Baird" written on it. With the other hand he raked his fingers through his wet hair.

He glanced from side to side, looking for something or simply trying to avoid looking at me. "I'll go back and get the name again. Sit tight. I shouldn't be long."

"Wait." I sat up. "Won't security in Lethe be tighter now?"

Brent was already at the apartment door. "I'm crafty. Don't worry."

"Are you crazy?"

His back was to me as he said, "It *was* wrong. This is business. Nothing more."

With that, he left, and I felt heat from my inner radiator, the hotness that had gotten me into trouble to begin with, swell within me. Suddenly, I was too hot with rage to be cold any longer.

"Our security cameras show that last night, two accomplices absconded with an undisclosed Deathlist from Reaper Head-quarters. Anyone who knows of the whereabouts of these two Stygians and does not report them will be prosecuted with a

Level Ten Offense for withholding information. I say to these accomplices, turn yourselves into Headquarters immediately for merciful justice."

Gerard and I sat inside of the tattoo shop, listening to Marin's biting podcast. The missing Deathlist came after a whole list of troublesome news for Styx. That morning, humans had announced a possible cure for heart disease, one of our most frequently used causes of death. But worse was the census report. The human population welcomed its seventh billionth member into the world last night.

"Might I remind everyone that tampering with the workings of Death is an offense worthy of eternal punishment in Erebus? It would behoove you to do as you're instructed. Do not deviate."

Despite the reasons everyone in Styx should be having one massive coronary, the only thing that boiled my blood was the Deathlist. Brent and I had agreed to write down the name of Eve's Reaper—Baird was all I knew—instead of pilfering the entire list, so as to leave no trace of our presence. Brent must have taken the list, perhaps even his own. There was no sneaking around with a missing list. The Deliveryman would know.

Whatever Brent wanted with his own Deathlist, assuming his was the one he took, it didn't mean anything to me. Not only had he reminded me how lonely I was by kissing me and then telling me it was wrong, he'd conned me into becoming a fugitive. It was only a matter of time before they found out who broke into the Registry Vaults.

I was, by my own stupid mistake, a rebel, and I was fucked for it.

The only consolation was that Brent wasn't captured, a

concern I had, since he had never returned.

"When you eventually surface, Hume," I grunted under my breath, "I'm going to kill you. Resurrect you. And then kill you again. That's what I'll do."

Someone tapped my shoulder.

I jumped. "I didn't take it!"

"Look busy. Charming Chadwick is back for more." Gerard didn't skip a beat.

Over my shoulder, I spotted Chad stomping out his cigarette outside of the shop. Fortune would be a kind goddess if she gave me some confidence so I wouldn't inadvertently confess my crimes to the creeper Eidolon. I'd have to be cool and continuously remind myself that Chad had followed me home and tried to attack me. We had history, and I was not about to give in to him like I had to Brent.

On my swivel chair, I rolled over to my station and fished my gear out of my backpack. It was Tuesday. Eve and her Reaper could have their fateful meeting at any moment. And Brent was probably halfway across North America by now, doing Hades knows what with the stolen property.

"Scrivies," said Chad as he glided into the shop. "You better be ready for some Deathmarks today. Head Reaper is in a foul mood."

"We can't go out and solicit Deathmarks," Gerard said, and it was the first time I heard him talk back to the Eidolon.

"Indeed, Gerry. I made sure that *Salon de Tatuoage* will be busy today."

"Did you do it by convincing everyone you saw to ask for pinups and skulls?" I hissed from my workstation.

"Exactly how I coerced your girlfriend to come here, yes, indeed." Chad's cigarette breath carried across the studio.

The stink was sickening. I was in no mood for smelly work conditions or this SOB scrutinizing our work.

"You're not supposed to interfere with the process," I said through my teeth.

"Silly Scrivie, what little you know."

For a moment, I saw him in my mind's eye with a Death-mark right in the middle of his forehead. It was a small tattoo, nothing impressive, but it was there and triumphant. Imagined victory must've been written in my expression because Chad's eyes flashed red to wrench me back from my fantasy.

"Rest assured, Eidolon," I growled before the image faded entirely, "you won't get any Master work out of either of us today, unless you want a pinup or skull on that butt-ugly face of yours."

Gerard was at the counter before I suggested a better place to put a Deathmark. "Ollie, don't argue."

"Am I supposed to let this fucker follow me home and harass me, too, Ger?" I was standing, but I didn't feel my legs. I felt nothing except the desire for everyone to leave me the hell alone—Brent, Chad, Head Reaper Marin.

"What are you talking about?" Gerard glanced between Chad and me.

"This champ harassed me after work the other night and then broke into my apartment." Chad's eyes turned red at my challenge and I grew confident. My hands matched his gaze. They were ready to do something—burn him or slap a Death-mark across his horrid mug. I would risk Erebus to show him I was not afraid. "Does the Head Reaper approve of bullying?"

"Ollie!" Gerard glared at me.

I hid my red hands behind my back. "Sorry. I'm having a bad week."

"No shit." He put a hand on my shoulder. "Go home. You can't do good work if you're unfocused."

My cheeks felt as hot as my hands as I held gazes with the Eidolon.

"Chad, excuse us, please." Gerard steered me toward the back room as Chad remained lingering in the shop, seething from my insubordination. I was tempted to put my fist in his jaw but stopped when Gerard wrenched me into his office.

"You have *got* to watch yourself," he whispered.

"He set Eve up. He is going to stick around until he catches me doing something, and you know it. I can't win, so I'm going to fight back even if it destroys me." My eyes were gritty, my hands red hot. Parts of me felt like they'd erupt or detonate with one more push from an outside aggressor. I did not fear anyone but myself at present.

Gerard's nostrils flared. "Take the day off. Go visit Eve. Say your good-byes and then make peace with it."

I wanted to go against the rules Brent and I had agreed to and tell Gerard everything—about the Registry Vault, the Deathlist, Brent's affection—but if I spoke, I would have burst into sobs. I wouldn't let Gerard see tears stream down my cheeks. He wasn't the type who knew what to do when someone cried, not even when his male clients sobbed during a tattoo session.

"Come back to the studio when you've cleared your head, kid." Gerard patted my shoulder again and stepped out of the room.

I listened to him smoothing things over with Chad before I took his advice. I slipped out the back door of the studio, leaving my tattoo machine and backpack behind. I would find Eve, and I would prepare for the worst.

Chapter Ten

"Congratulations, Stygians. The blog has reached a million hits in only four months' time. The voice of the stifled is mounting. Their murmurs are stirring the rebel fiend."

—HermesHarbinger.com, 2:30 pm 4 April.

15 APRIL

When I arrived at Eve's familiar, dilapidated apartment building in Saint-Roch, I started to push the buzzer for apartment 4B but put the moment on pause.

On the walk to her apartment, I had toiled with what to say, what to do, or if I should, in a roundabout way, tell her how much she meant to me, as our final good-bye. Everything from admitting that I was a Scrivener from the world of Styx to a simple hug went through my mind. Nothing felt sufficient. The only option was that I wouldn't let her die alone.

With a deep breath, I pressed buzzer 4B.

"*Oui*?" she called through the speaker after a few seconds.

"Eve, it's Ollie. I thought I'd come by after work to see how your Death—I mean, tattoo is healing. Can I come up?" I checked behind me. A row of streetlamps spotlighted parked cars and leafless trees. No Watchmen or Eidolons in sight.

Everything was tranquil—dissonantly so. I pressed my hands against my queasy stomach. I carried the same unsettled feeling as a child tucked away under a bed during a game of hide-and-go-seek. Only the stakes were higher than any childhood game I ever played.

The buzz and unlatching of the building's main door were a relief. I skipped several stairs until I reached the fourth floor. Barefoot and in a pair of jeans and a white tee shirt, Eve stood in the doorway to her apartment.

Fear zipped through me as I drew closer to my friend. She was pale, her eyes sunken.

"Mom won't get to see it healed if it keeps getting worse." Eve pulled her sleeve down over her viciously inflamed Deathmark and sank into the brown couch pillows. With brown bookcases, a tan rug, and auburn wood floors, Eve lived inside a chocolate truffle.

Inside her apartment, with lavender incense burning and Bad Religion playing in the background, it could've been so easy to pretend that this was just a sleepover between girlfriends and not a chance for me to delay her approaching death. My plan was to linger for as long as possible without appearing odd. I couldn't stop her from dying tonight or tomorrow, but I could be there as friend, to be by her side when it happened.

"Is there anything else I can do for it?" she asked about her tattoo, pulling me back to her reality.

My face hot with shame, I sat across from her, cradling a mug of coffee. She made it like she had at Le Nektar—only the whipped cream had melted into globs, and the coffee was lukewarm because I hadn't touched it in over an hour. "Some tattoos take longer to heal." *Some Deathmarks take longer to work, too.*

"As long as it does before Saturday." Eve balanced her elbows on her knees. A strand of blond hair fell over her brow. "Since you're here, Ollie, want to hang out and watch movies or gossip? Did you go out with that lumbersexual from the other day? Tell me details."

I was happy to accept her invitation. We had shared a few nights curled up on her couch talking about various patrons of Le Nektar. One last night doing what had helped build our friendship seemed fitting. "I don't kiss and tell, and you know it. But I'd love to hang out. Might even have to crash on your couch if it gets late."

"Right on! A sleepover," she said with a brimming smile.

I tried to mimic her glee.

"Remy and his friend, Nick, are coming over, too. The more the merrier, right?" She rose from the couch with renewed verve. "I'll get some blankets. You can crash on the couch."

When she vanished into her bedroom, I sank into the cushions. Here I was, with just a flimsy plan, and I hadn't accounted for Remy and his friend. There was precious little

I could do to save her if she suffered a massive coronary tonight. My plan was to protect from an outside threat—fire, electrocution, drug overdose, stumbling onto a kitchen knife.

I exhaled deeply until every molecule of oxygen drained from my body. My hands began tracing furious circles on my thighs, begging me to bail out.

"You can do this, Ollie," I rallied. "You're strong. You can—"

The doorbell rang.

There was a clamor from the back of the apartment before Eve rushed to the door and pressed the button to give her visitors access to the building. The pounding of boots grew louder and louder. She wrenched the door open and greeted Remy with a kiss. A tall, dark-haired companion followed Eve's boyfriend into the apartment.

"Well, there she is. The tattooist." Metal chains hanging from his pants' pockets, Remy strutted across the living room to shake my hand. "Nice to see you again."

"You too, Remy," I said.

"Ollie stopped by to check on my tattoo. I invited her to stay and hang out with us." Eve put her arm around me, as close friends do. "This is Remy's friend Nick. They met at a music festival last month."

Nick stepped around the coffee table to shake my hand. His grip nearly crushed the bones in my fingers. When his black eyes raked me from top to bottom, my blood ran cold. I recognized his expression—I'd seen the same one on the thugs who traveled Québec streets late at night. This guy was not the charming soul that Remy appeared to be.

"Nick, she's the tattooist who did my Day of the Dead

skull," Eve explained.

I felt for the ZZ Top belt buckle around my middle. Brent had left it behind last night after he abruptly left my apartment. I'd had to wrap his belt twice around my waist. No matter how irritated I was with how he betrayed my trust by running off last night, his belt was the only thing holding me together.

"Would you and Nick like to rent us some videos for tonight?" Eve nudged her boyfriend's side.

Nick gave her a cutting look. "Let's go down to the corner store and grab drinks first."

"It's late, and Eve isn't feeling well. Why don't you and I go, Nick?" Remy said after Eve started for her shoes and jacket.

Nick squared his shoulders. "They can watch for any trouble."

"What trouble?" I said before I could stop myself.

"Nothing you need to worry your pretty head about," Nick mocked.

Whatever trouble Eve and I were supposed to watch out for down at the corner liquor store, he wouldn't divulge. I had a good enough imagination to put together a few ideas, however, none of which I liked. I had agreed to stay by Eve's side. I would, even if going out into the night seemed to be the worst of options.

"What are we doing?" I asked Eve the second Nick and Remy vanished into the liquor store.

"We do this all the time." She never once looked at

me; she kept her attention locked on the empty dark street. Apartment buildings and corner stores surrounded us. The air was humid and icy, burning my lungs with each breath.

"What do you *do* exactly?" I nudged.

"It's not a big deal, you know. It's slightly criminal. Not like we're stealing Rolexes." Eve's attention drifted to her boot toes.

"Remy doesn't seem the type. Neither do you." I peered into the liquor store. Remy and Nick were at the register with their arms flailing and the clerk shouting at them. I wondered what it was they were arguing about. Eve, on the other hand, kept her eyes on her boots.

"This is Nick's thing, not ours." She lifted her head when the voices inside of the store grew louder.

"Do they usually argue with the clerk?" I put my face closer to the window, spying. Eve lost interest in her toes and followed my lead. She pressed her nose against the glass, too.

"Does the clerk usually get his gun?" I asked with a warble in my tone.

Her eyes were wider than I had ever seen, enough warning for me to grab her hand and run for safety, either in her apartment or some alcove far away from Remy, Nick, or the pissed off and heavily armed sales clerk. Eve squeezed my hand tightly as we crossed the street.

The pops of a fired handgun made us squeal. Our pace quickened.

From over my shoulder, I saw the liquor store door fling open and Remy and Nick spill out, dodging bullets. A heavy-set man in a green parka aimed his gun at us and fired again. With Eve's hand in mine, we ran. But all too quickly the men passed us by, their legs longer and their gait more generous.

"Goddamn kids!" shouted the clerk. Having been provoked enough to pull out his gun and make his point, I was sure he'd call the police.

Remy and Nick had already disappeared into a dark side street lined with homes and a canopy of trees. They whispered from the darkness "over here" and "come on." I pulled on Eve's hand, intending to vanish into the darkness with Remy and Nick. She resisted.

"Eve, come on," I urged. "Let's just get someplace safe."

She did not reply. With how hard we had been running, I didn't expect her to hold a deep conversation. Still, I slowed and looked behind me to see the nightmare I had been trying to avoid since earlier this week.

"What is it?" I screamed as I stared into the pale face of my human friend.

"I think…" She wheezed, "I think he got me."

I threw my arms around her and felt her back. Patting up and down, I felt nothing of consequence. However, adrenaline had a way of masking the truth.

"Is it bad?" she asked, her chin braced against my shoulder.

Just about to tell her she was fine and likely just winded, I paused on a spot on the left side of her spine. Part of my training as a tattooist and a Scrivener was to learn human anatomy. My heart, which pounded fiercely in my ears, slowed and slowed as the realization came crashing down upon me in the middle of a dark Québec City street at eleven in the evening.

Here was where it would happen.

Here was where Eve would die.

"Is it bad, Ollie?" she whispered again. Her breathing was shallow. As I chose to turn my inspection of her back into a hug, her body gradually began to sag in my arms.

"It's okay," I said, choking back tears. "You're going to be fine."

"You're lying." She tried to make that a joke.

I laughed. I had to.

"Eve, I'm sorry. So damn sorry."

"Eve!" shouted Remy. His boots on the pavement were like timpani drums against the syncopated rhythm of Eve's broken breaths. "Oh, my God."

My friend was wrenched from my arms. She collapsed when Remy took her from me. He did his best to keep her from falling to the cold asphalt, but his effort was for nothing. She was fading, quickly.

"Eve, baby! Eve!" Remy scooped her upper body into his arms and cradled her. He inspected his hand after he had touched her wound. Blood dripped from his fingers.

"Call the medics!" Remy screamed at me.

In some way, I was watching a movie—a fucking tear-jerker—as I stood above Remy and Eve's last moments together. I should have called an ambulance because that was the right thing to do, because Remy begged me to. With a shake of my head to snap me out of my stupor, I dug into my pocket to grab my phone. Someone could stop the bleeding. Eve could live, even if for a few more hours.

I made the call. I spoke to the person on the other line as if I were a robot. With the phone still to my ear and the voice on the line prattling on, I spotted Nick emerging from the shadows. It was his eyes that sent my world reeling into oblivion.

Gold eyes. Nick wasn't just a criminal punk. Nick was a Reaper.

My phone dropped to the ground at my feet.

"Baird," I said loud enough for Nick to hear.

He paused.

"Nicholas Baird," I added. "Reaper."

His gold stare grew brighter when I said the last part.

"Did Chad send you for this job?" I said as Remy screamed at us to help him with Eve's bleeding.

Nick never bothered to speak. His silence was answer enough.

My stomach roiled with a mixture of emotions. But sitting at the top of the concoction was wrath. Red anger flourished in my fingertips. I made no effort to hide my hands. I stood over Remy and Eve like a mother lioness over her injured cub. If Nick wanted to do his job on Eve, he'd have to get through me first, and then he'd have to contend with the paramedics who would save her. I knew they would.

My red-hand warning was what he needed to know—I was not human. The Reaper lunged at me. I ran at him, using my shoulder to stop him exactly as Papa had taught me to do. But even though I was fast, Nick got a hand around my throat, and the other clutched my dreadlocks. His grip was iron, fierce iron, squeezing out what air I had left.

"Nick, help us!" Remy shouted as he held his dying beloved.

The Reaper's gold eyes grew brighter, nearly blinding me, and my insides curdled.

How had I overlooked that he was a Reaper? None of that mattered when the horror that *he* was likely Eve's ferryman came over me.

Nick's grip on my neck tightened. I would soon pass out, and then he'd finish Eve. I had to stop him, had to bring him to his knees right now, not thirty seconds from now.

Not giving a damn about Level Five or Level One Hundred Offenses, I threw my hands—now bright red—around Nick's throat. He roared as the skin on his neck began to cook from my blistering touch. I only wanted to burn him enough to get him to let go. He didn't. In his eyes, I watched pain and pride in a fierce battle.

"Ollie," Remy's voice was a distant call as I forced more heat into my hands.

"Get Eve out of here," I gasped.

"Chad told me you'd try to intervene," Nick said, finally speaking.

The world spun. Black spots marred my vision. From behind Nick's dingy brown hair came the blur of a metal trashcan. Remy had left Eve's side long enough to take a swing on my behalf. The bin sent Nick into a stagger but didn't break his grip on my neck.

Those eyes of death went from yellow to a blinding gold. He turned on Remy. I couldn't move fast enough to stop Nick from snatching the trash bin from him. Metal struck Remy's face. Blood exploded over us as he crumpled to the pavement.

The attack on Remy gave me just enough time to throw an elbow into Nick's side. It was for nothing. He wouldn't go down so easily. Nick wrenched me toward the sidewalk. His target was the hood of a parked car.

Unconcerned that I might burn him to ashes, I swung my hot hands at his body. My fingernails dug into his flesh on his arms, burning off the topmost layer. I had expected him to throw me through a window or snap my neck. I would have preferred it.

Instead, he flung me face down next to Eve on the road. Her blood had already pooled around her. Her face was still and pale. Tears swelled in my eyes.

"I'm sorry. I'm sorry I couldn't save you," I cried.

A knee rammed my back, cracking a bone in my spine. I flattened onto my belly, defenseless as agony raced through my body.

It did not matter if Nick had realized ten minutes earlier or only just now that I was Stygian; his determination was all I needed to know that he recognized what I was and how to do proper damage.

Death teeming in his hardened expression, Nick turned on Eve. His eyes were locked on something that only he and I could see. The Deathmark on Eve's shoulder glowed through her yellow jacket. Fiery lines in the skull pulsated, beckoning her Reaper to complete the job. Nick curled a hand around Eve's thin bicep and the Deathmark. That small touch was what he needed to destroy what I was fighting to protect. His eyes sparked victoriously as he started to withdraw Eve's soul. And she couldn't fight back. She stared vacantly at her Grim Reaper as all humans did when it was their time.

The heat in my crimson hands charred the pavement when I pushed myself upright, leaving burn marks on the road. I climbed to my knees and reached after the enemy. Through my tears, the sparkling red orbs of my fists guided me to my victim.

I didn't feel the suppleness of Nick's skin. It singed too quickly. A saccharine tang of burned flesh enveloped my senses. It smelled of bittersweet triumph.

My eyes cleared when Nick bellowed, voice echoing.

Eve's spirit hovered half in her body and half in Styx, awaiting the remainder of her ferrying. There was no emotion on her soul's face as her body lay forgotten and bleeding on the ground. She was vacant. Lost. Stuck in purgatory.

But Eve wasn't dead yet.

When I finally confronted Nick, it was not his scowl that chilled my firestorm, but what was burned into his left cheek. My reddened palm print was stamped on his face.

And in the middle was my Deathmark.

Chapter Eleven

"The skull is Death. From it, you will help me recover the balance of life."

—Head Reaper Marin

The look in my eyes said it all. Nick's quivering fingertips feathered his cheek and quickly retracted when his skin sizzled.

The shape was crude, but it was definitely a skull, and it smiled triumphantly back at me. How had I done this? How had I transferred my Deathmark with only my hand?

I could burn Stygians, sure, but put Deathmarks on them? And *without* a tattoo machine? Gerard and Mama and Papa never told me about this level of skill. Gerard had always said only Master Scriveners could put a Deathmark on a Stygian, and to even try would cause trouble for me with the Head Reaper. So it had never occurred to me to go near any Stygian with my tattoo machine. But this was entirely different. This was a Deathmark put there by the palm of my hand and nothing else.

How was it possible unless…unless I actually *was* bound for Masterhood?

"You…" Nick paused. "You bitch!"

The skull elevated his wrath and understandably so. From what I knew, a Deathmark on another Stygian was no different than a Deathmark on a human. It hastened death. Nick would soon meet his maker because of my doing.

I had no idea what level of offense this warranted, but I was positive it would not get me a slap on the hand and community service. Erebus would be my next stop.

But as angry as Nick was about the mark on his face, my anger was equal to his. I wouldn't let this asshole have anything else. I wouldn't back down for his satisfaction.

I forced my bodyweight into him, and he went down, slamming into a nearby parked sedan. He flailed and struggled to find his footing. I used what leverage I had and pinned him to the car, standing face to face with him, my fiery hands clutching his throat. This time I was burning through his neck, not just the topmost layer of his skin. My fingertips sank down into his muscle. I would make my point. Here. Now. I would.

"Tell Chad and anyone else who will listen that I'm done following your orders," I said with a fierce voice I didn't recognize. "I am not your fucking puppet!"

Something sharp pressed between my lower ribs and I felt a hot wetness pouring out. I found a switchblade buried in my side, and Nick was forcing the weapon deeper.

That's when the pain registered.

I cried out as torment spread from my core, sending

signals to the rest of my beaten body to shut down—it couldn't take any more. But my hands grew more determined. The wronged Scrivener in me would not let him—or Marin or Chad—win. Breathing became laborious as blood flowed into my lungs. I closed my eyes, not to avoid the look in his, or the way his neck shed its layers beneath my clutches, but to focus my remaining energy.

"Ollie!" shouted a man. "Don't!"

Brent threw his arms around my waist and wrenched me from my prey. Nick collapsed, gasping. The switchblade dropped to the pavement. Brent released me as quickly as he'd snatched me away from doing further harm to Nick Baird. I stumbled backward, nearly losing my balance entirely, grasping my ribs and spitting blood.

Nick cowered against the car. Brent didn't transform into his dark alter ego to make his point. There was no action, no attack, simply electrified silence as he stared down at Nick, his red eyes ready to devour the Reaper whole.

Nick threw an arm over his face to avoid the Eidolon's grisly stare.

"You're lucky I stopped her," Brent growled. "Now get the fuck out of here."

Nick did not hesitate. I wanted to believe that this was only because of Brent's threat as an Eidolon. But the terror in Nick's expression was very real and very much directed at me.

In seconds, he was gone, leaving Brent and me standing over Remy and Eve's bodies. Eve was dead. Her soul sat like a lost child beside her body. Remy was unconscious judging by the slow rise and fall of his chest.

"You okay?" Brent asked me as I clutched my side.

I choked back the pain and nodded. It wouldn't be long before this wound would heal—minutes probably. Nonetheless, it hurt. A deliberate lungful of air stretched my ribs. The movement intensified the pain.

"You could have melted him," he said over my keening. "That's a serious fucking crime."

My head spun at just the notion of melting fellow Stygians, let alone the consequences.

"Here." He removed his jacket and then his flannel, which he wrapped around my ribcage. He tugged. I yelped. Then he tied a knot in the sleeves to lock the tourniquet in place. I gazed down at the flannel compressing my chest like a corset.

With each shallow breath, and the support of the makeshift tourniquet, my stab wound began piecing itself back together one layer at a time. I had regularly torn my knees from skateboarding accidents as a kid. I'd healed unnaturally quickly then. I expected a stabbing to heal slower, but it didn't, for which I was grateful.

If only the guilt would go away, too.

"Are you better?" he asked.

I blinked to clear the wetness from my eyes. "What do you mean by…melt?"

He put his hands on my sides for support. "Master Scriveners can melt Stygians. You are the ultimate destroyer. You could've obliterated him."

"You mean kill him?"

"Yeah. Exactly."

In my mind, ideas raced like a raging wildfire. I thought only Eidolons could kill Stygians like Scriveners and Reapers. But if Master Scriveners could kill Stygians, too, that explained why there were so few Masters around and why Chad wanted so badly to see me exhibit signs of such a skill-set so he could arrest me. As my mind filled with ideas, my head spun and my heart felt as if it would explode.

"We can't talk about this here," I said as I looked over at Remy and Eve sprawled out on the street. Sirens roared in the distance. Medics were coming to their aid. When they arrived, we would have to be someplace else.

Remy was still, his head bleeding from the hit. And Eve lay crumpled on the ground. Crimson rivulets spread like fingers out from her body. Their bodies did not haunt me. I had seen death before.

It was Eve's soul, sitting next to her body, staring, green eyes calling to me from a purgatory where she didn't belong, that tore my heart into tiny, meaningless pieces.

With a little bit of restored energy, I tried to break out of Brent's grip to crawl to her side. Brent held tight, dragging me back into his arms, too far from Eve to touch her. Her soul tried to stand and walk the ten feet to reach me but was drawn back to her limp body. She was joined to it at the hip, half-ferried, half-dead.

"Don't talk to her," Brent urged.

"Dammit," I cried out, the act stinging my punctured lungs. "I couldn't stop it. I couldn't save her."

"Let her go."

"She needs me." Eve's soul wavered through glassy tears as I wept.

"She doesn't know she's dead. She's confused." Brent pulled me upright. "You have to focus on yourself now."

"No, no, no."

"Listen to me." He shook my shoulders. "You've done

what you can. She's gone. Dead. And you will be too, if you don't work with me."

His white thermal undershirt was caked in blood. He wore a glazed expression, like this was far more horrific than anything he had ever seen. I found that impossible to believe. He was an Eidolon.

"We can't stay here." Brent's closeness felt good—comforting in light of our predicament. "We have to get out of Québec before this reaches Marin."

"I won't leave her like this."

Brent sighed long and hard. Surely he was trying to prepare a response I wouldn't want to hear. After a moment, he said, "Once the assigned Reaper starts a job, he's the only one who can finish it. Not even the Head Reaper can pick up where another left off."

I met his eyes. I needed him to hear me. "I *know* you can help Eve. Can't you go after Baird and make him do it?" I thought of those souls high above and how I'd once feared that Eve would soon become one, too. Now I feared that Eve would become a ghost who haunted the same place day in and day out, feeling forever connected to a body that no longer existed. That was worse.

Much, much worse.

Brent's grip slackened. "Baird won't come back after what just happened. He's probably already hunting down Watchmen to tell them what you did. The best we can do is leave her, Ollie. I'm sorry."

"*Please*. I will do anything you need for your rebellion. *Anything* if you help her, Brent."

He set his jaw. "Check her body for a pulse, just in case."

I flew to Eve's body and put my fingers against her

lukewarm neck. I focused as I waited for a heartbeat. Eve's soul leaned forward, observing her body as I tried finding some inkling of life.

An icy breeze brushed some dreadlocks from my shoulder. Eve had fawned over my hair. She had once touched it and quickly retreated as if she had gone past a personal boundary. It was only in her death that she had the courage to touch my hair again.

I pressed harder on her neck.

"She's gone," I whispered.

Brent's feet echoed as he made his advance. He knelt across from me. Eve's body lay between us, but her soul scooted alongside of me, stretching the tether linking her to her corpse. She put her hand over mine. As I gazed at her ghostly touch, I stilled. The tears hanging from my eyelashes didn't dare to fall.

"Give me your necklace," Brent said.

"Why?"

"Her body was her anchor. That's dead. I'll ferry part of her soul into your necklace as a new anchor. It's the best I can do."

"Then what?"

"Nothing. If Baird doesn't finish the job, she'll be stuck in your necklace until it is destroyed. And if it's destroyed… she'll be lost forever."

Sniveling, I put my fingers to the pewter lotus flower. It had been a gift from Mama when I finished my apprenticeship years ago. She had said that as a lotus grows out of muddy waters, I would rise out of the ugliness of my job as a Scrivener. I lowered the pendant into Brent's palm. The black leather cord coiled around the lotus.

He folded his fingers over it.

I knew of nothing worse for humans than remaining bodiless and straddled between two worlds. Eve would be that unfortunate soul forever struggling to find a home that was visible, but just out of reach. She would become a ghost story people whispered to each other in the dark hallways of derelict buildings.

That was no way to exist, not for the cruelest of spirits.

With her soul in the pendant, she would be with me. *I* would be Eve's home—the bearer of her soul.

Brent pressed the lotus to Eve's glowing pink Death-mark—the only thing on her body that was animate. Even that was waning.

"Are you *sure* you want this for her, Ollie?"

I had said I wouldn't let Eve die alone. I would uphold that promise.

I nodded at the Eidolon kneeling across from me. "Do it."

Chapter Twelve

"And when you fall asleep, children, do not look to the dark corner, for the Black Beast will be there, waiting to ferry you home."

—Marcus Bordeaux, *Bedtime in Styx*, circa 1945

The door to my bedroom closet hung ajar, allowing a partial view of Miss Piggy, my twelve-gauge shotgun. I stood in silence, holding my backpack, which was stuffed with clothing and the Interceptor—the four-by-four box that had provided me hours of Canadiens hockey games in lieu of Marin's doomsday broadcasts. I would not leave the Interceptor behind. I had a feeling it still had a purpose, yet I didn't know what exactly.

Now that I had committed a Level Ten crime, Brent and I had agreed that running was the only option. For the first time, Miss Piggy would be used for what it was intended—protection. What Brent and I would do once we found a place to hide out west, we didn't yet know, but somewhere remote, somewhere not high on Marin's radar seemed a worthy option until a better plan made itself clear to us.

"Hurry," Brent hollered from the living room of my apartment.

He had given me ten minutes to pack. It had only been five.

My thoughts kept racing back to Eve and how we had left her body and Remy in the middle of the street a moment before the ambulance and police arrived on the scene. The emotional truth of Eve's death had not yet crashed down upon me. Running overrode any chance to pause and reflect. Until now.

Determined not to think too long about Eve, I bent to grab the shotgun and winced. The flannel cinched my ribcage. The stab wound had healed. I was no longer coughing blood. So, I picked at the knot. It didn't budge.

Brent had made certain it wouldn't come undone, hadn't he?

After a deep breath, I paused. My fingertips glowed red, ready for the challenge. I put them to the soft cotton and burned through the fabric. The tourniquet unraveled. I finally had use of my entire lung capacity, and it felt as invigorating as sliding into a pool on a summer day.

"Ollie, come on."

I grunted vulgar words, grabbed Miss Piggy, but stopped in the doorway of my bedroom to take one last look at a lifetime of charcoal drawings tacked on the walls. Beaches, mountains. Freedom. A bucket list of dreams.

I backed into the hallway and made an about face for the door. But as I passed by the kitchen, I noticed the plate of chocolate chip cookies on the counter. The treats stopped me cold.

Mama.

Papa.

With everything that had happened, I didn't consider how they might feel. They needed to know what happened. They needed to know I wasn't dead.

"Brent, I can't leave Mama and Papa. I…I shouldn't leave at all. I should just tell Marin what happened, and maybe he'll give mercy."

Brent was cupping my face, his nose practically touching mine, before I even saw him move.

"No." His voice was dense with tension. "Marin won't show you a lick of mercy. You have to get away from Québec. We'll figure out everything else once we're safely outside of his radar. Do you understand?"

Eyes watering, I gave a reluctant nod.

"*Promise* me you won't consider coming back here until we have a plan." His hands were hot against my skin. Those eyes could've flashed red to emphasize his point. Those cerulean jewels, almost human-like, urged me to comply.

"I won't mention it again," I murmured.

He started to pull me into a kiss, but pursed his lips as if a thought diverted him. Instead he finalized his action with a kiss to my forehead. He lingered there for a moment longer and then backed out of our closeness.

I watched as he slipped a backpack over his shoulder and strode toward the door. He might have been a rebel for longer than I was alive, but I was a novice. I had familial connections and reasons to stay in Québec City. I wasn't ready for this.

"I at least have to let my parents know I'm leaving."

"Keep them distant." His voice was dry. "It's the only way you can protect them."

I ran my fingers over the green plastic blanketing the cookies. Mama loved colorful plastic wraps, embellished Ziploc bags, anything to adorn her culinary masterpieces. She had once scoured Québec City for a red Crock-Pot at Christmas. She had settled for a red-and-white pot that looked like an overstuffed candy cane filled with gumbo.

"We've got four hours until sunrise. Let's go." Brent was in the doorway. Dudley was at his side.

I made for the door, refusing to consider how long I would be gone. But I stopped halfway across the living room, struck by a thought. If I took the cookies, Mama and Papa would know I'd come home after the incident—which would surely be in Marin's noon report—and that I was okay…at least for now.

Rushing out with cookies in one hand, my shotgun in the other, and Eve's soul in my necklace, I made a hasty valediction to the apartment I had called home.

I was a gun-slinging rebel now.

Whoever or whatever made Brent Hume a car singer was a sick son of a gun. Everyone knows the type—they can't carry a tune, but they sing as loud as can be, leaving everyone in earshot cringing.

Brent's vocal straining distracted me from continuing the conversation that we had started back on the street where Eve met her end. What did Brent mean that I was the ultimate destroyer? Between lulls in the songs—when I could hear myself think—my curiosity about being a potential mastermind exterminator took over. How could I do it? Why had no one ever told me before now? Was it enough to scare Marin and his allies into leaving my family and me alone?

Another question came to mind, but it felt wrong, considering the turmoil swarming around me like a plague of grim locusts.

Why had Brent kissed me and then declared it a mistake?

Between Brent's singing and my inner mayhem, I'd found myself sketching a portrait of a screaming woman for the last nine hours. My sanity was summed up in her misery.

I hadn't felt right complaining because Brent had taken the first, second, and the third driving shifts. I wasn't keen on maneuvering a stick shift Dodge truck through mountainous roads, tweaked as I was. Brent didn't mind driving. He also didn't notice that I wasn't a fan of nineties pop music.

His singing started back at the United States border, where the Patrol Officer had asked us where we were headed. I said New York City because it would be easy to blend in there. Don't people go to cities to hide?

Besides, maybe Brent would find some nineties-themed karaoke bar so he could sing his precious heart out. Brent argued against it—not finding a karaoke bar, but rushing off to New York City. So, instead, we were heading to Beattyville, Kentucky, home of moonshine and Brent's family, so we could rest in a safe place, load up on supplies, and make for the west before the Watchmen caught on to our whereabouts.

We were still only in upstate New York however. I had

twelve more hours of my inner turmoil and him screaming the greatest hits until I was thrust into the middle of a Reaper family reunion. There was not enough sketch paper in the world to keep me from putting my charcoal pencil up his nose before then.

All things considered, I slammed a fist on the radio dial. A silver CD spat out from a slot. Robert Smith's homage to Friday stopped, and Brent's strained baritone petered out into a self-conscious chirp.

I looked out the passenger window at Holsteins and bales of hay as the American countryside flew by. The view would have been lovely had I been someone not on the run for committing multiple Level Ten Offenses against Death.

"Your singing is getting on my nerves," I said after a beautiful stretch of silence, the first in hours.

His knuckles whitened on the steering wheel. "At least you're honest."

"Speaking of honesty." I cleared my throat. "Why don't we talk about why you kissed me and then acted like it was a mistake?"

I spotted his discomfort in his iron grip on the wheel. He eyed the CD, seemingly intent on pushing it back into the radio, hitting play, and excusing himself from answering my direct query.

"Am I a bad kisser? Am I not your type? What?" I went on.

"It's complicated," he said.

I wanted the fucking truth. So, I let silence and my hard stare eat him alive.

He blew air from his nose multiple times, cracked his neck, and said, "Mixing romance and rebellion is problematic."

That made logical sense. "You could've told me that the

other night."

He chewed the inside of his cheek as if bracing for a screaming fit about playing with another's emotions. Personally, I had no energy to expound on the subject. There were bigger questions to pose. The inquiry over the kiss was just my warm-up.

"Now that we have that covered, let's talk about what you said on the street. Why am I the ultimate destroyer, huh?" There. Straight-fucking-forward.

He brushed his fingers though his hair. "What do you know about Master Scriveners?"

"Not much; just that they were all killed off in the Purge by Eidolons."

"Then you don't know about melting."

The image of my black neoprene gloves dissolving from my hands popped into my head. The smell was sickening. I hated that.

"If you go nuclear, you can kill a fellow Stygian—including Eidolons and even Marin, if you have an Eidolon to help you. It takes a significant amount of work, but Masters can do it. And it is scary as hell."

Maybe what I had witnessed in the past twenty-four hours had destroyed what was left of my emotions, but I was not as shocked as I was deadened. I rapped my fingers on my drawing pad, which I had folded to my chest.

"This skill must be what triggered the Purge," I said.

"You got it. Marin won't have anyone under his rule with the ability to melt him into nothing." His strong brow rose, creasing his forehead. "That's why Chad was after you. If he saw any sign of your potential, he would have taken you to Marin. You would've become a fine story for *Reaper*

Monthly."

I looked out the window at the blurs of cows and farm-houses as I thought about narrowly avoiding exile in Erebus for an innate trait that should have been considered a gift or talent, not a threat to authority. As I pondered what happened on the street outside of Eve's apartment, I couldn't help but think about my friend. Somehow I had convinced myself that Eve was alive, working at Le Nektar, and that I was on a classic American road trip.

It was the only way to get through.

"So I guess I can't go back to working at *Salon de Tatouage*, eh?" I joked.

"No," he said with no humor in his tone. "You will never go back to that life now that they know what you are."

I put my fingers to my beloved lotus pendant. Mama's cookies and hugs. Papa's visits to fix broken faucets in my apartment, and our late night conversations about life. Coffee with Eve. Discussing the injustices of Styx with Gerard. Walks with Dudley around the familiar nooks and crannies of my humble neighborhood. These things were never going to happen again.

Their loss had not yet hit me. And I cringed that it someday would. When it did, no mental preparedness would protect me from the fallout.

Chapter Thirteen

"Have a wild and woolly time."

—Beattyville Local Advertisement

16 APRIL

The remainder of our trip to Kentucky was conducted in silence. Well, save for Brent's long playlist of eighties and nineties vocal hits. Our lack of conversation troubled me until I accepted that, although Brent had been chatty at the outset, he wasn't one for idle small talk. Or perhaps he just wasn't comfortable with my ability to melt him into oblivion. To be honest, I wasn't comfortable with that truth either.

Could I accidentally melt someone I liked—maybe Brent?

And was I bound to Brent's side now? Would we get to the Rocky Mountains and then would he announce that we'd have to go our separate ways to keep off Marin's radar? If he did, I would not be pleased. For now, I appreciated

Brent's company, and the broad smiles he'd flash me when he'd catch me staring.

His smiles dwindled into forced cheer when I spotted the sign welcoming visitors to Beattyville, Kentucky. The welcome promised one thing: A Woolly Worm Festival. Brent refused to explain what woolly worms were. Unfortunately, we didn't spend enough time dawdling in Beattyville for me to ask the locals when the next woolly worm stampede was.

He had sped through the miniscule Southern town so fast I hardly had a chance to observe the handful of 1950's style two-story buildings, and the people milling outside of the shops. When I had asked what was the hurry, he mumbled something deliberately incoherent. I made out "Watchmen" and "hillbillies." That was enough to shut me up.

Once we hit State Route 52 and began climbing a hill, the truck's speed eased even if Brent's attitude did not. We were soon cruising through winding roads that would have been romantic if the swerving hadn't offended my weak stomach.

In spite of my discomfort, I still grew excited to see the young leaves sprouting in fluorescent green, not yet the deep emerald of summertime foliage. New birth and growth were encouraging. I rolled down the window to take in the springtime air—far warmer and more soothing than the briskness of Québec City, which hadn't left winter behind. I hung my head out the passenger window, a few dreadlocks flapping in the wind.

A robin sprang from her nest in one of the overhanging trees and swooped to one side of the road and then another before rising above the treetops.

That's when I saw it.

"Sunlight." I threw a hand out of the window and let the heat sink into my skin. We Stygians lived under an umbrella of cloudiness for good reason. But the sun…if we ever did see it in the brief breaks in the souls, it was a gift worth talking about for days. Feeling it against our skin for longer than a second was even more unique and more worthy of celebration. Right now, I was in some sort of euphoria from which I did not ever wish return. Sun. Warmth. It brought life and happiness. Without it, the world would wither into nothingness. No wonder it felt like a drug greater than sugar or coffee.

"Is the countryside less congested with souls?" I asked because Québec was never this clear, in my whole history of living there.

"Something like that."

I grinned, watching golden rays highlight my pale arms. A wet nose brushed my ear. Dudley was probably as tired as I was of the Cheetos, Twizzlers, and road trip funk. I hauled him into my lap and wrapped an arm around his waist so he could indulge, too. His neck stretched long and his little black nose twitched as wind whipped at him.

The truck slowed. We made a jarring left onto a narrow dirt path. Tree branches slapped at the sides of the truck. Leaves smacked Dudley and me in the face. Time to close the window. Dudley crawled into the backseat and groaned from renewed boredom.

The road was becoming less and less developed. Grass filled in where dirt left off and that faded into underbrush. Everything in the truck creaked and bounced.

Soon, the road wasn't there at all.

"Are we in the jungle?" I asked.

"We Humes live as remotely as possible."

Dudley flopped around on the backseat like a salmon in a boat. His ears bopped. Paws clung to the seat with no chance for grip. Stress filled his beady eyes.

"We're almost there, Duds. We *are* almost there, right?"

The truck came to a halt, throwing us forward. The engine rumbled and then died. A fallen pine tree blocked the trail.

"Get your stuff. We're hiking," Brent grumbled.

Dudley gave a pitiable whimper.

I scratched under his chin. "It can't be that much further, Duds."

Oh, how wrong I was.

Our journey turned into a three-hour scramble through dense brushwood. I enjoyed hiking, having gotten lost in the Québec countryside numerous times, but this trek was not any fun with Dudley stopping to pee on every tree we passed and Brent refusing to answer when I pressed him about where we were headed or why, exactly, we could see the sun in all its glory.

Every now and again he put his hand out, bringing us to a stop. He'd then scan the wilderness, put down his hand, and lead us onward.

When Brent stopped for what felt like the twentieth time, I lost the last of my patience.

"What in Hades are you looking for? Woolly worms? Because I can't help you find them if you don't tell me what they are."

He pointed across the web of trees. "There. See it?"

I followed the trajectory of his finger to observe exactly what we had seen for the last five miles—trees and more trees, with maybe a squirrel here or there.

"It sees us."

Being told something is watching you is unnerving, even for Stygians, who are typically the creepers in the woods watching unaware humans. However, nothing looked amiss. Birds chirped. No crunch of undergrowth punched out the rhythm of an approaching assailant. It was peaceful. There was...

By Hades, a soul hovered between two distant pine trees. It had to be as tall as Brent. "What's it doing there? Is it lost?"

"More like trapped." My perplexed expression was enough for him to continue. "These souls are similar to Eve, except they aren't in your necklace. They never made it to the next step because their Reapers never finished the job. They were probably arrested and sent to Erebus before they had their chance. Good ol' Marin's laws working against us."

Sadness for these souls crept over me. "Can't we help them?"

"The only way is if we convinced Marin to bring back those Reapers from Erebus to release their souls from hell." He started to walk, but stopped and looked over his shoulder. "Or if Styx had a Head Reaper who wasn't hell-bent on fascist control."

As he commenced his hike toward the soul hovering nearby, I admitted my confusion to myself and then to him. "What does that mean?"

"It means we need to remove Marin from power so Styx can start running like it should."

I tried keeping up with his pace, but he was several steps ahead before I could take even one. When he stopped, I had thought it was to give me a chance to catch up.

"Don't slow down, or the ghosts will grab you. They do that to pretty things like you," Brent said over his shoulder, after breaking again into a determined stride.

"What ghosts? You didn't say there was more than one!"

He didn't give details as to *what* they did once they'd grabbed you. I didn't need to know anyway. As we marched toward the figure, more and more apparitions appeared from behind the trees. Too soon it was a flash mob of ghosts. This was bad news.

I disliked crowds—even the ghostly kind. And I despised going to those corporate run haunted houses around Halloween because paying people to scare the shit out of me is not my idea of a good time. I poop on my own just fine, thanks.

I trotted behind Brent as the ghosts broke into a fit of melancholic wails. They swarmed Dudley and me as if we had something they craved. Howling wisps reached out to us. Hair floated around the souls' gaunt faces. Gnarled flesh pulled over their eye sockets and mouths. There were no eyes—no pupil or iris, but they apparently saw the fear in my face. And they seemed to crowd me all the more for it.

Brent said not to slow down. I didn't, but that did not stop the lost spirits from fondling my hair or the lotus pendant anchoring Eve's soul to me. Some teased Dudley's floppy ears as he kept one pace ahead.

"Brent."

A cluster of immaterial bodies crowded in front of me.

"Brent."

"Keep walking," he said, off in the distance.

Dudley went up on his hind legs, his front paws clasped

around my waist, looking at me for direction. His skinny body quivered. So, I scooped him into my arms and ran. The first spirit I blew through left me with a damp chill. The feeling got worse as I moved through the rest of the crowd.

"Brent!" My scream barely made it over the wailing.

Dudley dug his claws into my arms.

"Where are you?"

Between hazy shapes, I spied our escape. I put Dudley down. He was the first to rocket out of the ghost labyrinth. I followed close on his heels. We waded through a creek and over a small embankment.

Before us stood a two-story log cabin with a wraparound porch and open windows with floral curtains flicking in the breeze. To the side was a red barn, partly hidden behind the cabin, and a pair of run-down cars from the fifties stacked on bricks. Trees circled the homestead. The place seemed peaceful enough, until the wrong end of a shotgun pressed against my right cheek.

The man behind the double barrel was shorter than Brent, but twice as wide. His brown beard was flecked with gray. A green ball cap shielded his face from the raging sunlight, but it didn't hide his menacing stare.

"Whatcha doing here, little miss?" he asked in an accent far heavier than Brent's.

I started to push the strap of Miss Piggy from my shoulder until he cocked his gun. The slide and click was deafening. Maybe a point-blank shootout wasn't a good idea.

"Wallie!" Brent shouted from the thicket, somehow behind us when he had been marching ahead. The forest full of broken spirits was disorienting. Brent must have gotten snagged up in their curiosity, too. But if he had, the silvery ghosts allowed him to move freely now. They parted like stage curtains as he marched through the last of the pine trees. Once Brent cleared the woods, the souls filled in where he had trudged, each eyeless spirit watching from afar.

"Put the gun down," Brent ordered over their fading cries.

Wallie did, and Dudley and I took a collective breath of relief.

"What are you doing here, little brother?" Wallie stepped back. He smiled at me with a nice set of teeth.

"The herd is getting bigger." Ignoring his brother's question, Brent pointed toward the souls on the perimeter of the woods. They peered through the trees just as hostages peered through prison bars. I now understood why Brent didn't find the sun quite as special as I had. Those souls should be high above, floating toward their salvation, not in Kentucky, haunting a forest, waiting for Head Reaper Marin to take note of their plight. I felt mortified for soaking in the sunlight a moment ago—their suffering was the reason for the sun.

"The herd is only gonna get bigger if Marin doesn't do anything." Wallie's yellow eyes faded to a cool blue.

"He doesn't give a damn about anything but keeping himself in power," Brent hissed.

"Right, well." Wallie put his hand on my shoulder. "Welcome, Miss…"

"Scrivener Dormier," I said, feeling a little too formal for the circumstances.

"Aha, a Scrivener. Have you come here to help us then?" Wallie queried.

"We'll see, won't we," I said with a fake smile.

"That we will. You two wait here. I'll go hide the step-stool before Sue Ellen sees ya." Like that, Wallie dashed to the cabin, up the porch stairs, and then vanished behind the screen door.

"Stepstool?" I asked.

"If you see her carrying one that's painted like a Holstein cow, best you run."

What in the hell had I gotten myself into?

The cabin's screen door flung open and smacked against the siding. Her hair tied in a burgundy kerchief, Sue Ellen Hume—I assumed—shuffled onto the porch in a floral housedress far too fitted for her pudgy shape. She carried a black-and-white painted stool.

"Brent, don't make me come down there and slap you. Get your ass over here." She slammed the stool down, straining the integrity of its black-and-white legs.

Dudley sprinted toward the beater cars, evidently needing no further warning to clear the area. Brent laced his fingers with mine and started toward her.

"She has the stool," I said from the corner of my mouth. "Is she an Eidolon, too?"

He remained silent.

"Brent?"

Once we made contact with the porch, I peered up at Sue Ellen. Behind her, Wallie wrung his green ball cap, and his giant forehead glistened with sweat. One, two, three steps and Sue Ellen and I were face-to-face. I finally got the purpose of the stepstool. I was no six-foot tall runway model, but Sue Ellen was shorter than I was by several inches. The stool made it so we could stand eye-to-eye.

"A hippie." Sue Ellen's dark eyes raked me from head to

toe. Never had I been self-conscious about my dreadlocks, bell-bottom jeans, and white tank top until that moment. My style wasn't diverse by any stretch of the imagination. Jeans, an occasional tie-dyed skirt, and tank tops with sweaters for colder days were the extent of my wardrobe. I was a woman of convenience and comfort. Enough said.

"So are you a Master Scrivener?" Sue Ellen asked, eyes burning through me.

I was not sure how to answer because I didn't know for sure, so I said, "Yes, I'm a Master. Best one this side of the Mississippi."

"You are a spring chicken if I've ever seen one. All the Masters I've met have decades on you."

Instead of spitting out a witty comeback, I opted for silence as I tried to decipher this Reaper's brash personality.

"She's powerful, Sue Ellen," Brent said. "She doesn't need decades to prove herself."

Sue Ellen's lips pulled into a narrow slit. "We'll see about that."

After spending a good hour getting a tour of the Hume's little farmstead in the Kentucky hills, meeting various Reapers who were either relatives of Brent's or friends of his family, I could not get a proper feel for Sue Ellen. Brent's brother-in-law, Wallie, and cousins—Amber and Patrick—were quiet Reapers with nice smiles and agreeable dispositions. Their friends were too many to remember their names. I lost count after twenty. They needed nametags.

While I could not figure out Sue Ellen, I did catch on

that this group of Stygians was the first rebel cell I had ever encountered. The thirty or so Stygians surrounding the outside of the Hume's modest home proved that rebel cells were no myth or fabrication of the government.

Sue Ellen had warmed up to me during our tour. That warmth was shown with an arm around my shoulders. I was neither comfortable with her closeness nor convinced that it was meant to be friendly. Sue Ellen was obviously this rebel cell's leader. And she was incredulous of my skillset.

"According to my nephew, Scrivener Dormier can help us," Sue Ellen said, her voice vibrating my body. "We have yet to see her at her full power, but Brent assures me she can do the job."

Of course, I wasn't sure what job that was. I wanted to hear it from Sue Ellen and Brent. But I let her complete my introduction, as uncomfortable as it was to stand in front of a group of Reapers staring back at me with hope. If only they knew that I was just as hopeful they'd be able to protect me from my fate.

As quickly as the introductions and tour began, Sue Ellen pulled me into the home, where I walked into a living room covered in pictures upon pictures of the Hume family.

"Brent and Wallie have to meet with some of the rebels." Sue Ellen sat down in a wooden rocking chair. The furniture creaked as her weight settled. "This will give us time to get to know each other."

Trying to keep up appearances, I wandered from picture to picture, observing the faces of the Hume family from as far back as the Civil War. I carefully searched for a picture of Brent.

"You don't like me," I said, feigning confidence.

"I never judge someone until I know them, Scrivener. I don't trust you."

"Why?" I paused in front of a picture from the mid-1950's that piqued my interest. The man was very clearly Brent. The woman next to him looked to be his wife or girlfriend by the way they were holding hands.

"You are young. The rebellion needs an experienced Master Scrivener." Sue Ellen began rocking in her chair. The creak of wood against wood instantly created a grating rhythm.

"Who is she?" I asked, my interested locked on the picture.

"Isobel Flemington was a Master Scrivener, much like you, I'm afraid. She lacked experience, too."

I moved in closer. My nose nearly bumped the glass. Isobel Flemington was the one Brent had mentioned back in my apartment days ago. She was the Scrivener who gave tattoos of the sun and the moon.

"Isobel died on account of the rebellion. Brent was never the same after that, bless his heart."

The kiss, I thought. Had he regretted getting close to me for this reason?

"What am I supposed to be to your rebellion?" I pulled away from the picture and turned to make eye contact with Sue Ellen.

"There's a difference between you and Isobel. Sit."

I made my way to the couch next to her rocking chair. It was covered in a colorful afghan that had seen better times. Careful not to put too much weight on it for fear of ripping it in half, I sat on the edge of the couch. Sue Ellen waited until I was comfortable before she spoke again.

"Brent told me you put a Deathmark on a Stygian with

your hand?"

Nodding seemed a suitable reply.

"What made you do this, child?"

I formed my thoughts carefully before I dared open my mouth. "I was provoked."

"You were attacked?"

"Yes." In my mind I saw Eve's body lying on the pavement.

"Did you know you could put a Deathmark on another like so?"

"Nope." Trying to keep myself together was becoming a challenge as we sat face to face. Sue Ellen had a way of seeing past the bullshit. This skill was intimidating.

"Could you do it again?"

I smiled, cynically. "Depends."

"Let me rephrase my question, child." Her voice was cutting. "*Would* you do it again?"

Chapter Fourteen

"For how could this Scrivener be a terrorist?
This rebel is no radical, no dissident. She is our champion."

—HermesHarbinger.com, 11:05 am 17 April, Sunday

17 April

My brain was slow cooking in a bone crock-pot. Springtime Kentucky nights were far warmer than Québec's. My bell-bottoms dangled over the edge of the dusty mattress. A tank top and panties were all I could stand to wear in the stuffy barn loft. Though I was close to naked in another person's guest room, I was not self-conscious about it. Heat makes a modest soul do strange things.

Illuminated by a kerosene lamp on the banister of the loft, Brent sat shirtless and slumped in a wooden chair, his back to me, oblivious to my suffering as he stared out over the darkness of the barn below, keeping watch.

The golden blush of light swathed him from the waist up. I should have been spellbound by the rise and fall of his shoulders or the rope of muscles stretched over his large frame or how it would feel moving in and above me.

But I wasn't.

My attention was fixed on the tattoo between Brent's shoulder blades. Inside a Celtic infinity loop was a skeleton cupping the earth in one hand and a scythe in the other. The entire piece looked hours fresh.

I had no clock to tell me how long I had been staring. I tried to gather the courage to ask him about it. Stupidly, I clammed up every time. And yet, with this hesitation, I mustered the nerve to inch across the mattress and slink behind him to have a closer look, on the off chance he had fallen asleep.

Heat boils away common sense I suppose.

I squinted as I crept closer. The lines of ink were flawless. No imperfections that made human-done tattoos so endearing. Whoever had tattooed it was a master of her skill. And if I was correct, the lineage was Celtic. The filigree swerved and arched with purpose, telling an intricate story about Death and his duty to humanity.

"It's about eighty years old," he said.

Halfway across the bed, I froze in my elbow-crawl, butt in the air. He'd heard me coming.

"Looks good, doesn't it?" He started to turn around.

I accomplished my first back flip. But I had no time to celebrate the triumph of mind over body, as I was determined to conceal myself with the bed sheet.

"There's no sense in covering up," he said in a husky but lighthearted voice. "I've got a great imagination."

"Was your ink done by Isobel?"

He nodded. A sad smile stretched across his lips. His eyes glazed as people's do when they're thinking about a memory.

"Sue Ellen told me a little about her today," I said.

"Figured she might."

"I'm sorry that you lost her."

His chest and shoulders expanded from a deep, calculated breath. "I'm sorry I kissed you and then acted like it was wrong."

That gave me pause. "I thought you said romance and rebellions don't go together?"

"I did." In the faint lighting, I watched one eyebrow lift, egging my libido on. At the moment, hiding out in the middle of Kentucky, standing on the edge of a life of a rebel, I felt oddly connected to Brent. I knew enough to feel somewhat at ease in his company, but not quite enough details to let him see just how much I needed him.

"Why did Isobel give you that tattoo?"

"It was a test of trust. She could've put her Deathmark there," he breathed out as if he had a million things to share and only the air to speak my name. His attention drifted to my right side. "How's your stab wound?"

I noticed how he twitched when I lifted the hem of my tank top to bare my stomach and ribs. The reflex was not an effort to shy away from seeing my body, but from something more carnal in nature. I deduced this from the subtle flicker of red in his blue eyes. Even this Eidolon, the most powerful Stygian I had met, next to Head Reaper Marin, couldn't mask his desire.

"The wound is fine." I had healed hours and hours ago. He knew that. I did too. Exposing my body was not entirely fair, but felt just fine from my perspective.

"I was thinking about what happened back in your apartment." His voice was soft and low, like he had been formulating a way to talk about it without igniting a fight between us—or something more pleasurable. "I shouldn't have come on so strong. But you are…you're an amazing being, Dormier."

I said nothing, trying to continue being the stoic hard-ass who was baring her torso in effort to lure him closer.

"We shouldn't allow ourselves to get involved," he added as he rose from the chair. Those butterflies in my stomach sprang into jumping jacks as he moved toward the bed.

"Why not?" I stuttered when his knee dipped into the mattress.

"I don't want the same thing that happened to Isobel to happen to you."

I snorted a laugh. "I've fucked up my life without the help of a rebellion. No reason that should get in our way."

Thankfully, he laughed too, as if it gave him relief.

A smile tugged at the corner of his mouth as he peeled back the tank top over the rise of my breasts.

I was certain he heard those butterflies thumping my stomach walls. But I didn't care either. He needed to know that behind my snarky exterior, I wanted him as well.

He trailed fingers across the plane of my belly. I gasped when they crept northward and stopped on the new pinkish scar. His eyes settled where his fingertips sat. For a while, he stared, and I found it in me to breathe steadily. That ended when he put his lips to the scar.

Had he done nothing more, I would have remained satisfied. But his hands found my hips, and a jolt zipped from my toes to my head. That feral stare wordlessly told me what he was planning next.

His thumb locked underneath my chin to force my face to align with his. There was softness in his lips when they met mine. His tongue moved carefully, asking for entry. And with each pass, I opened wider, inviting him.

I slipped my cool hands around his neck and through his hair. With a burst of excitement, I noted that in this moment, in these conditions, I fully trusted this Reaper. So I pulled my top over my head. He released a strange but contented growl, hooked his fingers on my panties, ignoring the catch of my breath, and slid them down my legs. Tingling rushed through me as I lay naked before him.

He covered my breasts entirely with his palms, kneading them with careful attention to each moan that slipped through my lips. I had no chance to overindulge. Those hands, working out the tension in my body, skated down to my hips, and then were gone.

The sounds of rustling clothing brought an impish smile to my lips. I watched his jeans slide over his hips to reveal his swollen erection. A pass of my tongue over my teeth and I curled my fingers around him, noting that my grip barely encircled him.

A bass rumble emanated from a secret place when I began to caress him, learning every inch of his manhood with each stroke. I quickly struck a rhythm while savoring the spasms rippling through him. He pinned my wrists on either side of my head and covered me. His lips took mine hostage again. The pillow dipped when he pressed his forearms into it for balance. Our fingers interlaced as his hips, hard with muscle, glided between my legs, forcing the tip of his sex against me.

"I want you," he whispered into my ear.

My lungs screamed for air, but somehow I uttered, "I want you, too."

Brent followed through to the hilt, stretching me beyond expectations. I threw my head back into the pillow and cried out in a blend of passion and pain—two things I never knew could be so damn harmonious.

But he stayed motionless. Quiet. As if he was uncertain.

"What is—?"

"Shh." His hand covered my mouth.

I was about to reach for his shoulders when he flew to his feet and into his jeans. I rolled up, riveted in panic.

"Stay here." He buttoned his jeans.

He tracked around the mattress, his muscles flexing with the cadence of his stride, jeans hanging from his hips. He descended into the darkness as Dudley sprang out of it. The mutt rushed up the stairs of the loft with his ears pulled back and tail tucked between his bony hind legs. His bottom was the last I saw of him before he vanished behind my backpack.

I clawed at the floor for something to wear other than the bed sheet. I found my panties and Brent's shirt. I threw both on. The buttoned flannel hung to my knees.

With my shotgun slung over my shoulder, I raced down the stairs. The barn door was slightly ajar where Brent had slipped out. I peeked through the crack. Brent's backside was to me. The moon didn't have to accentuate his musculature any more than nature already had. In only jeans, he was a Greek statue.

And he was standing before a militia of Watchmen, their scythe pins glistening in the moonlight.

Chapter Fifteen

"Death is our mission. Not egalitarianism."

—Bill of Stygian Rights, Preamble

"She can't run forever," said a voice from the other side of the cracked barn door. "Turn her in."

"I don't know where she is." Brent's voice was deeper than I had ever heard.

"You'll be charged for a Level Ten for harboring a terrorist if you don't hand her over. We know you're together to overthrow Marin's seat."

I cupped a hand over my mouth. *A terrorist? Overthrow Marin?*

"You weren't listening, son. I said I don't know where she is."

"We have a warrant decreed by Head Reaper Marin to search any location on the basis of suspicion." In the crack between the doors, the Watchman moved into eyeshot. He was quite young, but his eyes shimmered as bright as the moon. He was primed for a fight. "Let us search the property, and we won't make further trouble for you."

Brent hooted with laughter. "You are going to make trouble for *me*?"

"We'll do what we have to, Eidolon Hume." There was no mistaking his trepidation.

"What's going on?" Wallie was outside the barn, somewhere I couldn't see.

"You are not allowed on this property without permission, Watchmen." And there was Sue Ellen.

"We're here for Scrivener Olivia Iris Dormier, ma'am."

Brent left no opportunity for further conversation before he shifted into that lightless phantom. Sue Ellen's yelp echoed when a gang of Reapers swarmed him.

I started to pull the barn door open to help, when a hand found mine. Yellow eyes, like the headlights of a far-off car, stared at me. The rebel's grip was unrelenting as he dragged me across the barn toward a door that hung ajar. Another pair of yellow eyes peered through the door, waiting for us.

"Come with us," a teenage female Reaper murmured, grabbing my hand to help her young ally steer me toward the forest behind the barn.

I glanced over my shoulder, thinking of Brent defending a Scrivener from a hoard of Watchmen. Surely he could take them, but there was no dignity in running if it meant leaving him to fight my battle.

I resisted the young Reapers' pulls. "I've got to help him."

"No," one cried. "Brent told us to hide you if they come."

"We have a spot where they'll never find you," said

another voice from behind me. I turned to see yet another Reaper helping to shuffle me off into hiding.

"Brent knew they'd come?" I said.

"The Watchmen always come looking for trouble."

I stole another glance at the barn. A flash of black and white galloped toward us. Dudley's tail circled like a propeller. Thank Hades he made it.

"Come on." One rebel coiled her arms around my waist and pulled me toward the forest where Dudley had already disappeared.

One leap over a cluster of branches and we were encircled by a fortress of trunks, underbrush, and weeping spirits. Foliage scrabbled at my limbs. Twigs snapped underfoot. Disembodied hands of the ghosts grasped at us. The three young rebels knew the forest well, guiding Dudley and me over logs and patches of woolly moss.

My heart soared into my throat when I spotted a pair of yellow eyes. A Watchman closed his hand around one rebel's throat and she screeched.

I put the stock of my twelve-gauge against my shoulder when I came to stop. Having never shot anything that breathed, I didn't know about injuring Watchmen with gunpowder, but it was a damn good night to discover if it would work.

"Let her go," one rebel screamed. She and the male flanked me.

The Watchman tightened his grip on his victim's neck.

I cocked the gun.

"Turn yourself in, and I won't harm her." The Watchman's tenor was bitter.

My finger hooked the trigger. Could I get a shot in

without hurting my ally?

Behind him, the cooing spirits grew interested. Hands brushed his shoulders and the tips of his hair. He threw them off with an elbow but to no avail.

"You'd hurt innocent Reapers just to get to me?" I asked.

"Better to cut off young fruit than spoil the lot."

I took aim at his forehead. "I'm going to count to three and then I'm gonna see what triple-ought buckshot will do to a Watchman."

The rebel coughed as the Watchman's grip constricted.

"One more chance. Let her go," I said in a voice that didn't feel like me.

The rebel's arms flapped like a bird's against the hunter's body.

Through the forest, more Watchmen raced toward us. The ghosts cluttered their path, slowing them down, but they weren't enough to stop them entirely.

I aligned my shoulders for impact and squeezed the trigger. The gun's kick threw me off only by a little. A crack reverberated in the treetops. The Watchman's grip loosened, and the rebel fell forward but caught herself with her hands.

"Run!" I screamed.

The pair at my sides wrenched their friend to her feet and scampered behind me.

The Watchman's headless body crumpled to the ground. Curious souls gathered around him, uncertain at first. Was he going to join them or rise into the sky? Was he dead? When his spirit didn't lift out of his body, the souls picked at what was left of his head, pulling out blood vessels, possibly getting back at Death for being so cruel to them.

I cocked the gun again. The click ricocheted inside the

cathedral of trees. I had enough shots to take out most of the advancing Watchmen, if my aim was accurate. I locked the muzzle on one as he broke from the pack and closed in. This one was effortless. He went down, and a clique of souls peeled away to inspect him.

"Come on," cried the male rebel.

"I said hide," I barked.

He disappeared back into the undergrowth.

My attention went to another adversary in time to aim and fire again before he reached me but I missed. Until now, I had never missed a shot in my target practice—moving or stationary. I went to readjust my aim but was thrown to the ground. My shoulder blades slammed against a rock.

A red-eyed phantasm looked down at me. For the second time in three days, I was looking into the face of an Eidolon, the black beasts that all Stygians dreaded.

Tonight was the first time I didn't fear the closeness of an Eidolon.

"Stay down," his fiendish tone commanded.

"Hume!" Watchmen shouted in warning.

Brent circled to meet the enemies. His mass blocked out sight of the approaching enemy. The only thing in my view, sprawled over the forest floor nearby, was the headless body of the Watchman, thumping and rolling back and forth, entertaining the spirits. If the sight hadn't struck me as funny, it would have been excellent nightmare fuel.

"Eidolon Hume, we *will* subdue you if you force us."

Brent's miasma intensified, adding the weight of ten men over me, as numbness danced up my legs, creeping toward my core. Soon my legs and hips were submerged in nothing. The pressure grew heavier. I started to panic. My fingers and toes were the first to feel a tug, pulling me toward him like matter drawn into the singularity of a black hole.

So this was what his victims endured? Terror drawn into a noxious vacuum? While my power turned me into magma, Brent's turned him into arctic death. We were opposing forces, in some ways balanced by our divergence.

I recognized the drop of Brent's jaw and clapped my hands over my ears, having heard those Eidolon screams more than enough to keep me from sleeping soundly for the rest of my life. In conjunction with that vile chorus were the cheering spirits, watching like bloodthirsty hockey fans from the sidelines. It was too much to bear.

But I had to see him in action.

I craned and stretched my neck to see skin unravel from the Watchmen's bones as they drifted toward Brent. But as his power grew, I lifted from the ground, drawn into the dark vacuum as well. There was nothing to grasp onto. A second later, I crashed into his backside.

What should have been his spine and muscles, the same muscles I had run my hands over in passion earlier, was gelatinous. I wriggled my fingers and was quickly thrown back by a powerful force. I landed on that cursed rock again. The iciness receded. Voices quieted.

As I lay before Brent, my hearing didn't instantly return. The trees, the animals, the souls—everything—paused in awe of the power we had witnessed. Brent's shadow drifted away. Soon he was his human form. The skeleton tattoo, holding the scythe tenaciously in his grip, gazed down at me.

I swore he gave me a wink.

Brent stood over what was left of his prey. At his feet were three shriveled, discolored corpses stuck in their death screams. When Brent breathed out, their remains collapsed into a pile of ash at his feet.

Sue Ellen had a wicked eye on Brent, and she wasted no time expressing her discontent. She marched up to him, grunted, and struck him in the jaw. The controlled turn of Brent's head worried me. Would he take Sue Ellen out in front of her children?

"We never destroy Watchmen!" she yowled. "Marin will *ruin* us for this."

I was on my feet, with hands around Brent's forearms, before he could make a move on Sue Ellen. Wallie and a few nearby rebels threw themselves in front of her, but which one they were protecting I did not know. We were kidding ourselves though. None of us could stop Brent. The proof was in the Watchmen dust at our feet.

"This rebellion is not about injury to anyone but Marin," Sue Ellen said.

"I had to do it," Brent hissed.

"I know." Sue Ellen spun away. She was halfway to the porch when she shouted, "Wallie, we have to leave. *All* of us have to leave *now*!"

Wallie bowed his head. "Marin will send reinforcements once this gets back to him. We can't let him find us."

The three teenage rebels who had helped me escape from the barn slowly emerged from the shadows. Each gave me a passing glance of pity as they returned to their camp-sites. Others followed the same course, heads low, fear in their faces.

"Where will they go?" I asked Brent.

"Anywhere but here."

"You didn't have to take them out like—"

"I had to," he barked. "You are the only Master Scrivener we have. That makes you our only hope to bring Marin down. You are irreplaceable, Ollie."

My throat tightened upon hearing this. I had to touch Brent's shoulder to keep from falling to my knees or passing out. "I can't handle this pressure, Brent."

"You have no choice anymore. If you turn yourself in, he'll destroy you. If you stay with me, I'll make sure you never know what Erebus is like. I promise."

I liked knowing he was on my side. And perhaps he liked knowing that I was on his.

"So what do we do now?" I said.

"Get out of Dodge." He squared his shoulders. "But there's something I need to do first."

When he ripped the Mossberg from my shoulder, I didn't bother asking him what he had planned. Who asks a raging Eidolon with a shotgun about his intentions? Not this Scrivener. However, I chased Brent. So did anyone nearby that overheard him.

The ridges of his shoulders were awash in indigo moonlight as he traipsed through the woods and into the yard. The shotgun hung from his shoulder with the same ease that his jeans hung from his hips. He would have been beautiful if it were not for the maniacal lilt in his stride. He approached the rundown cars stacked on cinder blocks and put a fist through the rear window. Glass rained over the backseat.

The glare in his eyes was far more unsettling than anything I had seen from his beastly alter ego. He grabbed a gas can from the car's backseat. I scarcely had a chance to jump out of his way when he circled to the barn.

Several rebels raced down the steps of the cottage,

followed by Sue Ellen and Wallie.

"Brent, what are you—" she silenced when he passed her by without acknowledgement.

The Eidolon's back flexed in an expanse of muscle as he yanked the massive barn door open. He splashed gasoline over the straw covering the floor and shouted, "Ollie and anyone else, you have one minute to pack your things before this place gets blown to kingdom come."

I went into action without paying attention to anyone else but myself, my feet barely touched the ground as I ran. In the loft, I tossed everything into my backpack and didn't pause to slip on pants or shoes. There was no time. Brent hurled the gasoline can aside, where it landed with a hollow thud as I shot out of the powder keg.

The incoherent chattering from outside was filled with worry. Wallie and Sue Ellen stared with dropped jaws.

Brent's ire was impossible to ignore. And I didn't want to get in the way of it. So Dudley and I scurried off to one side, safely out of reach. Dudley crowded my legs. He knew trouble was afoot.

Brent put the gunstock to his shoulder, cocked it, aimed it at the kerosene lamp perched on the banister to the loft, and pulled the trigger. The lamp shattered and rained burning oil onto the gasoline. The resulting detonation sent us stumbling backward. Wood lit up like kindling. Smoke swirled from the orange and red flames. Heat burned my face, arms and legs, but left my backside cold.

Something is behind me.

The souls hovered at the forest's edge, and they watched with interest. I refused to fully look at them. I didn't want to see their pain or have it burned into my memory. But when the barn was fully engulfed in flames, creating a fire large enough to light the night sky, they drifted toward us.

Hundreds of them filtered into the clearing, down the creek, the embankment, and toward the inferno. I was motionless as a silent infantry of ghosts floated around me. Their chill was filled with relief, not despair. And I smiled inside.

The first souls to reach the barn moved into the fire. Their disembodied shapes intertwined with the smoke and flames before they shot toward the sky, at last united with the swarm of souls soaring above. The blend formed a kaleidoscope that if witnessed by human eyes, would merely appear like the smoke of a large pyre. We knew better.

Brent's attention was glued to the barn as I crept to his side.

"Fire reminds them of what it was like when they were alive," Brent said, somberly.

"Will it lead them home to the Afterlife?" I asked over the fire's crackle and Sue Ellen's wailing.

"Not directly. It'll only get them out of this place. With any luck, they'll find their way back to Québec with the other unferried souls where hopefully Marin will let them cross over, but probably not." We looked at the sky, now clouded over in souls, the way the sky should be when spirits were on their way to meet their destinies. The sun and the stars were beautiful, but they were gifts that were never meant for us. Overcast skies meant Styx was working as it should. And now in this small corner of the world, it was.

"Could you have done that for Eve?"

"Eve was half-ferried from her anchor. For one reason or another, these souls were never given directions to the

Afterlife. It's different. In many ways, worse."

The truth made me all the sadder for their suffering.

"Let's hope Marin is in a good mood, if they make it to Lethe." He shoved my shotgun back into my hands. I dropped everything to catch it. His gaze settled on my bare, muddy legs. "Put on your pants and boots. We've got a long hike back to the truck."

Chapter Sixteen

"All voting is a sort of gaming, like checkers or backgammon, with a slight moral tinge to it, a playing with right and wrong."

—Henry David Thoreau

"A continent-wide search has begun for a confirmed rebel uprising. Only hours ago, it was reported that Master Scrivener Olivia "Ollie" Iris Dormier has gone missing from her post in Québec City.

"Speculation is that Scrivener Dormier has united with known rebel Eidolon Brent Rutherford Hume to protest Head Reaper Marin's attempt at peaceful restoration of balance between humans and Stygians."

Brent's fist crushed the radio, reducing the background noise to just the hum of rubber tires on asphalt.

"I hate that they're calling us terrorists," I said as I flicked the corner of my drawing pad with my fingertips. The result was a click, click, click, as I unleashed my anxiety.

"They think it's terror if you piss yellow and shit brown." His eyes were hidden behind mirrored aviator sunglasses as the sun rose higher. "Out west there's pervasive contempt for Marin. We'll be fine there. Don't worry about what you hear on the radio."

Easy for him to say. He had learned to live with being a rebel. I hadn't.

I thought of Wallie, Sue Ellen, and all the other displaced rebels. We had come into their safe, happy home and, with the help of Marin's Watchmen, we tore it apart. "What will happen to the rebels?"

"They'll find other cells to hide out with. That's how it has always been. We get chased from place to place."

"Doesn't sound like much of a life."

"It's hell. One of these days it's gonna stop, even if I have to take Marin out alone."

"You can't take him out alone, though."

His aviator sunglasses snapped to me then back to the road.

"So how does it work exactly? I mean, taking out the Head Reaper." Not that I was interested in pursuing this cause. Least not yet.

"Since he's the top guy, the rules are specific. A Master must put a Deathmark on him. And an Eidolon must ferry him."

"Well that sounds easy." I snorted a laugh. "Let's go back to Québec and knock on his front door."

"*Cracker Barrel*!" Brent's hungry outburst caused him to lose control of the truck for a second. Dudley and I sought stability in seats and door handles.

Twenty minutes later, Brent was gnawing on Necco Wafers as we waited for our table for three at *Cracker Barrel*. We perused assorted knickknacks in the gift shop seasoned with Yankee Candle's Fresh Linen Spice. Brent had sweet-talked the hostess into letting Dudley join us. He told her Dudley was my service dog, who kept me composed in crowded social settings. Since the restaurant was packed from one wall to the other, the hostess hadn't objected.

We settled on jumbo checkers to pass our time as we waited. Buried deep under Brent's down jacket for warmth, I scooped the red pieces. Brent took the black. Both of us monitored the area for Watchmen.

Dudley sat at our feet. He groaned—he wasn't a fan of board games, just tennis balls.

"Mama loves *Cracker Barrel*." The everlasting knot in my stomach tightened an inch. "Maybe I'll grab a knickknack for her. Some memento from…what state are we in?"

"Missouri." He skipped a black chip over one of my red ones and then surveyed for Watchmen. "I hope you were kidding about going back to Québec."

I moved a red chip out of the line of fire. "I wasn't."

"We can't go back until we're ready."

"Marin should go down today, not a year from today."

"Crown me."

I scratched my head and then flipped over the game piece to make his plebian chip a king. "How did you do that so fast?"

"Used to play English Draughts back in the day. I'm *that* good."

"Pin a rose to your nose." I bounced a red piece over two of his, taking his players for my spoils.

He grimaced. Brent was a sore loser. Then again, so was I.

"What was life like back in the day?" I asked, hoping to distract him long enough to cheat my way to a chip's crowning. That's how Mama and I rolled. Papa always objected to playing board games with Mama and me for this very reason.

"Life was hellish," Brent said with a sigh. "The worst was when Marin assigned me to the Eidolon Naval Unit. I don't like the water and the things in it."

"Like krakens?" I had grown to love krakens after watching *Clash of the Titans* in sixth-grade history. Who wouldn't get excited to see a colossal lizardy monster devour a ship? It's epic.

"Krakens are mythological creatures. They don't exist."

I gave a shrug. I wasn't sure if his know-it-all attitude was for fun or for real. I twirled a dreadlock between my fingers as I strategized my next move. Cheating in front of Brent wasn't easy, even when he scanned for those scythe pins. "Where did you sail?"

"Shipped out from Le Nouvelle-Orleans in June of 1945, bound for the West Indies."

"Did you hunt krakens there?"

He looked at me like I had two heads, or several tentacles and an appetite for pirate ships, and said, "Spent more time raiding rum distilleries than working. That lasted ten years before Marin put an end to it."

He jumped his king over one of my pieces. Another red chip down.

"Did you get to travel to other places?" I asked.

"Was stationed in every continent besides Antarctica." From the lift in his baritone, he liked talking about his past, at least the more pleasant parts of it. "My favorite place was northwestern Montana, along the continental divide in the Rockies."

"Why?"

Melancholy crept into his contemplation. "If you've ever wondered if there is something greater than the world as we know it, visit Montana. All that untouched land shows you there's more than you and me, that we aren't just employees of Death. It levels the playing field between humans and Stygians. We're just souls, and we're happy for it."

That was not the answer I expected. "Could you be happy in Montana?"

"I'd be happy anywhere that makes me feel less like the monster I am."

I felt the same. Partly human. Mostly monster. "Are we going to Montana then?"

He tossed a black chip across the board, surrendering his impending win to me, and leaned back in the rocking chair. "I haven't seen mountains or breathed their air for too long. I want to see that before we face the heat."

I stared, for I couldn't speak. There was nothing I could say to make his dream a truth. And there was a niggling suspicion that the "heat" he referred to wasn't for our crimes, but for something greater, something that would change Styx—and us—forever.

"Dudley, party of three," the hostess boomed over the intercom.

After a fairly silent breakfast, we stopped at the gas station next to the restaurant to fill up before the ride west. I wandered around the station's shop for foods to keep us satiated once our feast would no longer tide us over. Had we been health nuts, this place would have been a nightmare.

I grabbed what I could carry and waddled to the register. Bags of Cheetos and Funyuns, bottles of soda, Pixie Sticks, and several Kit Kat bars blanketed the counter. The potbellied clerk didn't flinch at the pile of decadency. With my reddened eyes, dreads, and bellbottoms, he would assume I had a bad case of the munchies.

"It's a long drive to Colorado." I gave a flirty smile.

He went about scanning the barcodes for each item with the urgency of a stoned tortoise.

Great. This is going to take forever.

I folded my arms and gazed through the shop's glass door. Still wearing those aviator sunglasses, Brent was in the midst of filling the truck's gas tank. His chestnut hair rustled in the easterly breeze. He almost had me believing he was calmly apathetic through and through.

I fingered a wad of paper in the pocket of Brent's jacket. It rustled differently than the masses of empty candy wrappers strewn about in his car. The paper felt heavier. I withdrew it along with a couple of twenty-dollar bills. My heart fluttered when I read "Deathlist" on one corner of the crumpled mess.

The one he stole from Lethe?

"Come home. Please," a distraught voice said, and my eyes snapped up from staring in disbelief at what I was holding. My heart thudded violently in my ribcage as I looked around for the familiar woman's voice.

"He'll send us to Erebus," the woman spoke again.

A massive pressure took shape in my forehead. I shoved the Deathlist back into the jacket pocket when the clerk shifted to one side and revealed, from behind that distended belly, a small television with an antenna.

I didn't see a sports game or whatever he was watching. There was no collective cheer from fans or sportscasters giving a quick rundown of the plays.

What I saw stopped time.

Mama stood in front of a microphone. Papa was behind her. His eyes turned down like they had at his Meemaw's funeral years ago. Mama's face was creased with anxiety. Her hair was messily swept together in an orange bandana. I had never seen them so damaged and browbeaten, not even at the loss of their family members.

"Please come home." Mama's voice broke.

"Olivia," Papa urged. "Please help us."

My stomach lurched. I was "baby girl" and sometimes Ollie. Not Olivia.

"Stone and Lorelei Balanchine have been formally charged with a Level Nine Offense. Head Reaper Marin has given Scrivener Dormier forty-eight hours to return to Headquarters, or the Balanchines will be sent to Erebus," a reporter said as the image of Mama and Papa lingered. "If you come into contact with Scrivener Olivia 'Ollie' Dormier, do not attempt to apprehend her. She is dangerous. Contact your local Watchman immediately."

A picture of me smiling, as if the photographer caught me in a laugh, flashed onto the screen. My green eyes sparkled. It was not a sinister photo you would expect of a fugitive terrorist. The picture was from Mama and Papa's collection.

I doubted it would inspire panic in the hearts of Stygians. My inability to frown in front of any camera lens played to my advantage for once.

"That'll be twenty-two sixteen," the clerk said.

Startled by his words, I pressed a trembling hand to my chest, my breaths shallow.

"You okay, miss?" he asked.

I couldn't speak. I couldn't tell him that I had just found Brent's Deathlist and discovered that my parents were facing damnation. I wiped the tears from my eyes and nodded.

He dumped the last of my pickings into a brown paper bag anyway. His belly moved back in front of the television screen.

I slapped the two twenties down on the counter and muttered, "Keep the change."

The shop door swung shut behind me. I dove for the truck's driver's seat, tossed the bag of food in the back with Dudley, and patted at the ignition. The key slot was empty.

"Motherfucker!" I pounded the heels of my hands on the steering wheel.

"Looking for this?" Brent slid into the passenger seat with the truck key pinched between his fingers.

I plucked it away and rammed it into the ignition. I knew enough about driving a stick shift to put the car into neutral before turning the engine over. That was the extent of my experience. But I would tear through the gears to get the truck back to Québec City.

He covered the hand that death-gripped the shifter, slowly crisping the leather and melting the steel. "Why are you shaking? What happened in there?"

Tearful, I shoved him away and clutched the steering

wheel.

"You don't look right." He threw his hands around my wrists and gave a tug. I lost contact with the wheel before I could melt it into a defunct blob. "What's going on?"

"It's none of your goddamn business, Brent."

He didn't reply or back down, though I was sure I looked set on administering a Deathmark with my glare. Even as he fought the sting of my heat, he wore the stare of a militant soldier. He had years to perfect the gaze. I wouldn't conquer it in seconds. So, I blew air from my nose and gazed into the rearview mirror.

"I can't do this," I said at last, and felt no better for it. "I'm not a rebel. I'm a fuckup. Mama and Papa are going to be sent to Erebus unless I go back in the next forty-eight hours."

Those sapphire eyes became slits. "Get out of the driver's seat."

"No!"

"You'll get out by your will or mine."

I steeled myself. "This is *my* choice. Not yours. I have to save them."

"It's a trap, Ollie. The moment you step back into Québec, Marin will arrest you and banish you in one fell swoop."

"I don't fucking care. I won't let them go to Erebus on my account!"

"They'll go regardless. And you will, too, if you go back. Your parents don't want you to go down. They'd want you to stand up for yourself."

"Bullshit," I screamed. "It's bullshit. I have no choice."

We sat listening to Dudley's rustling in the backseat. Every one of the ten minutes we stared each other down, I wanted to yield to his influence. But when I thought of what he might suffer if he remained at my side, what everyone might suffer if I didn't go back and stand up for Eve and Mama and Papa, I reestablished my resolve.

"You're more naïve than I thought if you believe that Marin would show you or your parents any mercy," he hissed.

"I have to go back," I said, "and you can come with me or continue to hide out west."

Cussing under his breath, he climbed out of the truck in a huff and slammed the passenger door so hard, a crack slithered across the dirty windshield. I waited until he disappeared into the gas station shop and then I put my hands on the steering wheel. This was my chance to peel off without him. He may not be able to catch up if I cranked through the gears.

For a second time, the tang of burned leather filled the truck cab.

"Son-of-a-bitch!" My fist made contact with the dashboard. Bones crunched.

I wouldn't run from Marin and let everyone I loved die for my mistakes. There was no valor in it. Sooner or later the Watchmen would find me, and I would face my fate. I wouldn't spend a lifespan hiding away, yearning for the comforts of what I had thrown away while carrying the lost soul of my friend around my neck.

Screaming inside the truck was not adequate. I climbed out, slammed the door with a force comparable to Brent's, and kicked the sides with my hiking boots.

Dudley watched through the truck window with his ears pulled back.

I pumped my reddened hands when a bell tolled with

the swing of the shop's door. My hands in clubs, ready to serve up justice, I spotted Brent with a roll of silver Duct tape and a pair of oven mitts with "I heart Missouri" screen printed onto them.

"That's not gonna work," I snarled.

"It is merely ceremonial," his voice rattled with fury. Stalking toward me, he ripped off a strip of the tape with his teeth.

I knew I wasn't in trouble of becoming his prisoner, but I took off anyway. I was on my stomach with a knee in my back within ten feet from the truck, my right cheek squashed against the concrete stained with gasoline and oil.

As I writhed beneath him, he slipped the oven mitts on and taped them into a crude set of handcuffs fit for a Scrivener. He had my ankles bound before I could kick a body part he treasured. Brent was proficient and unnaturally quick.

"Fuck you, asshole!" I growled.

"Love it when you talk dirty." He wrenched me from the gasoline-stained pavement with one hand.

"Let me go."

"Never."

Chapter Seventeen

"Our powers do not reside in our Deathmark alone, dear daughter. May you have the fortitude to see that when you've flourished into Masterhood."

—Master Scrivener Richard Dormier on his execution day, January 1st, 1987

Brent held out a jelly jar. The campfire glistened like tawny crystal through the clear glass.

I tucked my knees to my chest. I had vowed to keep my eyes on the fire or the truck or the campsite Brent had whipped up somewhere in the prairies of eastern Colorado— anything that wasn't him. I wanted to go east. Brent wanted to go west.

And here we were, a couple hundred miles from the Continental-fucking-Divide.

My plan amounted to "make east with hell and fury on my ass." In my plan, Brent would either have to keep pace and join me, or risk getting burned like Nicholas Baird. But Brent was whip-smart. He'd know how to get around my fiery touch, which meant that I'd have to preempt him. Somehow.

"I'm not thirsty," I grumbled to my supposed friend.

"Drink it. This is the last time I'll ask nicely."

Mumbling curses, I kicked my legs straight and groaned. Clear liquid splashed around in the glass. I sniffed what was inside and gagged.

"Bleh. What is it?"

"Moonshine."

The fumes made my eyes water.

"It happens to the best of us, Ollie. We wig out and want to run back to our mommies. This isn't a happy life we're living, but it'll get easier as long as you stay focused and have a drink."

"I don't *want* to run home to Mommy because I'm scared. I have to go home to stop Marin from sending Mama and Papa to Erebus. There's a big difference, Bunyan." I whiffed the moonshine again, and it didn't seem quite so bad the second time around. But it was still revolting.

"I told you, the situation with Lorelei and Stone is a trap."

"How do you know? Did you read Marin's mind?"

"I know Marin. If he banishes them, he has no leverage over you, and right now, that leverage is all he has. Your position is better than you think."

I sighed, flaring my nostrils.

He pointed to the moonshine. "Do yourself a favor. Suck that down. You'll be higher than a kite in minutes."

"Why do you want me higher than a kite?"

"You need to relax, because you could go nuclear if you

keep up this anger."

"Isn't that a good thing?"

"It's only good when it serves a purpose, like melting bad guys."

I was gripping wrath with all I had, but looking at Brent made this difficult. Anyone could understand that, in his mind, he was protecting me from myself. His intentions were sweet. His execution was callous.

Still, drinking moonshine would soothe the anxiety forming a cancerous knot inside of me. I needed relief, if only for an hour or so.

"There's nothing you can do for anyone tonight," he said. "Take a load off and drink. Enjoy that we're in the middle of nowhere without a Watchman in sight."

I struggled not to spill the drink when I took the first sip. I coughed, but it didn't lessen the burn that rocketed from my lips to my stomach. The effects began instantaneously. My body melted into unconcerned tranquility. A moment later, my mind followed the same delighted path. I chased it with another drink.

He plopped down at my side and threw his legs out in front of him.

We watched the snapping campfire flames in silence. Dudley was curled up nearby. The sky spread out before us as a black and gray quilt of hazy spirits. Between the gaps in the souls were sparkles of starlight, exposing us to the heavens.

This was the nowhere.

There were no Watchmen patrolling the countryside, no scythe pins. We were two people sitting in a field. This must have been what Montana was like—a friendless, vacant place I would have wittingly lost myself in if I wasn't running for my life. This would be my future with Brent—a glimpse of what our shared fantasy would be, should we run for it.

I sipped the liquid fire again when I started to get feeling back in my hands and feet.

I didn't want to feel anything.

"So," I said several minutes later, enough time to ease the coil of muscles around my bones. I was moonshine's bitch now. And it was luxurious. "Are you going back to Québec with me?"

"You know the answer to that. Neither of us is going back until we're ready."

I wriggled my fingers and toes. I couldn't feel them. That cancerous knot? Benign and reduced in size. I generally tolerated a couple of beers before I started wailing Foreigner's "I Want to Know What Love Is" at the top of my lungs, but I had no clue what this five hundred-proof spirit would do if I took another sip. Screeching a cheesy love song was bad enough. Doing it in front of Brent was not my idea of holding myself together. Besides, I only needed a minor buzz to persuade him to loosen my wrists before I set off on foot for Québec with or without him.

I shoved the bottle at the Eidolon. "Since you're the experienced one here, what do rebels do with their downtime?"

"Drink. Fight. Screw. Drink some more. Get damned. What do you want to do? I'm not game for dying tonight."

I gave each option due thought and said, "Since fighting is on the list, want to learn how to give a face-buster? I promise it won't hurt…for long."

"If you fight anything like your papa, I'd rather not."

I studied his chiseled profile. "Sounds to me like Brent Hume is scared to lose a fight to *la petite mademoiselle*."

A dark eyebrow lifted. "I don't want to humiliate you in front of Dudley. Dogs remember these things."

"Well, what else is there to do?"

He didn't mask the bleed of yellow into the sapphire gems of his eyes. A pass of his tongue over his lips confirmed that he was thinking of that list of rebel activities, but he was clearly not interested in fighting, drinking, or dying.

I looked over myself. Sex appeal didn't ooze off of my getup of his flannel, my jeans, and muddy boots. I was anything but a coquettish minx.

"You know, Brent, I had lots of time to think about what we didn't finish in the barn loft earlier this morning. Kind of a shame we were interrupted, eh?"

That yellow gaze was on me. "An hour ago, you called me a lying sack of shit with rat testicles for balls."

"Sure, but I don't *hate* you."

His laugh revealed his skepticism.

"There are Pixie Stix in the bag in the backseat," I said. "Maybe you'll…"

He was over at the truck rummaging through the paper bag on the backseat before I finished my sentence, which was good because I forgot what I was saying. Over the crackle of paper, he mumbled that he was starving and then he backed out from the truck brandishing an array of Pixie Stix like a multi-colored lightsaber.

With one blue Pixie Stix hanging from his mouth, he sported an expression like a cat's as he teases his prey before he eats it. I grew uneasy until he threw a hand around the back of my neck, spat the Pixie Stix on the ground, and pulled me into a powerful kiss.

Despite his succulent kiss, all I could think about was

that my sweating hands were still bound, and I was, for the moment, at his mercy.

"I want you, Ollie," he whispered in my ear, his lips nipping at my earlobe. The remainder of the Pixie Stix plummeted to the ground, scattered at our sides.

"Then what's stopping you from having me?"

His hands cupped my cheeks, and he pulled me toward him, closing the space just enough that his lips brushed mine. I decided Styx could survive without my guilt and self-sacrifice for a few hours, because I wanted him, too.

All of him.

Brent peeled his flannel from his shoulders. His black T-shirt separated me from his skin. He pulled the shirt off in one smooth tug, unnecessarily flexing muscles in the amber glow of the campfire.

I put my lips and tongue to his chest. Tasting his body barely eased my frustration. My hands hungered for parts of him I couldn't reach, until his jeans sagged to his knees, exposing his straining masculinity. I passed my tongue between my teeth, biting the tip to control my need.

His reply to my obvious desire was unbuttoning my jeans and flannel shirt. I wriggled free from my clothes. But the flannel hung around my forearms, tangling as a mass of cotton around my wrists. As he undressed me, I explored the contours of his chest with my mouth—learning his body in place of my indisposed hands.

Brent cupped a breast in each hand and gently squeezed, but he didn't linger. There was more to explore. His hands travelled along my sides and over the arc of my back. With a hook of two thumbs under my panties, he lured them down my hips and thighs.

He leaned back and gave a growl that was not human, but dark and wicked, with the promise of doing exceptionally amazing things to me.

His gold eyes ran up and down my nude body. He was plotting his next move.

Before I could show him what I wanted, he put his lips to my collarbone and suckled his way down to one hardened nipple. I burrowed my fingernails into the cottony mitts when he bit down, simultaneously sliding a pair of fingers inside me.

My mind raced as I succumbed to his prowess. This splendid bit of exquisite musculature had fought and killed for me. This body belonged to a man who exuded raw machismo that made every last inch of me feeble at his touch. He had said I was amazing, but I hadn't the chance to tell him the same before I melted into his grip.

His tongue probed my stomach until it finally met the junction of my inner thighs. He looked at me, not for an invitation, but as a warning. I gasped when his tongue captured my womanhood in a hungry kiss. Somehow my legs were yanked out from under me. Our heap of discarded clothing broke my fall when I landed on my back.

I gave in.

I abandoned the struggle as every swirl of his tongue on my hot flesh drew out my essence for his own survival.

Moaning, I arched my back to deliver more to him. And all I could do to steady myself in case I fell off the earth was to put my mitted hands on the top of his head and steer his tongue to send me toward that blinding, pulsing release.

But I didn't close my eyes.

I had to watch his proud frame dance with my body. Only

his tongue worked me, and yet his whole body flexed and strained to satisfy me. The vision left me breathless. My head fell into the bedding of our clothes. My heart rate tripled.

Every last inch of me was powerless from total surrender.

"Brent, now," I cried out. "Please."

He took one last, intoxicating draw before moving between my thighs. He took his time, like we had a million years to reconnect. Our eyes locked. And then he fully sheathed himself. The barrier between us was gone. The daunting world I had been living inside of faded into insignificance. Our bodies were joined as they were meant to be. This connection was the safe haven I craved.

I buried my face into the crook of his neck. I tried to lure him closer as he hovered above, our hips joined together, but our lips distant.

"I want to watch you enjoy this," he said.

His long fingers curled around both of my wrists. He pinned them to the ground above my head and reclaimed my mouth with his. His kiss was voracious, and it told me he was barely holding on.

I didn't fight.

And because I didn't, he started one slow, deliberate stroke. I moved to accept him. After slipping inch by inch, his control gave way to a thrust.

He peeled his lips from mine and balanced on two straight arms. There was no hiding my face. He saw every flutter of my eyelids or bite of my lip. As I reveled giving in, he reveled in watching me enjoy our closeness as he rocked us toward that pinnacle.

Time stilled as he increased his tempo. He was everything I needed at this moment. I craved his love. I was one part of a whole with a friend who meant life and death to me.

"I can't hold out," I said in a harsh and uneven breath.

I locked my legs around his waist. He lifted my hips from the bedding as he delved deeper. Pacing was abandoned for that growing swell of satisfaction. I held on. I fought the heat brewing in me.

My body rippled in synchronized explosions in one final beat of passion. I couldn't see or hear anything, as if I was lifted into the cosmos. I didn't want to come down from it, though every last fiber of my being ached.

As I throbbed in ecstasy, he gave a growl before he burst. Shuddering, he slammed against me in his climax, twitching from a frenzy of his own pleasure.

This was what sent humans and Stygians alike into battle with prayers of life on the other side. This was the change I hoped for in my life. I had felt it, if only temporarily.

The symphony of crickets and crackling fire lured me back down to earth. My vision returned to the black firmament dotted with stars and souls. Brent appeared back over top of me, blocking eyeshot of the heavens above.

Accomplishment and satisfaction were embedded in his smile. His eyes were a cool blue.

His lips, sweet with my wetness, pressed to mine. Too soon, he sat back onto his heels and combed a hand through his hair, dripping with sweat. I propped myself on my elbows, feeling empty now that we were no longer physically engaged.

This perfection was what I had to look forward to in Montana.

Too bad I would never get to see the West's mountainous beauty.

Chapter Eighteen

"We must find this Scrivener.
We must find her Eidolon accomplice.
They will lead us."

— HermesHarbinger.com, 2:45 am 18 April, Sunday

18 APRIL

Brent was used to sleeping outside. The proof was lying before me, fast asleep as the fire roared beside him. He appeared just comfortable and relaxed as he might be on a recreational camping trip.

As for me, the idea of closing my eyes didn't appeal. Sleep was elusive.

There were many things I wanted to do. Cuddle next to Brent. Wake him up and ask for another round of intimacy. The strongest pull came from the slip of paper I had found buried in his jacket pocket earlier in the day.

His Deathlist.

Carefully watching Brent for signs of movement, I slipped my hand inside his jacket that lay discarded on my sleeping bag. The paper crackled when unfolded, but nothing that the pops from the fire couldn't mask. I gave Brent a close inspection and, just for good measure, a little nudge of his side.

He didn't budge.

I hustled to the other side of the fire where flames would hide my reading material should he awaken. There would be just enough of a gap to cram the Deathlist into my jeans pocket if he did.

Another glance across the fire—all was safe—and I turned my attention to the list.

Deathlist for Brent Rutherford Hume, Eidolon Reaper

I took in a deep, controlled breath to steady my shaking hands. I had never dared to read over another's Deathlist. It felt sacrilegious, disrespectful. Yet…

The topmost name on Brent's Deathlist gave me pause. I peered over the top of the paper at Brent at rest.

Jacob John Jackson

William James Jackson

Marcus Theodore Ruth

Derek Theodore Jackson

I stopped.

With a full breath, I dared to read the name I saw out of my periphery.

Olivia Iris Dormier

I read it over and over as incredulity swelled within me.

Olivia Iris Dormier

Olivia Iris Dormier

A sudden tightness in my chest left me breathless and dizzy. The Deathlist fluttered to the ground when I slapped both hands at my sides to stop the stunned heaviness from dragging me through the ground and into hell. Air would lighten my shock, I thought. It would clear my mind. Only punctuated gasps came to my rescue.

I should not have looked. It was stupid. What did I expect? Nothing good comes from Deathlists. And I would have been happily unaware of this one if I had more control over my curiosity.

Was Brent so desperate to escape Québec because, in the end, he'd have to be the one to end me? Would he fulfill his obligation if forced?

As the myriad of questions raced inside of my head, I found myself grabbing my belongings as Brent remained still by the fire. The only personal items I kept were a bag of clothes and the Interceptor. Everything else, I would leave behind. I wouldn't need much at any rate. Some cash, clothes, maybe my jacket.

I checked Brent periodically, but he was fast asleep as I dashed around him, my world turned upside-down for the third time in a week.

Sitting next to the truck's driver side door, Dudley's ears pulled back when I approached him. He must have known what I was up to. Dogs are intuitive creatures.

Tears welled in my eyes, I scratched Dudley behind his ears and then kissed his forehead. Dudley had represented stability and unconditional friendship. There was no possible way to repay him for all he had given me. But I couldn't take him with me.

Dudley whimpered.

"I have to go back..." Because if I didn't, Mama and Papa would go to Erebus, and there was a good chance that if I didn't plead their case and mine, Brent would eventually have to honor the job it seemed he was dragging us away from.

Those hound eyes blinked unhappily. He knew...or rather *I* knew what I was going to do was wrong, that it betrayed the bond between Brent and me. But sometimes we have to go against our hearts to save others, no matter how much it hurt.

The time is here for someone to make a goddamn difference.

I'll end it after bringing Marin to his knees. Somehow. With or without help.

I repeated the mantra for hours after reading Brent's Deathlist. Had someone been sitting next to me in the truck, they might have thrown a straitjacket around me. Traveling cross-country alone opens the mind to a surfeit of thoughts. Some are good.

But most thoughts eat away at your dying confidence.

Just as when I'd left Québec and Papa and Mama, I was sick for having left Brent behind, despite knowing about our lethal destiny. He could have taken me out at any moment. He remained by my side instead, protecting me however he could.

Anxiety had had its hold on me since leaving Québec after Eve's death. Today, it sent out rapid-fire attacks on my stomach. Soon, the unease would spread outward, taking my heart and lungs as its prisoners. It wouldn't be long before I succumbed entirely.

By the time I hit Buffalo, New York, at ten at night, I was beyond exhausted. My legs were stiff, buttocks raw, eyes crossed. And I had several more hours of driving ahead. Going against better judgment, I pulled into the Sisters Café, a greasy spoon that had seen kinder economic times and wasn't bustling with diners like the IHOP across the street.

I looked at my lifeless phone on the empty truck seat next to me. I had turned it off when we left Québec two days ago. Only now did I give it any thought. I pressed a button to give it life, because in some small way I hoped Mama or Papa had escaped Marin and were trying to call and tell me. The low battery light screamed for attention behind the log of missed calls. Mama had called fifty times. Papa had called fifty-four.

I ripped open the glove compartment and tossed the phone inside. The phone landed on top of a crumpled hat. I paused and plucked the discovery from the glove box. The deep blue garrison cap bore the United States Navy emblem. Sewn into the sweatband was *B. Hume*.

I was a history buff—human history, that is. I loved anything that shed light on their curious behaviors, which explained my reality TV habit, but the World War II relic lost its intrigue when I lifted a brown leather booklet tucked into the back of the glove compartment. The cracked spine groaned. Inside was Brent's recognizable, chicken-scratch handwriting.

"November fifth, 1944," I read aloud. Below the date was a sketched map in varying shades of black and blue ink, some of it drawn long ago, and some lines that could have been added yesterday. Written in faded black were the only two words I recognized:

Registry Vault.

I flipped the page to find a passage.

Château, main entrance. Across from elevator is left stairwell down to bottom floor. Another left. Employee door. Make another left, down a flight of stairs. Entrance is at the end of the corridor, around the boilers.

The headlights of a passing car startled me. I chucked the booklet back into the glove compartment and slammed it shut. The red sedan circled around the parking lot and then drove off, heading back toward the highway.

A figure—a woman—dashed away from the window of the Sisters Café when I looked up from the truck. She hustled back behind a counter.

Every car and person...*everything* felt like the enemy.

The aviator sunglasses would at least keep part of my face hidden for the brief minute I'd given myself for coffee. Maybe whoever saw me would think I was a movie star and not a harbinger of death wanted for a gazillion Level Ten Offenses.

I walked through the door of the Sisters Café with my guard on high alert. On either side were rows of empty red booths bound together with neon pink piping. Straight ahead was a bar covered in red menus, napkin holders, coffee mugs turned on end, and sugar dispensers. "The Girl from Ipanema" played softly from a speaker by the cash register.

Behind the counter, a busty woman in a pink uniform, with blonde hair pinned into curls and brows arched in black pencil invited me with a warm smile to come and sit. I noted the woman's nametag from across the diner—Clover. She was the one who had dashed from the window.

I strode to the counter with my head down. "Coffee to go, please."

"To *go*?"

"That's what I said."

"This ain't downtown Buffalo, honey. We don't have those paper cups like Starbucks. We do make a fine pot of coffee." A baby pink porcelain mug was flipped over and filled to the brim before I could protest. "Cream?"

When she poured the perfect amount of milk to turn the coffee a honey brown, just as Eve had always done, I halted my retreat. I put a finger to the lotus pendant. Eve. Mama and Papa. They needed me.

"Caffeine keeps me going on quiet nights like this," Clover said, unobservant of me inching away though I so badly wanted to snatch the mug and fly like the wind. "We have a lot of quiet nights now that everyone goes to IHOP next door. Most people who come in here are trying to avoid the crowd. What brings you here so late?"

She lowered the carafe to the counter. I turned toward the door.

"You… You aren't going back to Québec, are you? The Watchmen are looking for you there. You won't get far. Best you stay away."

I stopped. A surge of heat rushed into my hands. I looked over my shoulder at Clover. "What did you say?"

Her smile was replaced with wide-eyes when I slowly stalked toward her. Good. She knew she pushed too hard. "It's that… I recognize you under those glasses. It's your mouth. It turns down so prettily. Just like it does in your pictures on TV."

I scoped out the lay of the land again. No watchmen

appeared from a dark corner to slap me with an arrest warrant. No white vans pulled into the gravel parking lot. It was a muted television hanging from the ceiling to Clover's right that sickened me.

My face—and freckles—were on it.

"Shit!" I stomped my foot.

"Oh, dear!" She swung her full hips around the countertop and hustled toward me. "Please, don't go. You're safe here. No need to get upset."

"Stay back." I threw out my ruby hands. "I can mark you if I want."

"I know. *Everyone* knows." Her pink and black Skechers left streaks on the checkered tile when she skidded to a stop. "I'm on your side. We've been looking for you."

"*We?*"

On the television over her shoulder, there was a picture of me at Mama's niece's wedding that then scrolled to my visit to Montreal for my birthday, hiking at Gaspe Peninsula months ago, and at *Salon de Tatouage* with Gerard. It was a goddamn marquee of my life.

I snapped back to Clover. "Are you an undercover Watchman?"

"Heavens, no. I'm not a loyalist." Her eyes were glued to my fiery red hands. "I was given a message by a rebel cell out of Kentucky to be on the lookout for you, that we should help you if we find you."

I lowered my arms a little. "You're a rebel?"

"My whole life," Clover touted. "My sister, Violet was also a rebel."

My butt was an inch from the barstool when I stopped and said, "Violet Magby?"

Clover looked away, at the floor.

Violet had been executed for failing to meet her soul quota. But more importantly, she was believed to be part of a rebel cell.

"The Sisters Café. You and Violet are *the* Sisters," I said as an afterthought. "I'm so sorry." I didn't know what else to say. Sorry didn't feel sufficient.

"Violet went down with pride." That sounded as if she wasn't convinced of it yet.

Clover's raised eyebrows made her look sympathetic and sad for her sister, but there was a trace of grit that spoke to her want for revenge. I was facing a true rebel, one to replace the one who had fallen.

Rebellion is systemic. One day it would take over Styx.

One day was not soon enough to save me.

"You're the top rebel," she said. "Public enemy number one. Marin has every Watchman from here to California looking for you. He doesn't care if we commit one of his offenses because he's so desperate. Reapers are using this as a free pass. They love you for it."

She slid the cup of coffee toward the edge of the counter like someone attempting to coax a wild animal to the peanuts in her outstretched hand. "Here. Have something to drink."

I settled down over the cup of coffee with its perfect amount of cream. Clover began to fill me in with what she knew of the various rebel cells scattered across the country as I sipped my favorite drink from the ghastly pink mug. The coffee was as delicious as Eve's.

"How many of these clubs are there?" I interrupted after twenty minutes of her chat about monthly meetings, the Hermes Harbinger blog, and a history of the rebel cells that had been around since the early 1950's, after Scrivener Buddy Hennessey, Styx's Godfather of Revolutionaries, was executed for terrorism.

Had he not slipped up or slowed down, he would still be alive today. For all we knew, Buddy Hennessey could have deposed Head Reaper Marin. And he had been called a terrorist, like me. He was our Guy Fawkes.

What did that make Olivia Dormier then?

"Marin is raiding Reaper communities looking for anyone who smells like a dissident." Clover leaned over the counter and stuck out her round bottom.

I would have given a lot to have a quarter of her backside to fill my jeans.

"He's trying to bring down the blog, too. That's harder to regulate. No one knows who the author is, not even some of our top rebels. It's a mystery. They'll probably never find out. Did you know, yesterday the site reached five million visits? I don't think there are five million Reapers. I'm telling you, Ollie, if you want to unite everyone, get on the television or Internet and make a plea. We'll listen if you talk to us."

"You think that's all the rebellion needs?" I was incredulous but curious.

"The rebellion needs a voice. And you—"

"They're coming! I heard so over the radio scanner," a man with an Indian accent yelled as he raced across the Café at us, swinging a spatula high in the air.

I jumped and gave him a wild stare. He lowered his spatula.

"I mean you no harm," he said to me. Wearing a white apron covered in splotches of dried egg, the thin man was dark-skinned with a curly black beard and a navy blue turban.

"Who's coming, Azim?" Clover nudged.

There was an engaging hope hidden behind the alarm in Azim's round eyes. He stared at me as if he wanted to ask me a million questions, though there wasn't time to even properly introduce himself. "The Watchmen…"

Motherfucker.

"Hide, Olivia," Azim urged.

Car headlights washed over our faces.

"Hide behind the restaurant." Azim tucked his spatula under his arm and took my hand. "We'll take care of them."

Before I knew what he was doing, he had steered me to the rear of the restaurant, thrown open the backdoor to the café, and shoved me onto a square patio.

Chapter Nineteen

*"One cup of powdered sugar (three cups of sugar if serving
Reapers), One teaspoon each of baking soda, citric acid, and
tartaric acid, Two tablespoons of Kool-Aid.
And a pinch of extra sugar."*

—Lorelei Balanchine's Pixie Stix recipe

Azim closed the steel door, shielding me from whatever
was about to come down on the Sisters Café. I prickled with
anxiety. I was exposed outside.

I scanned the area to quiet my fears.

My choices for hiding spots were a dark barricade of pine
trees twenty feet away, a thirty-year-old beige Oldsmobile,
and a Dumpster appropriate for discarding a dead body…or
ten. I would have to make for the truck to escape.

With my back flat against the brick façade, I padded
toward a corner and inspected the parking lot. A familiar
white utility van—the Watchmen's paddy wagon—parked

alongside the truck nixed any thought of running for the vehicle and peeling away.

Fuck. Fuck. Fuck.

What I would have given for Brent's company at the moment. If I hadn't left him in such a hurry, I might have been in Buffalo and the Sisters Café with *him* by my side. He would know how to get from the rear of the café to the truck, and he'd do it without second-guessing himself like I was now.

"I have no idea what you're talking about," Clover's voice came muffled from the other side of the door. "We haven't seen anyone. No one ever comes to the diner anymore. They go to IHOP. Have you met Darlene there? She'd help you find someone. She's a nosy one."

I dove behind the Dumpster and rolled to a stop in a perfect, crouched position.

Metal creaked as the café's back door swung open.

Careful not to kick up gravel, I stretched out so that I could watch from under the Dumpster, maintaining a push-up in case I had to spring into action—not that I had a clue what I'd do if it came to that. I spied Clover's pink and black Skechers. She rolled one foot from side to side. Next to her, a pair of black wingtip shoes stepped confidently onto the little patio. A floodlight shined down on them, casting the shoes' stitching in dramatic contrast.

"See. Nothing. I told you," Clover said. "Now, would you care for a slice of pie? We're known for our pecan pie. Imitation sugar, of course. But you wouldn't notice the…" Her drivel faded when the door clicked shut behind them.

I let out a tense sigh and collapsed to the ground. From under the Dumpster, I spied the truck. I scrambled to my feet so my back was against the brick wall. I eyeballed my next move.

This check revealed a second Watchman standing next to the van, hands at his sides. He wasn't a towering Reaper, probably an inch or two taller than me.

The punk wore skinny jeans, loafers, a brown leisure jacket, and was far too blasé to sport his scythe on the lapel of his jacket. Instead, it was hanging from his belt loop at a slant.

"We haven't seen anyone like that," Clover shouted from inside the café.

"We've been on her tracks for days. We know she passed through here."

"I haven't seen her."

"Are you willing to testify in front of the Head Reaper that you haven't?"

A two-ton weight landed in my stomach. I'd have to make my move soon to keep Clover and Azim from trouble. I put my hip to the brick. My pocket crackled from a Pixie Stix.

I ripped off the top of the wrapper with my teeth, took in one big breath and, out of the shadows, trotted across the gravel parking lot toward the truck. My heart thudded so hard, I feared it might crack my sternum.

"Don't lie to me," shouted the Watchman inside the café.

"We haven't seen her." Her voice was strained.

"Hey, buddy." I called out to the Watchman.

Two gold dots locked on me before I sent a typhoon of sugar granules whizzing into the air. His eyes disappeared underneath an assault of sour apple Pixie dust. I rammed my shoulder into his chest, running full speed.

The impact threw the waif Reaper into the side of the van as he cried out from the assault. My hands broke into a luminous ruby glow. One gold eye popped open when my fingers went for his throat. His Adam's apple instantly collapsed, crushing his windpipe.

"I'll burn a Deathmark onto your neck if you fight me. Get in the van."

The café door hurled open and out ran his comrade.

"Stop." I barked. For some reason, he did. "I'll burn through his neck if you come closer."

The punk's wail and his singeing flesh backed up my warning.

"You can't fight two of us," the black-suit said, hands raised.

"I wouldn't test me on that, Grimmie."

Clover and Azim peered through the foggy café window. I spotted Clover's cheek trickling blood. Azim cupped his chin like his jaw might be broken.

"Get in the back of the van. Both of you."

The suit didn't move. But I wasn't about to send him a personal, handwritten invitation.

"I'll mark him. Do you want his hastened death on your conscience? Because that's what'll happen if I mark him."

"No," the suit growled.

"Then start moving."

Giving me a chilling death-stare, he strode to the back doors of the van. I wrenched his ally to his feet, my grip scorching his throat. The suit slapped two hands on the door latch and yanked the van open. My boldness withered from what I saw inside.

Five sets of eyes stared out at me from the dark van, terror in each watery gaze. I stared back at the five captives.

To what lengths would Marin go to catch me?

I saw brilliant shades of red. Wherever boldness went to hide, rage didn't give a shit.

"What were you going to do with them?" I demanded of the suit.

"Take them to Head Reaper." His voice was biting.

"Then what?"

The greenhorn Watchman howled. My hand had turned garnet. My fingers were set on eating away my captive's throat exactly as maggots devour rotting flesh from a bloated carcass. I tightened my clasp.

I wanted to watch my hand melt through the son of a bitch's neck as I slowly decapitated him. But his squeal snapped me out of it. I loosened my grip enough to keep from choking him and asked of his companion, "What will Marin do with them?"

"He'll send them to Erebus."

"Why?"

His eyes narrowed into citrine splinters. "Because of your rebellion."

I departed the Sisters Café in the white van. Locked in the back, the Watchmen were tied into statue-like immobility thanks to Azim's talent with rope. They had divulged, after an interrogation, that Marin decreed anyone who had contact with me, or was under suspicion of having contact, were to be returned to Lethe for due discipline. In other words: banished.

This left me terrified, evidenced by my death-grip on the

steering wheel, and enraged, evidenced by said death-grip slowly melting away said steering wheel. Maybe my hands knew more than I cared to admit. Maybe they were ready to deal out justice, and I hadn't quite caught up.

I wasn't sure if hunting Stygians was how Marin treated every rebel or if I had something extra special on other insurgents. All I was certain of was that I had sorely underestimated him.

He either knew my weakness, or he was damn lucky. I had lived long enough to prepare myself for what he would do to me alone. I couldn't watch those around me become his victims, too. I had helped snuff out enough souls. Too long I had slaved to Marin's megalomania.

No more.

I had left the five prisoners at the Sisters Café with a promise from Clover that she would see them safely to their homes straight away. I prayed I had left Clover and Azim with thoughts of a better world, because I was uncertain of it.

Suppose if they held out hope, maybe hope would return to me as I continued on the last leg of my expedition into a version of hell on Earth.

As I drove, the only source of companionship, aside from the gagged Watchmen groaning like two whining teenagers, was Marin's arid voice over the radio.

"I am well aware of the unrest that runs through Styx today. I say to you, be patient. I seek balance in these troubling times. I can only achieve balance with your assistance."

"Too little, too late, jackass," I groaned.

From the back of the van came muffled chirps.

"What's that?" I asked, checking my prisoners in the

mirror. "You've gotta pee?"

I jerked the wheel to the right. The Watchmen slammed against the side of the van and then hit the floor in a no-contact equivalent of a face-buster.

Papa would be proud of that one.

"In other news, fugitive rebel Master Scrivener and possible HermesHarbinger.com author, Olivia 'Ollie' Iris Dormier is still on the loose. Authorities have picked up on leads in the American states of Kentucky, Missouri, and now New York. It is only a matter of time until this terrorist will be caught and disciplined. Be patient, fellow Stygians."

The brief instant between the total darkness of night and the soul-cloudy dawn over Québec City was sacred to me. The city's stratified buildings, old and new, were stacked alongside the Saint Lawrence River as if rising to kiss the souls flowing over the crests of Levis and the Isle of Orleans.

This daybreak would've been beautiful if I weren't driving east on Autoroute 40 in a Stygian paddy wagon with two baddies in the back, and a steering wheel melted down to the metal ring.

The view of Québec reminded me of how much I'd missed the home I had spent a lifetime longing to escape. I had been gone a few days, and yet the city looked vibrant. Flowerbeds of tulips and English ivy sprouted life. I wove through the narrow streets of old-style buildings painted in a rainbow of colors. I passed by familiar places that had been landmarks on my daily walks to work. The Laundromat. The coffee shop.

I put my hand to the lotus pendant.

An Eve-less Le Nektar was open for business. My throat ached as I thought about her. I'd never again go into Le Nektar to find her standing behind the counter.

Eve was gone.

And the worst of it? I could not have saved her, because she had an enemy I could not have anticipated. Me. If Marin had his way, I'd soon follow in Eve's path.

Going straight to Erebus would be my well-deserved penance for failing my friend.

Not far away from Le Nektar was the tattoo parlor I had called home for years. The lights were low; a "Closed" sign hung in the window. Everything looked at a standstill from my drive-by.

I had thought to run straight for Mama and Papa's apartment. I was sure I'd find Watchmen there who'd lead me to Head Reaper Marin. But first, a little surprise for Marin—the Interceptor stowed inside my backpack. To put it to use, however, I needed tools and a self-taught crash course in overcoming my fear of heights.

I parked the van a few streets away and checked my captives for any loose ropes. They were as secure as when Azim had first tied the knots. Thank Hades that, as mere Reapers, they couldn't burn their way through them like I could.

The back door of *Salon de Tatouage* was in an alley wide enough to fit two slender people side by side. No one travelled through the passageway unless they worked or lived in the bordering buildings, so it kept me adequately concealed. The flat gray door was what I needed to get inside and out of view. I couldn't get to it fast enough.

A slip of the key and I was in the back room awash in

shadows. I tiptoed toward Gerard's office, where he kept a sizable toolkit that he used for odd jobs around the shop. That and some basic technology were all I would need to supersede Marin's daily broadcasts with my own.

Well, I prayed it was.

I was going to climb to the eighteen-story-high roof of Le Château, where the main Stygian broadcasting equipment was located, to rig the Interceptor to the Stygian antenna, interrupting Marin's mandated broadcasts with my own call to unite the rebels—one that would surely set Styx on the road to a full-on insurrection.

But I was still inside Gerard's office, not a hundred-and-eighty feet above the city. The soft green glow of Gerard's desktop computer pulsed like the beam of a tiny lighthouse, bringing me back down to terra firma. I was inches from the computer desk when my boot slipped out from under me.

I sailed into the air and squealed before I landed on my backside. The desk chair skidded across the floor and slammed into a file cabinet. I pressed my hands on the tile and lost traction again. My arms splayed out. My noggin cracked against the tile.

The pain wasn't as bad as my injured ego.

Hades only knew what else would fail me—brains, courage, bladder? I ran my hands down my face. At least no one saw this. If Brent had, he would surely...

What the...?

I inhaled a metallic pong. I rose, trying to get my feet underneath me. One foot slid over a plane of water, but I caught myself when I threw my shoulders over the desk. I yanked the lamp chain. A glow of forty watts illuminated the back room.

Painted from floor to ceiling and everywhere in between was a mosaic of bloody handprints in what looked to have been a sadistic fight. My foot and hand prints had streaked the red film blanketing the floor.

"Gerard?"

I started toward the door. My knees collapsed, and I crashed into a file cabinet. Over and over I attempted to stand, until I spilled out of the office and into the storefront. An amber blush cast the walls of black and white tattoo flash and workstations in early morning warmth.

But it was not a beautiful, welcoming picture.

Gerard, bloody and weak from a beating, was held upright by Chad's single-handed grip. Behind them was a pair of Watchmen, arms folded over their chests and those damned scythes pins winking at my predicament.

Chapter Twenty

"Scriveners are my curse."

—Head Reaper Marin

19 APRIL

"Lookie here," Chad sneered, and all feeling drained out of my body. "The Scrivie returns."

Gerard's strained face reddened from Chad's tightening grip. His fingernails cut into my mentor's throat, and though I had no personal experience with Chad's power, I was confident he was displaying only a smidgen of what strength he possessed. The two Watchmen lingered, seemingly waiting for Chad to give his command.

My muscles were reduced to paralysis. Firing on all cylinders, my mind begged me to dash out of the shop and run for safety. But my heart, pounding like a trapped, wild animal inside my ribcage, urged me to stay and fight. Gerard needed my help.

I couldn't let them see my fear, even if it had flashed across my face in the instant I walked into the room. I had to hide it, mask it, and convince myself that I was a warrior hell-bent on protecting Gerard, while inside I was screaming for a quick death.

My hands throbbed with heat like they had hours earlier outside of the Sisters Café.

"Don't hurt him," I uttered a plea for my mentor and friend, wishing I had enough air in my lungs to speak more persuasively. My knees buckled slightly when I attempted to root my stance. The shift of the Watchmen's eyes told me they noticed it. "You want me to turn myself in?"

"Ollie, don't," Gerard grunted.

Chad's grip constricted an inch. Gerard gasped. I couldn't help but wish Gerard could call on his own power or heat to help himself. One clamp of a singeing hand around Chad's neck would be a sufficient attack. But Gerard, bloody and weak, had nothing in him, no life force powerful enough to save himself. And as far as I knew, he wasn't a Master.

However, my own heat rose like wildfire up my arms and toward my shoulders. Rare was the occasion when this talent in my hands outsourced itself to the rest of my body. Now that it had, I peeled my jacket away, letting it drop to the floor at my feet. The hawk eyes of my adversaries followed my every move. My ruby-colored arms were certainly an unsettling vision, or so I assumed, because just as they spied uncertainty in my weak knees, I spied something in them. Hesitancy? Regret? Fear?

"Let him go, and I'll turn myself in," I said with confidence I didn't know I had.

"See here, Scrivie, I don't have to negotiate with you," Chad bit back. "You have no leverage."

The shift in the Watchmen's faces told a slightly different story. They didn't want to get near me; that much was obvious. Touching this Scrivener would risk burns, and if they knew anything about Nick Baird's fate, they knew what I was capable of. Or so I hoped.

But Chad's threat on my life and Gerard's was greater than anything else.

I needed help—Brent and Clover and Azim. No, I needed a whole army to help me put an end to the senselessness. Alive or dead, it wouldn't matter. Marin would continue his tyranny, and his loyalists would enforce it.

The next move was mine, and my primary concern was seeing that Gerard walked away unscathed. I put my hands into the air to show my intent to surrender. A drop to my knees was my laying down of arms. Just as I began to bow my head and tell them that I was giving in, I watched Chad's gray eyes transition into Eidolon death-red.

"No!" I shrieked.

The time between the air leaving my lungs and my legs propelling me upright was sufficient for Chad to draw out Gerard's soul. In one vile inhale, my mentor of twelve years, the only other Scrivener I knew, my friend, and the man I turned to for advice, was gone. Ash collected on the floor where Gerard once stood. In an instant, Gerard became a memory, all because of my choices and actions.

There was no logic, or hesitating, or thinking. What little sense I had was gone. I threw myself at Chad, knocked him to his back, and clamped my red hands around his throat as my lungs poured out a murderous screech. In the reflection of the shop's window, I caught a glimpse of myself. I didn't recognize this Scrivener, this beast in a red bodysuit filled brimful with insurmountable rage.

Chad wasn't quick to let me have my way. I had no doubt that he had encountered a Master Scrivener's full-blown ire before. Unlike Nicholas Baird, he had skills beyond the average Reaper. So, I held onto his neck with all my might, and I willed death upon him as the Watchmen pulled at my shoulders and legs and hair to remove me from my prey.

Chad didn't need their help, however. My grip slackened when he morphed into that vaporous, horrid blackness that I had seen before. He was just as horrifying, just as brooding, and just as commanding as I remembered. The two Watchmen and myself were thrown across the shop by an unseen force. The brick wall separating *Salon de Tatouage* from the hair salon next door broke my fall. I slid to my buttocks but wasted no time scraping my feet against the blood-covered floor as Chad's dark alter ego advanced.

This time his hand found my neck. My feet came off of the floor while my back and scorching red arms pressed against the brick wall.

Chad's red stare bored into my wide eyes.

"Now I see why Brent Hume had his eye on you." Pinning me to the wall, he raked me from head to toe with his contempt. "Too bad you'll go to Erebus before you realize what it means to be a Master."

My arms and hands struggled to find grip on the brick wall. I felt what should've been mortar and stone fuse together into an impervious barrier of liquid fire. The wall was melting from my touch.

Or was it disintegrating?

Or—when I felt cool air brush my palms—was it vanishing?

I wanted to see, to know what was happening, and I got a chance when I fell backward through the wall. I slid across the floor of the hair salon, slamming into a stylist's chair. Bricks crashed to the floor of the dark, unopened shop. The liquefied portions of the brick wall dripped from the hole I had burned through it.

Without giving much consideration to this newfound skill, I grabbed the nearest object—a metal can of hairspray—and hurled it full-force at Chad's misty shadow and then threw my weight against the salon's front door, setting off the alarm. The chill in the air was hard on my lungs as I ran from Chad and the Watchmen. I ran hard and fast until my body couldn't run any longer.

In the back alley of two brick buildings in Haute-Ville, I stopped and hid behind a green Dumpster, huddled down like the fugitive I was.

Chad and the Watchmen had been close behind me, but they lost my trail when I used Québec's winding streets to my advantage. They weren't completely gone, however. Their voices could be heard some distance away.

I peeked around the edge of the Dumpster to gauge the scene. I waited an extra beat of silence before I turned around to see red eyes peering at me. A pair of hands covered my mouth as I drew in air to scream.

"Shh." Brent's eyes scanned the end of the alley for pursuers.

I shoved his hands away and whispered, "What are you doing here? How did you find me?"

"I had a damn fine idea where you took off to." He matched my volume and tone.

"Where's Dudley? Did you leave him behind?" I had to know. People I loved were dropping dead at my feet. Dudley's safety mattered.

His heavy brow furrowed. "Don't change the subject. What are *you* doing here? We have sex, and then you ditch me? That's shitty."

"You know why I had to come back," I argued.

He rose to his feet, obviously no longer concerned about detection, and so I followed his lead and stood up, too. "Fine, Ollie. We'll play the game your way."

"Damn right we will." I tamped down my regret and guilt for Gerard as I faced Brent. I had grown used to guilt eating away at me. Another soul on my conscience wouldn't break me.

I was already broken.

"Chad took Gerard out," I said. My throat constricted and eyes watered thinking of Gerard's fate. I should've done more. I should've saved him.

Brent sighed. "He'll take out your parents next if he's their assigned Eidolon."

"I know. But at least he can't take me out since *you're* the only one who can."

He looked at me as if I could read minds.

"I read your Deathlist. I know that I'm on it," I said, to answer his quizzical expression. I set my attention on him and waited for a reaction.

"Then you know why I was trying to get you as far from

this place as possible—so that Marin couldn't capture you, put you on trial, and then have you sent to Erebus. I couldn't bear to be the one to send you, Ollie." Brent leveled his gaze on my defiant stance. But I couldn't read his expression. Was he upset? Angry? Ready to turn me in for betraying my promise to him?

Never mind his thoughts. My plan hadn't ended. It was just impeded. I had to get the Interceptor mounted, and then I'd speak to Styx and, more importantly, Marin, on behalf of my parents. I couldn't let anyone else suffer—Mama, Papa, Brent. I wouldn't.

"I want to protect those I love," I said, not as a plea, but as an unwavering vow. "It's not my fault that you are afraid to honor your Deathlist."

"Listen to me for a moment. I read my list after we got back from the Registry Vault. I almost told you, but I needed to get you out of Québec because I knew if you stayed, I would have to fulfill the assignment." He spoke in a soothing tone, combating the tension in my body. "I couldn't say it sooner. I just…just didn't have the words."

I didn't know how to channel my frustration, how to tame it now that it was pushed into overdrive. I couldn't ignore the urge to rip everything I loved and hated apart, starting with Marin. Anger was a budding malignancy working its way through my heart. What was I supposed to do with it?

"Ollie, I'm sorry. Give me a chance to figure things out, and then we'll come—"

"I have something to say that everyone in Styx needs to hear. I need your help though." When our eyes met again, he saw it—the fire in me, the Scrivener who would first burn through brick walls and then the world to make her point. He knew I could do it. Only now did I feel I could do it, too.

"Whatever your plan, it involves the both of us," he said, trying to pull me back to practicality. "Your decisions affect me. Let's talk about this."

"Nothing can change what you'll eventually have to do, Brent. Help me stand up to Marin and save my parents. Please."

There was a familiar tension in Brent's face. The same strain he carried at Cracker Barrel and the gas station; the same edge that he used against the Watchmen in Kentucky. Thinking he would offer up a rebel's handshake, I was surprised when he instead pulled me into his arms. Those familiar flexed muscles held me tight to his chest. His head fell to the skin between my neck and shoulders. My flesh blossomed with goose bumps from the brush of his beard. I buried my face against him and breathed him in.

"I will go to hell and back for you," he whispered into my neck.

My arms tightened around his body, drawing him even closer as his words rooted themselves in the core of my soul. I wanted to tell him that I felt the same, too, but I couldn't form the words. Not before I spotted, through glassy tears, the newest danger approaching from the opposite end of the alley.

"We have trouble," I said, unfurling from him.

An engine that sounded like a semi-truck boomed to life at one end of the alley. A silver sedan screeched to a stop in front of us, reverberating the ground under our feet. The tinted gray passenger window wheezed as it rolled down. A blast of thudding rap music—Snoop Dog, maybe—threw me back.

"Turn it down," the female passenger snapped.

The music quieted a second later.

"C-Clover?" I stammered. "What are you doing here?"

Her beam spanned from ear to ear. "*Bonjour*, Olivia."

I did a double take of the sinewy Reaper behind the wheel. Azim had shaved his beard, but still wore his blue turban and that brimming grin. I would recognize him from miles away.

"Why are they here?" I asked Brent.

"Doesn't matter. We have to get out of sight." Brent flung open the back door. He shoved me inside the car. I slid across cool leather, making a note of the Mercedes Benz logo embroidered into the headrests.

Brent tapped Azim's shoulder and slammed the door. The car took off, roaring out a lion's call, and threw us all into our seats.

"Would someone please tell me what is going on?" I finally had the ability to formulate words.

"I followed your trail," Brent answered, keeping his gaze set ahead. "I met Azim and Clover shortly after you left Buffalo."

"We thought we were too late when we drove past the tattoo parlor and saw it was destroyed," Azim said.

The sedan rocked as he swerved in and out of traffic. Azim's talent for staying unperturbed didn't surprise me. Back in Buffalo, while he had tied up the Watchmen and dumped them in the back of the van, he prattled on about the latest blog post on Hermes Harbinger—and he had done it with a smile.

The car veered onto Autoroute Dufferin-Montmorency.

The Isle of Orleans, with its humble ridges, was on our right, coming into view through the morning fog billowing over the Saint Lawrence River. The island grew larger as we approached Pont de L'Île D'Orléans—the only bridge that linked it to Québec City.

"Why are we headed toward the Isle?" I gazed out the windshield.

"Québec City's rebel cell is having an emergency meeting," Clover said. "And you're the guest of honor."

Chapter Twenty-One

"We must find this Scrivener.
We must find her Eidolon accomplice.
They will lead us."

—HermesHarbinger.com, 2:45 am 18 April - Sunday

The Isle of Orleans was an island of rolling hills blanketed with vineyards overlooking the Saint Lawrence River and Québec City. Most locals visited for a quick escape from downtown. I had come here plenty of times when I was a kid, climbing trees and sneaking grapes from the vineyards.

We arrived at a quaint cottage with a painted red door and white stucco siding.

"This is where the rebels are meeting?" I'd imagined that the Québec City rebels would meet in some forgotten factory building miles from downtown.

"Yes, ma'am," Clover replied, balancing a mountain of Sisters Café sweatshirts in her arms. She and Azim had crammed the trunk full of them to pass out as a sort of rebel uniform. Brent had called it Death Swag. He wasn't that far off.

Nonetheless, the clean red sweatshirt I was buried under brought warmth on the chilly spring day.

"Best we not stay out here for them to find us. Everyone get inside," Brent demanded and we—all of us—obliged without delay.

Uneven wood floors as old as Québec groaned under us as our parade entered the cottage, which was reminiscent of a northwestern mountain lodge that had gone forgotten. The furniture was pieced together from scrapped tree parts. A dusty moose's head hung above the fireplace. And all semblance of a lively rebel meeting stopped.

More than two-dozen golden eyes fixated on me simultaneously, each pair glistening in the light of the crackling fireplace.

Brent and I stood side by side, fingers interlaced. I wasn't convinced that somehow we'd been duped into a trap fashioned by Marin, but I eyed everyone, plotting how we'd escape if this were indeed an ambush.

But then something gave me pause.

The clicking of nails on the hardwood floors started after I took several long breaths. Dudley trotted past all the pairs of legs toward me. He reared up, tail slapping from side to side when I dropped to the floor. Those beady hound eyes bulged. I pulled him to me and gave him a suffocating hug.

"Duds," I said to my furry companion. He licked my cheek, a habit I didn't like because I knew where that tongue had been. "Was Brent good to you, buddy?"

"He was treated like royalty," Brent answered from

behind me.

My legs drove me upright when a male Reaper with a steely gaze peeled away from the group and made his approach. Blond hair scraped his wide shoulders. He was as tall as Brent and as filled out. A scythe was pinned to his crisp black shirt collar.

I looked around. Everyone, including Azim and Clover, stood in awe of this Reaper, except for Brent, who looked like he was two seconds away from snapping him in half.

"Scrivener Dormier, I am Garik, Head Watchman for the First Precinct of Styx. As you know, every Watchman in the Province of Québec reports to me." His thick French-Canadian accent melted each vowel into the next. He had a commanding air about him. "I am also the head of this rebel cell."

A floorboard creaked when Garik took another step toward me. Brent inched closer to my side like the steadfast soldier he was. Garik stopped. His simple good looks remained cool. No smile. No frown.

"Thankfully, one of us discovered you before Marin did," he said, giving Brent a sidelong glance. "Now that we have you, we need your help."

Right. This wasn't a "Hey, let's have punch and cookies while we talk about how to make Styx a better place" type meeting, was it?

"You want help with deposing Marin." I already knew. No sense in wasting air.

"Then it seems we are on the same page," Garik said with a cunning smile.

I squared my shoulders. "So long as we play by my rules, we are."

Garik stared pointedly. Perhaps he didn't expect me to be quite so demanding.

"Will you do what I say?" I needed to know the answer and *now*.

"I cannot promise we will agree to your orders, Scrivener Dormier."

"I think you should," Brent interjected. "Dormier knows what she's doing."

Garik raised one eyebrow. "Would you do what she says?"

Brent squeezed my hand. "I trust her. So should you."

Every Reaper in earshot muttered comments to each other. Faces that were glum smiled. Voices that had seemed hesitant were energized by what they heard. Brent Hume's loyalty to me seemed to be enough to earn their conviction, or at least their interest.

Garik waited until they quieted down before he spoke again. "Let's hear your plan then, Scrivener Dormier."

After telling the rebels my plan, which amounted to putting myself in the public spotlight to call on the union of anyone who opposed Marin's fascism, they weren't keen to help. They wanted me to say that I would run headlong into Lethe and boil the flesh off of Marin's bones. That's all they cared to hear.

I acquiesced to their pleas after hearing their counter proposal, however. I would make my public broadcast, and then Brent would help us get into Lethe. From there we would stop Marin for good. While I wasn't entirely certain that I could, I needed the rebels to help me speak out and, in the end, save Mama and Papa.

But after a couple hours of plotting and strategizing, I needed air. I slipped out the back door and onto a little concrete patio where new grass sprouted through a myriad of cracks. An upturned lawn chair with rusted legs would have been a lovely place to sit and stare out over the expanse of naked vineyards nearby, if I didn't have so much on my mind.

I finally had time to process everything that had happened in a few short days. Eve's death. Mama and Papa's capture. And now the most recent—Gerard's banishment to Erebus.

I put my hands to my face and breathed in as deeply as I could.

Enough was enough.

By capturing Mama and Papa and banishing Gerard, Marin was making it clear he meant to bring me to my knees in front of all of Styx. Before now, he wouldn't have had a single person to answer to about injustices like these. Until Hermes Harbinger had popped up.

Until today.

I tore at a hangnail with my teeth. Papa would have given me a disapproving glance if he saw me now. He had always said I had pretty hands—that I shouldn't hurt them. I tucked them into the kangaroo pocket of my sweatshirt.

"I'm going to destroy Marin," I said, hopeful that those I loved could hear me from across miles and dimensions.

The back door cracked open and Brent poked his head out. Clutching a mug of tea, he stepped outside. We stood quietly for a moment, our red sweatshirts from Azim and Clover binding us together as rebels. Against the springtime

chill, steam from the drink spiraled out of the mug like miniature spirits rising toward the sky.

Brent offered me the drink. A whiff of lavender swept
over me. I took a sip.

"Lavender is calming," he said.

"I'd need a vat of this stuff to calm me down."

"Or maybe just a keg of beer."

"That, too."

We laughed, but it was a tense, forced laugh.

Brent ran his hands down his face and dropped them to
his sides. His expression lost its lightheartedness. His brow
carried the stress of the world. Had I the power to kiss that
stress away, I would have, but the best I could do was set the
tea down on the patio, take his hand, and pull him toward an
age-old maple tree that reminded me of one I had climbed
every summer in my childhood.

"How did you escape Garik's lecture?" I gave his hand
a squeeze to assess his mood.

He returned the effort by interlacing his fingers with
mine. His grip tightened then, as if I or my hand might run
away again. "Garik's got his head so far up his ass, he probably can't see that the Reaper sitting in my place is five-foot-
two and female."

"You don't trust him?"

"I don't trust anyone who plays both sides." Brent's eyes
narrowed as he spied the maple tree I was steering us toward.
The branches were filling in with bright green leaves. Without asking, he put his hands on my hips and lifted me onto
the lowest branch. I didn't need the assistance, and he knew
that. Brent just wanted to touch me—a fact I welcomed.

As I settled onto my perch, feet dangling a couple feet

above the ground, Brent sat next to me, his shoulder pressed against mine. How appropriate that as we gazed across the vineyards back toward the house, the sun began its descent.

We sat in silence, listening to the ambient noises, squished together on the branch like a pair of teenage lovers. This stillness was the peaceful center of the hurricane. The storm was coming. We would be in the thick of it sooner than I wanted to acknowledge.

This fleeting ceasefire was paradise.

"Are you ready for this?" he asked, in reference to the plan of attack.

My eyes fluttered shut in an effort to keep the world of Styx and rebellion separate from the tranquility of the moment. "I have no choice, whether I'm ready or not."

"Guess that's how rebellions work."

"Suppose so." I looked back at the sky and then at Brent, where I caught a fleck of anxiety in his expression. His confidence slackened, like he wanted to drag me through the earth's core and all the way to China, miles from this mess.

My cold fingers barely felt his beard when I drew him in for a show of thanks. For once, I was cool and calm as he enfolded me in his arms, deepening our kiss as the sun set on our slice of peace.

Chapter Twenty-Two

"There is probably no pleasure equal to the pleasure of climbing a dangerous Alp; but it is a pleasure which is confined strictly to people who can find pleasure in it."

—Mark Twain

27 APRIL

The morning sun was bright and vibrant over the Isle of Orleans. Brent darted in and out of the cottage, loading the Mercedes's trunk with ropes, harnesses, and tool chests that we had acquired from the rebel cell. I wrung his World War II cap in my hands, my only sign of disquiet.

Brent swept a hand across his sweat-covered brow. "What do you have in that brown toolbox though? Thing weighs a ton."

"Some tools." I stuffed the garrison cap inside one of the giant pockets of my navy blue jumpsuit, which had "Zooey" embroidered across the chest pocket. Brent, Azim, and Clover wore the same costumes, except their suits were named "Juno," "Boris," and "Rebecca" respectively.

The Mercedes creaked when Brent dumped the last of the goods into the trunk. "The weatherman said it'll be sunny until early afternoon. We should get moving now, because it will be more difficult to install that doohickey to the roof if it is raining or snowing."

"It's an Interceptor," Azim said, standing next to the driver's side of the Mercedes.

"It's a *doo*hickey."

In the hours since arriving at the Isle, Azim and I had to remind Brent that the Interceptor, the square metal box, was our key to seizing Styx's main broadcasting system. Hooked up to the antenna, it would be our means to connecting to the masses.

Brent checked the sky. "We better hurry."

"He's correct. We can't delay," Garik said as he climbed into a white Watchman van.

Towering over Québec City in verdigris copper and russet stone, the fairy tale stronghold atop a mountain, Le Château Frontenac, awaited our arrival. The wide central tower of the Château looked taller than ever when we made our final turn into the hotel's courtyard. In minutes, Brent and I would be dangling from the top from a blue rope the diameter of my pinkie. The notion turned my already unsettled stomach.

Brent, Clover, and I climbed out of the Mercedes and

left Azim sitting at the wheel, prepared to make our getaway. We agreed that blending with humans would hide us from Watchmen. Or at least it would confuse them long enough for us to make our escape.

Around us, flags representing ambassadors from France, Great Britain, and Italy flapped in the brisk April wind. The Québec City flag, with its four white fleurs-de-lis and a cross embedded in royal blue, saluted us from high above.

The bellhops retrieved luggage from the row of guests' cars. They never knew that three citizens of Styx walked past them. We hustled one by one through the turnstile doors to step into Le Château's lobby for the first time.

Panels of mahogany adorned with sconces and chandeliers encased us. Together, we stood in front of the revolving doorway as blasts of cool air swatted our backsides, inviting us to retreat. Granite floors were blanketed in Persian rugs. The elaborate furniture looked too elegant to be comfortable. Ebullient workers trotted around the lobby in their pressed suits and red bowties, assisting guests. Dressed in our navy jumpsuits and army boots, toolboxes in hand, the three of us Stygians were plebeians among human monarchs.

I tucked my hands into my jumper's pockets. "I can't believe I've never been here."

Brent hooted. "I can. This place isn't for the poor."

"I'd have to start charging for the Café's sweatshirts to stay one night here." Clover eyed a rather handsome bellhop wrestling a suitcase onto a brass dolly. "It might be worth it if I can take one of those home."

Brent stared at Clover as if she was intriguingly bizarre to him.

"Well," I sighed. "It's business from here on in."

Brent's mirrored sunglasses reflected the bustling atrium. His jaw was set, shoulders squared, and lips showed no hint of nerves. I fed off his bravery.

"Clover, you know what to do." Before I finished the words, she was off toward her station in the rooftop chef's gardens, where she would be our eyes should any Watchmen try to make a move on us.

I made for the concierge desk with Brent bringing up the rear. Behind the counter, a man with snow-white hair and a mustache curled at the ends was my target.

"Can I help you?" the concierge asked, sporting a nice grin under foggy eyes.

"This place is busy isn't it?" I asked.

"Indeed it is."

"I wouldn't be able to tell a ghost from a human being in here. It's gotta be good for business. Anyway, I'm Zooey, says so on my badge." I pointed to the name embroidered into my jumpsuit. Brent bumped my shoulder.

"So," I went on, "my colleague spoke with Marcus, who reported a leak in the roof on the tower." I flashed a badge from our fictitious repair service, Aloft Roofing. Aloft Roofing had emailed the hotel that morning to make a sales call.

Yesterday evening, a hotel worker by the name of Marcus had met with Azim over coffee and had given him pertinent information—most importantly his email address, which was promptly hacked by yours truly.

The old man studied us. Then the flesh around his milky brown eyes crinkled with a grin. "Ah, yes, Aloft Roofing. I remember. Marcus sent me an email this morning. Shall I have someone—"

"Not to worry. We already know the way." I was pulsing

with relief.

"I assume you have keys to the eighteenth floor and roof access?"

Brent yanked a set of decoy keys from his jumper and dangled them in front of the concierge, giving a silent, curt signal that we were equipped.

"Very well. Please let us know if we can be of any assistance, Zooey."

And like that, we penetrated Lethe's luxury façade. There was no resistance or deadly fight, no rules to skip around. It was straightforward.

Almost too straightforward.

Only once we slipped behind the burnished gold elevator doors, out of view of the lobby of humans, did I breathe. Brent didn't.

I rocked from toe to heels, clutching my toolbox. "I didn't get to ask you earlier. World War II, huh?"

"Yup."

The elevator dinged as we reached the fourth floor, and we rose a little higher.

"Whose side were you on?"

"Styx's."

"Styx fought in the War?"

"I gave Reapers direction in battle." His barrel chest puffed up like a bulldog on alert. "Otherwise they would've taken out the wrong human soldiers, and the war might've ended differently. We control the course of human history, not just their deaths. It's important we get it right."

"Oh."

The elevator dinged, signaling floor fourteen.

"At least you have experience in battle. Being here

scares the hell out of me, and this isn't war," I said. There was no time to go into theoretical ideals.

"Experience tells me what I should be frightened of, Ollie. It's not always for the best." A slight lift followed by a drop, and the elevator doors opened to the eighteenth floor. "Besides, this *is* war."

He slid off the elevator before the doors finished opening. I padded onto the maroon carpeting. I wore the hat Brent had donned as general in World War II. And I chose to follow his lead. But when we came to a locked door with roof access, and he grabbed my hand, I hesitated to follow him.

"What?" he asked.

"We don't have a key." I fixated on the steel door that kept us from our goal.

Brent, who appeared unfazed by metal and locks, cracked a smile. "I'll half-death us through it."

"Half-what?" The word "death" coming from an Eidolon like Brent did not inspire confidence. In fact, it made me want to spin on my toes and make for the elevator.

"Half-death. That's how I presumably got us into Lethe last week. I would have had to ferry you through the bedrock wall noted on my map. Of course," he snickered, "you don't remember. I don't either. But I have a lovely vision of a polka dot g-string, and I don't know why."

I would have preferred a vision of a polka dot g-string to the brief memory I had of being awash in darkness as ice zipped through my veins. The former left a nicer imprint on the mind.

"So, you're gonna half-death me?" I was regretfully putting the pieces together and dreading what he would have to do to get us on the other side of the door.

"Yup." He drew me closer to him, his body already cold to the touch. "Ready?"

I sighed, took a deep, calming breath, and then I tried not to think about this next part.

"Look." Brent demanded for the umpteenth time. "The city is gorgeous from up here. There's the Isle of Orleans and the mountains off in the distance. This is the way to see Québec."

I locked my gaze on the Interceptor that he was fastening to the base of Styx's antenna. Staring at his work was easier than watching the souls whizzing around us, rattling structures I prayed weren't the ones anchoring us to the eighteen-story roof.

Contrary to Brent, being above the city, secured by a thin rope tied to my seat harness, was not my idea of grand entertainment, especially not when ghosts were buzzing around us like gigantic flies. That Brent kept insisting I take a look at the roofs of Québec City through the souls wasn't doing anything but aggravating my acrophobia. This was precisely why I never mounted the goddamn Interceptor on my own roof before now.

I gripped my blue lifeline and looked down between my boots, which were pressed to the copper sheeting of the roof.

If I puked, would it discolor the roof? Would it bother the spirits?

Brent aligned the drill. "Last bolt and then you can hook the rest up."

Wrapped around his leg and ankle was the remaining

length of the blue rope. The fancy little auto-locking belay device—what he called it after I called it a piece of scrap metal—was set so that if he had to lower me, he could pull on the lever and send me steadily back to earth. We were tethered together, but he held the control.

Too quickly I had forgotten that he was my Grim Reaper. With Brent's hand on the brake of that belay device, it would be an unfortunate moment for him to decide to honor his Deathlist.

Brent leaned into his harness, tipping backward an inch. I grasped his arm and yanked him upright.

"I won't fall," he said with a smile that was sensual enough to divert my panic for a millisecond. Brent's eyes were brighter than I had ever seen them. It was the slivers of sunlight peeking through the souls that made them sparkle like this, wasn't it?

"What's next?" A soul floated next to his head. He flicked at it as he would a bug. If a bodiless soul with no face could grimace, that one did before it floated away.

"Next I hook up the wires," I said, gripping the rope.

The process was simple. Remove the input to the box that transmitted the signal to Styx's main broadcasting center and then insert my own, which would both continue Stygian programming uninterrupted and allow my broadcast to override theirs at my chosen moment. Somehow, I managed to do this with only one hand.

"Voila." That was the most enthusiasm I could offer in the circumstances.

"That's it?" Brent must have expected me to give a hex, summoning forth wind, rain, and fire to make the Interceptor work.

"Maximus?" Clover's voice crackled through the walkie-talkie.

Brent withdrew the walkie from his pocket. "Go for Max."

"I'm in the rooftop garden below you. I saw some suspicious people."

I got dizzy when I looked down twelve stories to see Clover's navy blue blotch on the rooftop gardens encircled by the brick walls of the Château.

"There are three Watchmen heading toward the stairs in the main tower," she said. "One of them had red eyes. An Eidolon."

Brent and I exchanged looks. Neither of us bothered to mask our alarm.

"If it's Chad, it's bad news." Brent shoved the walkie into the pocket with the drill.

"It's set. We can go." I pried my hand from the jumper box, letting it go as a mother lets go of her firstborn at preschool. "Let's climb."

"We can't let them see the box, or they'll remove it." Brent's sudden interest in the distance to the ground turned my horror scenario into reality. "If they're using the stairs, others are using the elevators."

My mouth turned pasty. "What are you saying?"

"We can't go back the way we came." He reached for the blue coil around his leg and pulled the knot. The rope unraveled, spinning in a downward pirouette over the lip of the green roof. Hades and Brent only knew how far the rope descended. "Do you have that knife I gave you?"

I clutched his shoulder with one hand. "Don't do anything crazy."

"Do you have it?"

"Uh-huh." It was in my zipped pocket.

"Good. When you get to the bottom, cut the rope. You know where to find Azim and Clover from there." He brought my lips to his for a kiss. As he attempted to push me back, I clung to his shoulder and I breathed in his scent, holding him against me until time stopped. I should've kissed him harder and longer.

"Find them and get out of here," he said in my ear and then pried my fingers from him. He grasped the rudder of the scrap metal that locked me in place at his side.

"Don't let me go."

"*Je t'aime*, darlin'."

"No. Brent, wait!"

His sapphire eyes and the twinkle of the steel belay device were the last things I saw before my stomach shot into my throat as I plunged toward the earth.

Chapter Twenty-Three

"United we will live forever."

—HermesHarbinger.com, 3:30 am ET 26 April Tuesday

I stopped screaming when I realized I had feeling in my limbs. Adrenaline pulsed angrily from my toes to fingertips. I was dangling a few feet above the rooftop garden of the Château. The rope was long enough to send me into a harrowing controlled fall with a soft catch over the same place Clover had been standing seconds earlier. She was gone, racing to the car by now. I looked at the blue lifeline toward the roof. I couldn't see Brent, but the weight on the rope told me he was still attached.

"Ollie, cut the rope!" He shouted down to me. His voice was strained, as if he was engaged in a fight.

The knife, I thought. We were tethered to each other; the rope was looped around the television antenna that was anchored to the roof, with one of us on one end, and the other on the opposite end. Brent would fall if I cut the rope, just as I would have fallen if he cut the rope from his end.

But he had told me to cut myself free. And to trust him.

"Okay?" I screamed back at him on the off chance that he didn't mean what he had said.

"*Now!*" was his command.

"Fuck… fuck…" I fumbled with the zipper's tab and dug for the knife in my left pocket. The blade glistened. I sawed at the taut rope. Blue fibers frayed bit by bit.

Before I'd finished cutting, an object sliced through the air above and came to a crashing stop. A large stone urn cracked underneath the impact of a body in a black suit. His pant legs danced with his twitching limbs.

A Watchman.

I sawed at the rope with added ferocity. One last tap of the blade severed my connection with Brent. The landing from a fall of a few feet still knocked the air from me. There was no time to linger, sprawled on the garden terrace looking to the sky in wonderment of what I had survived, or in worry whether Brent was okay.

I climbed to my feet, wobbling on jelly legs, and raced for the exit from the garden. Inside the hotel, I followed the red *Sortie* signs without concern for who might be behind me or if I was running into the thick of an ambush. I didn't care if I had twenty people after me. Looking back to *see* twenty people would not yield any advantage. It did not help the victims in slasher movies—it wouldn't help me.

Each sign sent me past door after door of guest rooms until I came to a sterile gray stairwell. I flew down the steps.

They'll be waiting. The car would be ready, possibly rolling away when I ran to it.

From a few flights above came the harried voices and stomping feet of the enemy. I soared over the last remaining steps, landed in a crouch at the base of the stairs, and lunged at the door in front. It dumped me into another empty hallway.

My feet carried me left, toward the busy hotel lobby. I followed the polished wood walls for three turns until my feet hit stone. I burst into the foyer. The revolving brass doors spat guests in and out of the hotel. I shoved through a group of humans as I made for the exit.

"Hey. Watch it," they complained.

"Scrivener," shouted someone behind me.

I couldn't resist the urge to look over my shoulder, even though I knew better. I glanced to find a number of black suits flapping like grim streamers as the Watchmen made chase. Then I slipped through the doors. The April air bit at my hot cheeks. Flags cracked overhead. A car horn drew my attention to the Mercedes parked twenty feet away. There were only two heads in the car—Azim's turban and Clover's massive blonde mop. Brent hadn't made it down from the tower. The Mercedes started rolling away as I closed in.

"Come on, come on!" Azim shouted from the cracked window.

I wrenched the back door open and dove across the backseat.

"Where's Brent?" Clover screamed.

Not waiting for an answer, Azim screeched the wheels, and we took off. Through the rear window, I watched five Watchmen race out of the hotel. Two leaped over a collection of suitcases. Another tripped, sending luggage sliding over the pavement. Nearby humans glanced about, motionless in their confusion.

I looked out the rear window for Brent. In my head, I had hoped that somehow he'd be in the car before me. But he wasn't, and I couldn't bear the thought that he had been captured, too.

No matter the risk, I wouldn't leave him behind. I never would, not as long as I had authority over my mind and body.

"We can't leave him!" I wildly searched for a navy blue jumpsuit amidst the chaos. "Stop the car, Azim."

"He said get to safety. That's what I'm doing." The Mercedes sped up. We flew under an archway that spat us out onto rue des Carrières, running parallel to the Saint Lawrence.

"I said stop!"

Evidently, Brent had his own secrets. Azim had made a promise that he would protect me, but promises didn't supersede the end of my nine-millimeter pressed to his ear. That was *my* secret back up plan.

The car hydroplaned on melted snow before it came to a halt. We flew forward.

I thrust the back door open and sprang out. Watchmen ran at us, not impeded by the distance we had gained. There was no sign of Brent. But I wouldn't accept that he was stuck on the tower, nor would I accept that they had captured him. He could have transformed into his Eidolon form and done away with a handful of them at once.

"Olivia," Clover shouted. "Don't."

The Watchmen kicked up their knees. I ran. I'd blow through them as a tornado of blazing fury if I had to. I pumped my arms and hands. With several feet to clear, I saw my heat's reflection in the yellow glint of the Watchmen's eyes.

The collision of our bodies offset my balance. I went down on my back, gasping for air. Hands pulled at my jumpsuit, but as soon as they did, they let go. I was too hot to pin down. So, I clawed for anything I could—clothing, skin, and hair.

"Hold her down," shouted a Watchman.

Scythe pins shimmered as we wrestled.

"Get her legs."

Two navy blue jumpsuits raced toward me.

"Subdue her before Head Reaper shows up," someone said.

"What about Hume?" someone asked.

"They sent Chadwick after him. Get her underground."

Several Watchmen grasped my jumpsuit and yanked me onto my feet. Azim and Clover were shoved alongside me, their faces awash in fright. But the chorus of an Eidolon battle cry boomed off the midday tussle. The ground rumbled, sending our footholds off kilter.

A blinding darkness overcame me so fast that I lost sense of what was up and what was down. Bone on bone clashes, grunts, ripped clothing, and that godforsaken howl flooded my ears.

"Run." Brent's baritone shouted, inches from my ear.

My feet pounded solid ground. The rubber soles gripped the pavement. I was running. The dark haze that had clouded my vision faded into clarity. Straight ahead was the Mercedes, its muffler smoking. Azim and Clover leaped into the car. Cool leather caught us when Brent and I dove into the backseat. Then Azim hit the gas.

I yelped when I saw Brent's jumpsuit. Blood gushed from his stomach. Redness pooled over the backseat, dripping onto the floor mats. The Eidolon...the powerful, indestructible hero...was hemorrhaging blood.

"I told you not to worry about me." His face twisted in agony. Brent wasn't supposed to feel pain. He was an Eidolon, trained to take whatever Marin and his cronies would do to him. Brent shouldn't *know* pain. "They'll use me against you like they used Lorelei and Stone against you. Instead, you stuck around and almost got a face-to-face meeting with Marin."

"I had to help you." He pushed my hands away when I reached out to him. "Let me see."

He peeled his hand from his abdomen, opening the torn jumpsuit. I grew faint at the frayed tissue, the sight of his innards oozing out of his body. He put a hand over his stomach to hide his injury, but it was too late. We saw.

Clover threw both hands over her mouth. "Oh God."

An injury like that wouldn't have time to heal. Brent was bleeding out too fast.

"Chad and some of his friends jumped me after I fell eighteen stories. I'm toast."

I grew sick. He fell because of what I had done. He had become vulnerable to an attack because I had saved myself. "Brent, I thought you meant for me to cut the rope." He also should have been able to turn into his dark Eidolon alter ego and save himself.

"I did. I also said to get out of there. You shouldn't have

waited."

"How did they do this to you?"

"Eidolons can take down other Eidolons. I was lucky I got away at all."

I pressed my lips together to keep tears from rolling onto my tongue and turning the flavor of this moment any more bitter than it already was.

"Where should I go? We don't want them following us back to the Isle," Azim said, as his attention danced between the road ahead of us and the road behind us.

After a series of shallow breaths, Brent glanced through the back window as Azim increased speed. Garik's white van was catching up. Every time an enemy van attempted to pass Garik, he swerved to one side, nearly tipping his own van to do so. There was little hope of us outrunning the Watchmen if Garik couldn't hold them off. With Brent injured as he was, we would not get away if they intercepted our course.

"Brent, please." My voice was mostly air. "Don't give up. We'll get you help."

"You can't…put me before everyone else."

"I won't leave you." I touched his shoulder. This time he didn't shrug me off. I watched my hands pull at his jump-suit to cover his injury, to stop him from bleeding out. But the effort was meaningless. No cleverly designed tourniquet would be enough this time. "Azim, get to a hospital. They'll stop his bleeding."

"You do that, and I'll drain you," Brent hissed. "Head for Pierre-Laporte Bridge."

Azim's eyes flickered, recalculating our getaway.

"I'm the boss here," I bit. "This is *my* plan."

"*Don't* listen to her, Azim."

"You don't get to do this, Brent." I fanned my hand over his knee and put the other to his shoulder to hold myself in place as our car zipped through the city streets. Pierre-Laporte Bridge appeared at the foot of the escarpment.

Silent, Brent stared ahead, his head bobbing with the potted road. Over his shoulder, the white vans were careening in and out of traffic. Our destiny was about to bear down on us, and I couldn't face it with Brent giving up.

So he saw the bigger picture—the Stygian revolution—come to pass. But in the end, it didn't mean anything if he did not see the mountains again. He deserved that. He *earned* it after what he'd endured.

The tires of the Mercedes made contact with Pierre-Laporte Bridge. A small bump jostled everyone in the car. Clover let out a hushed sniffle.

"When you get to the middle of the bridge, stop. I'll take over driving."

"What are you going to do?" I asked.

"Distract them long enough for you to get away."

"No. That's stupid. Come with us."

The sloped beams of the suspension bridge passed overhead. Those white vans flew down Cape Diamond. This nightmare was unraveling too fast. I had no time to prepare—but for what? Escape? Erebus? Surrender?

"I love you, Ollie," Brent uttered.

"We're almost there," Azim said.

Soon, the car skidded and stopped. Traffic veered around us. Horns blared. I looked through the rear window again. The vans made it to the far end of the bridge. When I turned back, Brent was gone, and Azim wrenched me out of the backseat.

"No, Brent." I fought Azim's hold. He and Clover tried to help me stand.

The driver side door slammed. Brent was behind the steering wheel.

I dove for the handle. "Don't do this."

Azim threw both arms around my waist as I pounded my fists on the glass. Brent didn't flinch when the window cracked. The Mercedes engine revved. The car flew backward, spun in a half-circle, and took off.

Dread fluttered violently in my ribcage as I watched my lover—my Reaper, my friend—barrel toward the enemy with our luggage and dreams stowed in the trunk. At my feet was a pool of his blood, left behind to remind me why I had to let go, that he would likely die whether he stayed with me or saved us from danger. I put my hand to my chest because if I didn't, my heart would spill out.

"We have to run." Azim grabbed my hand.

"The river," I said, ignoring the fact that I wasn't much of a swimmer.

Azim's olive eyes danced between a bridge truss and me. "Then we jump."

"Jump?" Clover squealed.

The Mercedes collided with one of the vans, sending it spinning into oncoming traffic. Brent would do as much damage as he could. It's what I would have done—snag up a mess worthy of the front cover of *Reaper Monthly*.

"We can't leave him," screamed Clover as Azim hoisted her onto the bridge truss.

"Olivia, come on." He climbed beside her.

I put my hand to my necklace to feel for Eve before I grabbed the steel truss. I gave one last glance at the anarchy

Brent caused and then down at the ripples of waves of the Saint Lawrence River, a hundred feet below—the same river Brent and I had plunged into from the bowels of Lethe a week and half earlier.

If you can hear me, Brent, I love you, too. I will come back for you—I promise.

Azim took my hand in his.

And we jumped to our escape.

Chapter Twenty-Four

"A populace never rebels from passion for attack, but from impatience of suffering."

—Edmund Burke

28 April

"Head Reaper Marin has brought terrorist Eidolon Brent Rutherford Hume back from the brink of death. The Head Reaper's loyalists are now able to interrogate Hume on the whereabouts of Master Scrivener Olivia Dormier and several accomplices who have yet to be identified. Eidolon Hume has been formally charged with treason, a Level Ten Offense. This charge follows a list of offenses including sugar trafficking, list pilfering, harboring of a terrorist, and refusal of duty."

The news telecast was drowned by a cacophony of shattered glass and complaints that stretched from one side of the rebel cottage to the other. In the middle of the chaos, and in direct eyeshot of the television, I sat, and I said nothing.

"Marin's keeping him alive until he sings," someone roared over indecipherable shouting.

"You're wrong. Brent won't give up information. They want him alive long enough to lure us out of hiding." Garik's accent wasn't as smooth as usual. He was on edge.

"They'll torture him if we make him wait," one said.

"He'll be lucky if they show him mercy like they did Violet Magby," a Watchman mumbled.

Clover put her hand on my knee. Her fingers were little heat sticks.

For hours, in the cottage on the Isle of Orleans, everyone tried to coax me out of my stupor with words of encouragement, and then embraces when words failed. When that hadn't worked, they turned to quarrelling, fussing about who was to blame or what to do next. The television became white noise to our despair when they had no more to say to each other.

"Marin is going to inject fear into us by publicly destroying Brent and the Balanchines." Garik paced in front of me, rhythmically blocking out the television screen.

I ran my fingertips over Brent's flannel, draped across my knees. Clover had given it to me, having said something about keeping faith. It smelled of a spicy, masculine cologne. I tried convincing myself Brent would come back and slip into the forgotten flannel, proving that he hadn't been thrust into Death's spotlight and that I wasn't guiltily sitting in the cottage, numb to the horror. I wanted to believe I'd have a chance to tell him the things I hadn't.

I had failed Eve. I had failed Gerard and Mama and Papa.

I wouldn't fail Brent, too. I just wasn't sure how to help him.

"*Head Reaper Marin has called for an immediate trial for Eidolon Hume and for Stone and Lorelei Balanchine, Dormier's foster parents. He fears for Stygians' safety since Dormier and her rebels are still at large and could make a violent attack on innocent Stygians at any moment…*"

I rolled Brent's velvety flannel between the pads of my fingers. I didn't have to try very hard to imagine his muscles beneath its softness. He was still so fresh in my memory, like Eve, Mama, Papa, and Gerard. All had faces, lives, homes, and each had my love.

Death despises bartering, I thought.

Lethe. That's where they had him. That's why the place was secret. No one could save their beloveds if no one knew where to find them. But I knew. I had a map. I was there just last week.

"Garik, what are we going to do?" asked someone.

"Hermes Harbinger has gotten over a million hits in the last few hours," Azim shouted from the back corner of the living room. He had lingered behind the pixels of the Internet void for the entirety of our hours of preparation. He had given us updates on the website, treating it as a measure of Stygian interest in rebellion.

The fabric stilled in my hands.

There aren't one million Stygians. People must be revisiting the website.

"This proves Stygians are ready more than ever to unite and make a stand," Azim continued, with growing sanguinity. "What we need is a kick start. We need someone to be the leader. A voice."

"No," Garik snapped. "We don't have our guide into Lethe. Without Brent, how will we find Marin and stop the banishments? Marin wants us to rush to Le Château to meet his soldiers head-to-head."

"Then let's siege the hotel," someone suggested.

"Or riot. That might sidetrack Marin from the trial," said another.

Garik wouldn't budge. "We wait. Patience is our greatest ally now."

"I'm not waiting," I said after a moment of silence. The room grew instantly quiet. "I'm going to get them."

I clutched Brent's leatherette journal to my chest. I didn't remember rising from the chair or fishing the journal out of my backpack, or what words I uttered first. But I did remember Dudley greeting me with a wiggly dance.

"Scrivener Dormier," Garik began, "I think it is best if you—"

"For Hades sake, shut the hell up!" My hands reddened. The journal fell to the floor. Clover scooped it up before the rebel Watchman grabbed it. She gave him a fiery glance, and he backed off. "I'll save them with or without your help," I continued. "I have a map. I know how to get into Lethe without Brent."

"You are foolish to think you can do that," Garik volleyed. "It's meaningless to try."

"They're not meaningless. I'm not meaningless. Styx isn't either."

"I didn't say that."

"You implied it with your passivity." I turned to the gathering of slack-jawed rebels—the ones who needed to hear me more than Azim and Clover. I already had their support. "You want a guide into Lethe. I'll be your guide. I'll get you there."

"Even if you have a map, you're just a Scrivener." Garik fanned his hands over his narrow hips. "Your only power is in Deathmarks. As admirable as your offer is, Deathmarks are not going to get us inside."

My stare was poisonous, but Garik didn't back down like the other Reapers. He was a leader. He had every reason not to believe in my abilities. I wasn't sure *I* believed in them. But dammit, I would try. I would die trying.

"If you don't help, I'll go into Lethe regardless, and *when* I return, I'll show each of you what sixth-degree burns are like."

Clover gazed down at Brent's journal. Azim was the only Reaper in the entire room who dared to look at me with resolve, with the determination to see through whatever mission I had planned.

I gave Azim my sincerest, wordless thanks when Garik lowered himself to the couch as people do when they are about to agree to an idea they'd otherwise discard. I walked stiffly across the living room.

"How long do they have?" I asked Garik.

His attention was locked on the Navajo rug where I stood. After a moment, I realized he was staring at my combat boots. "The trials have probably already started. They'll be found guilty. Marin will see to it."

"When will they banish them?"

"As soon as the verdict is read."

My knees yearned to buckle. I fought it with everything I had. "Azim, is the Interceptor ready?"

"All it needs is something broadcast. It's waiting for you," Azim said from behind his laptop. His words hung on heavy air.

It's waiting for me.

Nothing that carried the burden of a world was more simply said.

They are waiting for me. Brent is waiting.

For years I had gazed upon the roof of Le Château, staring up at Styx's broadcasting antenna. Never did I think I would send out my own personal message from that transmitter. But the gears were waiting for me to set them in motion. My plan had arrived as stealthily as Brent had established himself in my life.

And in this singular moment I marveled at how terrifying it was.

"Where is the camera?" I asked Azim.

He pointed at a white cube the size of my palm next to the laptop on the coffee table. In the center was a glass eyeball of the camera. This little object was all I would need to reach Stygians. It was so small it was embarrassing.

"How will they hear me?" I asked.

"The microphone is built into the camera," he answered. "You can start anytime."

A scared little girl inside of me screamed to run into the nearest bedroom, curl up with Dudley, and weep instead of throwing myself out there through electromagnetic television waves to be rejected or loved. She posed a compelling—safe—case. But I licked my lips to wipe away the fear. Styx already knew me. As Clover had said, I was public enemy number one.

It was time I acted like it, dammit.

"Let's discuss what you'll say first," Garik said, his attention on my face now and not my boots. "This could mean life or death for us. Don't be hasty."

I thought to reply. I took a step toward the couch instead.

He started to stand, but a male rebel with thick shoulders shoved him back down. Garik bounced on the couch springs.

"This is her moment. Let her have it, Garik," the rebel said.

Clover placed Brent's journal in my hand. She gave me a knowing smile.

Reapers cleared the way as I pulled up a chair in front of the camera, brushed the hair from my tear-stained face, and placed my hands on my knees. Still in my jumpsuit, soaked in Brent's blood, I was not primped and polished like the newscasters.

But I wasn't a newscaster.

I was a revolutionary.

"Are you ready?" Azim asked.

Every rebel stilled. No one breathed. No one dared to.

I gave the slightest nod.

Azim's sigh was thunderous. "You'll be live in three."

I couldn't back out now. I wouldn't.

Courage, Ollie, a voice whispered in my head.

"Three, two, one," Azim said.

From the corner of my eye, the cottage's television flickered from Brent's violent interrogation to me, perched on the chair with swollen green eyes. I gasped because…

It worked!

I wanted to throw my arms around Azim or do one of Dudley's welcome-home boogies. As an alternative, I paused and let my excitement settle into dignified poise. I recovered with a smile and looked back at the camera, vowing not to give the television any more of my concentration.

I sighed and said, "*Bonjour*, Stygians. I am Olivia Iris Dormier. I put a Deathmark on a Grim Reaper. I fled Québec City. I am a rebel. And *I* am a Master Scrivener."

My jitters eased with each word. Even so, I took another deep breath before continuing.

"Years ago, Master Scriveners were annihilated. Marin got rid of most of Master Scriveners because he feared their power. Scriveners work tirelessly to help Reapers, and Reapers work tirelessly to maintain the balance. But Marin doesn't help us, does he? He demands more souls and doesn't equip us with the tools to meet his requirements. And if we don't achieve his quotas, we go to Erebus for eternal damnation."

I stole a glance at Garik and then back at that eyeball.

"Marin hides from us because he fears our retaliation. He hurts those we love. He manipulates us to get what he wants. Day after day, Stygians are brought up on charges and quickly sent to Erebus. Soon all of us will meet again in Erebus, if Marin has his way.

"I ask you, why does Marin punish you with his List of Offenses for jobs you can't possibly do with the small number of Scriveners who are currently serving Styx? And why do we allow our leader to instill so much fear in us? It was Marin who killed off the Master Scriveners—the only beings that could kill him, with the help of a willing Eidolon. He killed the Master Scriveners to protect himself from being dethroned as Head Reaper. He did it to stay in power, not to help Styx. Marin doesn't care about us. He cares about his position and abusing it for as long as we will let him. But not any longer.

"I don't wish anyone harm. I put a Deathmark on

Nicholas Baird to protect myself. Now, Marin calls me a terrorist. Self-defense isn't criminal. Saving those you love isn't terrorism. This is why I ask that you help me, and I will help you in return."

From Brent's leatherette journal, I held up the picture of him in his World War II uniform, standing in the woods of Kentucky, grinning. Styx viewed the heartwarming smile of the accused.

"Along with my foster parents, Lorelei and Stone Balanchine, this Reaper is considered a terrorist. But he saved me. And he believes in a world where Scriveners and Reapers are balanced again. He wants to restore Styx to what it once was. His desire for Styx isn't unique. *You* need help finding your Assignees. You need Scriveners to do that."

I paused, inwardly laughing because it was the same theatrical silence Marin used whenever he gave his daily speeches.

"Someone once told me that Death despises bartering. But Death needs a challenge. I ask you to stand up with me and let your demands be heard."

I ran my thumbs over Brent's picture. His smile challenged my composure. But I wouldn't let Styx see me weep.

Rebels don't cry.

I turned back to the camera.

"I still believe in you, Styx. Please, believe in me."

Chapter Twenty-Five

*"We began a contest for liberty ill provided with the
means for the war, relying on our patriotism to supply
the deficiency. We expected to encounter many wants and
distressed…we must bear the present evils and fortitude."*

—Major General George Washington, 1781

"Press the button on the transmitter belt before you start
recording." Azim positioned the tiny camera against my
chest. Pushed through the buttonhole of my jacket, the camera floated over my sternum and blended perfectly with the
hunter green garment. He leaned into the backseat of the
white van and observed it from a short distance. "They'll not
be able to tell you have a camera on you. I'll have the computer on standby to transmit the signal when you are ready."

"I want you and Clover to promise you'll steer clear if
things get messy," I said.

My job was to get into Lethe and use the power of

technology against Marin to save Brent, Mama, and Papa. If Marin didn't buy into our blackmail or if anyone was banished, Marin's sequestered little world would go live with a push of a button. And by revealing his secret location, Marin would lose his hideaway, and Stygians would flock to his underground lair to barter for souls and Deathlists and Obols and whatever else Stygians saw fit to barter for. It would be a nightmare for him. And ultimately, his power would be stamped out once a Master Scrivener and Eidolon came along and removed him from his seat of corruption forever.

Lights from the line of cars trailing us on the highway washed over Azim and Clover's tense faces. I glanced through the rear window to see our small convoy of white vans.

Clover reached around Azim and squeezed my hand. Her palm was clammy. "Don't worry about anyone else, honey. Focus on Brent. He needs you now."

Dudley sat between us with his ears pulled back. Clover had assured me she would take good care of him—after this was over, watching over Dudley would be her only Stygian job. He would have all the blueberry pancakes he could want at the Sisters Café. And knowing Clover, he'd put on ten pounds before summer.

Garik was behind the wheel. Another rebel sat quietly in the passenger seat. Both had grown quiet ever since we crossed the bridge carrying us away from the safety of our provisional residence on the Isle of Orleans.

The front end of the van scraped the pavement when we merged onto the steep avenue of Honoré Mercier that met the top of Parliament Hill. My skin rippled in goose bumps. At the top of the hill, we would be in eyeshot of Le Château Frontenac—our destination.

Streetlights stooped overhead, flickering to life as pink and orange ribbons festooned the dusk sky. Over the limbs of leafless trees, the front tower of the Parliament Building rose out of the ground as if standing to salute us. At last, Fontaine de Tourny, with its three tiers of cherubs and nymphs, came into view as the Oldsmobile crested Parliament Hill's highest point.

Garik pulled the van to the side, leaving it sitting outside of the hotel. Three similar white vans packed full of rebels pulled up behind us.

Crisp air bit at my cheeks. I was standing next to the car gazing blankly at the verdigris roofs of Château Frontenac without realizing I had climbed out of the car. My body moved before my brain accepted information—a frightening notion.

I looked around for Azim, Clover, and Dudley. They were gone—off to hide in the coffee shop across from the hotel as we had discussed. Once Clover and Azim set up their position and the signal from his laptop, and I gave the sign, every Stygian near a television would see what was happening from a first-person point of view, starting first with Garik's rousing speech.

I fingered my belt for the transmitter and powered it to life as Garik made his last preparations.

"Are you ready?" I asked Garik.

He nodded.

"Good evening, Styx," Garik said into his handheld microphone, facing the camera lens on my jacket. "We come together as one to speak out against Head Reaper Marin. We need our leader to hear us when we say we will no longer live in terror of missing our quotas, that we will take control back. We will stand united against him.

"The Head Reaper does not want to hear our complaints. He has concealed himself from us for centuries. We have speculated where he has been hiding. Tonight, we will uncover his refuge and bring a voice to our overworked Reapers and Scriveners."

My fingernails cut into my palms as Garik spoke. It was happening. The rebellion was in motion, and there was nothing I could do to stop it.

"Hermes Harbinger spoke of the need for a rebellion weeks ago, and now, *tonight*, we have our chance to speak to our leader face to face…"

As Garik's speech continued, I worried that we were too late. Failure had not come to mind until this moment. Confidence had been a chemical high I had ridden long enough. It was unavoidable that I would think of the worst.

Garik pointed in the direction of Le Château. The orange brick façade of the hotel trembled from our unified stare. We were few, but we were strong, and the hotel knew we were coming to relay the message to Marin that Lethe would no longer be the unknown city of Death—that it would not be forgotten this time.

With his speech complete, Garik and other rebels flanked my sides as we made the final approach. Footfalls beat like war drums inside the same courtyard Azim, Brent, Clover, and I had fled from hours earlier. Our steps quickened from a stride to a march. The turrets of the Château scraped the twilight sky and soon fell into shadow.

The bellhops and hotel guests watched in shock as thirty Stygians flooded the courtyard. And there was nothing the humans could do. One by one, we fed through the hotel's revolving brass doors. When I stepped into the lobby after Garik, I stopped.

Off to one side, indifferent to the humans marveling at the hotel's architecture, were enemy Watchmen blocking the staircase we would need to descend to get to Lethe's front door. I glanced at Garik and then at the chain of yellow eyes and black suits.

"Traitor," said one loyalist to the Head Watchman. "All this time you've been working against us."

"I am no traitor to Styx, only to fascism." Garik's posture grew taller from his forced self-assurance. "You will let us by, or we will go by force."

"Give us Scrivener Dormier, and we won't turn your names to the Head Reaper."

"We can take them," a rebel growled, itching for a good fight.

"What is going on here?" cried out a bellhop, who was the only hotel employee brave enough to take us on. "What is this? A protest?"

"We're here on business," Garik replied.

"No one told us there would be—"

Garik interrupted the bellhop. "Olivia, get everyone you can into Lethe. We'll take care of the Watchmen and the little guy." Rebels filled in behind him, matching the numbers of loyalists. And the bellhop, taking a cue, stepped back from the confrontation.

Once the human was out of the way, the masses charged. The wave sent Marin's loyalists back into the hallway of souvenir shops and polished wood paneling while the rest of us stormed down the stairs leading into Château's basement. Marin and anyone in Lethe had to have heard our trumpeting footfalls.

At the bottom of the stairs was a set of double-doors with a push bar and an explicit EMPLOYEES ONLY sign. A pair of Reapers kicked the door in ahead of me. I followed as the rest of the insurrection filtered through, two at a time, on my determined heels. I veered left, down a hallway bordered in brick.

This was my chance to show Styx where to find their Head Reaper. I thought of that tiny camera pushed through the buttonhole of my jacket. Azim and Clover were nearby transmitting the uncovering of Lethe. All I had to do was rip the door off its hinges, and Styx would finally have a place to go to barter with Death.

In the basement, I made a quick right around the colossal boiler locked behind a chain-link fence. I gazed down the long brick hallway with three fluorescent light fixtures hanging above. At the end was the door to Lethe.

And my spirit—my confidence in Brent's map—deserted me at what I saw.

"It's a brick wall," screamed a Reaper after he threw himself against it.

"This is the door, Scrivener?" another demanded. "Is this some kind of joke?"

I said nothing—no explanation or reason why I thought we would face anything other than a brick wall here. I couldn't remember anything that went on in Lethe—no one could. And Brent's journal didn't mention this part. I had assumed there would be something that marked an entrance. A window. A vent. Hell, a scrap of chalk so we could draw the damn door onto the wall and go through like magic.

I stared blankly at the barrier. Had Brent been at my

side, he would have half-deathed me through it. It was that simple.

But I was a Scrivener. My power didn't transcend Deathmarks and burning through cups of coffee. And the Stygians at my side didn't wield the kind of power that Brent possessed. There were no Eidolons to help us. Just incensed Reapers and one Scrivener.

I grew faint. The churning acid in my stomach threatened to erupt.

"What is this?" a male Reaper jumped in front of me, blocking my view of the brick obstacle. "You lead us into a dead end. This isn't Lethe; this is a mistake."

"What is going on? You promised us you'd lead us to Marin."

I was aware the camera focused on their disappointed grimaces. The world watched. I put a hand over my chest, careful not to block the view of those viewing from afar. I wouldn't cover anything — not even my failure.

"Why won't she say anything?"

"She doesn't know what she's doing. This is a mistake."

The complaints increased in volume as more Reapers crammed into the narrow tunnel. My followers turned venomous, when moments ago they had been unbreakably united in my cause. Amazing how quickly they turned.

When shouting wasn't enough, they started pushing and shoving each other. I was forced out of the wrestling match by a set of hands. So, I stumbled to the wall. I glared at it. Those red bricks and gray mortar betrayed me.

"Everyone quiet." A baritone roared over the pandemonium. No one heeded the demand.

I touched the brick. It was cold like my hand.

"Olivia," Garik barked over my shoulder. "You said you could get us in."

When I didn't reply, Garik spun me around to face him. His fingers cut into my biceps. "I should not have let this happen. This is it. Marin will have our heads for this, and it's your fault."

A rebel's mace-like fist sliced through the air and caught Garik's chin. Garik let go of me, but pain and embarrassment lingered.

"Give her space to figure it out!" The rebel put a mitt around Garik's neck. "Did you think that Marin would've left the gate wide open? This is Lethe, not a goddamn revolving door."

I couldn't stand to face the deluge of stares that crowded the tunnel. The brick wall in all its imperviousness was a preferable opponent. Again, I turned to it with as much disheartened gloom as before. The rebel and Garik continued exchanging heated words and then fists, as the rest of the following Reapers chimed in with their own criticisms and physical blows.

I put my hands to the wall. It was as cold as brick wall below ground should be.

But my hands were not.

"Let's get picks. We'll bust through it if we have to," said a voice that sounded a million light-years away.

"He'll have his guys on us before we can get anywhere. That's why we needed Hume. He could've gotten us in quickly."

Stale basement air made breathing laborious, but I filled my lungs with a deep breath. It calmed me. Mama had always said breathing was nourishment for the soul. "Be mindful of your breath, babygirl," she had told me time and time again. She knew something I didn't. So, I held the air in my expanded lungs, feeding the cells that made up my body.

My hands turned from a rosy blush to crimson. The heat travelled toward my wrists as if gravity was pulling it through me and into the ground. But the power didn't stop at my wrists.

Inch by inch, the sleeves of my green jacket flaked away into smoke and ash, receding up my forearms as hotness advanced like a victorious infantry. The display danced past my elbows, setting a course for my biceps and shoulders. Had I burned through the jacket and the rest of my clothing to stand naked before the rebels, I wouldn't have cared.

I gave my hands another inspection. They were no longer that striking, shimmering red, but indigo and my fingertips a blinding white. My fellow rebels backed away, coughing from the smoke and intensity, unable to stand the heat my hands were giving off.

So, how could I stand it?

Could the brick wall syphon off my heat?

My attention lingered on this manifestation. I stood in wonder. As I tried to pry my hands from the wall for fear I would melt the foundation of Le Château and raze it to the ground, I couldn't.

Instead, I stepped forward. My boot toes didn't strike the wall as they should have.

I took another step. Still, I didn't come into contact with the barrier. And when I felt liquefied rock under my hands, I understood.

My God, I'm melting the wall.

I'm walking straight through it.

But how far would I go? How long would my heat hold out? Would it give out or would I turn into a miniature supernova right here at the juncture between life and death?

I continued onward as flaming brick surrounded me. And I laughed. Holy Hades, I *laughed*. I gazed out at my blue and white hands instead, wondering when they would dissolve.

All fascination for this new power vanished when I looked ahead of me.

There was no more of the wall left to melt. It was gone. A crystal chandelier gently swung back and forth, illuminating blood stains on the cream and gold damask wallpaper. This had to be the entrance hall to Lethe. And in the center of the Victorian nightmare, smoke plumed around three slack-jawed, blond men in red jumpsuits and black military boots.

Son-of-a-bitch.

"We've been waiting for you, Scrivie," said one of the three, with a half-cocked smirk. Those gray eyes had become too familiar.

Chad. The Eidolon.

I pivoted back to the passageway I had created, set for a full-on retreat. But Garik squeezed through the narrow opening, his clothing and skin smoldering as they scraped along the molten walls. My heart was a lead weight. Only one body could pass through at a time, setting up these Eidolons for a self-serve banquet of Grim Reapers.

In so little words, I was fucked. So was everyone else.

I slowly turned back to face the adversaries licking their chops for dinner.

"Me-oh-my, the Scrivie burned her way through Lethe's

door," said Chad, the leader of the clowns from the bowels of hell. "Good to see you again, *ma cherie*."

His friends sniggered, though they held the stance of two alert Marines.

"You should've knocked before barging in," he said.

Garik stepped beside me to allow more Reapers to move into the room, but none of them walked beyond me to challenge these three. Their fear was rampant, and it must have smelled delightful to these fiends.

"Let us through," I said with a warble in my voice.

Three sets of empty eyes grew wide. They didn't expect this, did they?

"If you don't have an invitation, you *don't* get in."

"I'm asking you politely to move out of the way." The longer I held out, the more Reapers could funnel into the vestibule, and that meant a bigger problem for these guys. Strength in numbers, right?

Chad's leer revealed a set of rotted teeth, not from smoking too much, but from never putting a toothbrush to enamel.

I swallowed hard as I tried to keep my mounting concern for my loved ones under control. If I allowed myself to think for a second that they were dead or in great agony, I would not be able to carry forward. I needed to keep focused if I were to ever see anyone again.

Moreover, my breath—I had to use it.

I glanced at my sides to see who would be my frontline soldiers, but in that instant, the two sidekicks altered into shadows and sprang onto the damask wallpaper, leaving Chad grinning down at me like he had a perverted secret. I shuddered when the dark shadows peeled off the walls and dove into the bodies of two of my allied Reapers.

The Reapers stiffened, electrocuted with vile energy. They were possessed by the pair of Eidolons. I knew what that felt like. Brent had done it to me when he half-deathed me through the door on the roof. It was agonizing, like being frozen from the inside out.

The possessed stretched their hands out before them, worked by the will of the Eidolons. One at a time, they snapped their fingers in half. Bone popped out of flesh. This was knuckle cracking taken to eleven. The sadistic glee in their smiles was not theirs, but their waterlogged eyes told me of their anguish.

"Stop!" I yelled.

"Sure, Scrivie." Chad's mad eyes flitted between the possessed. "You heard the Scrivie. Stop them."

The half-deathed Reapers jumped to attention and saluted, while the rest remained paralyzed in fear of what they would do to us. When Brent had half-deathed me into Lethe, I never imagined it could be used for such wicked purposes. What made Brent different from Chad and the other Eidolons was that he used this Eidolon skillset for good and Chad and company used it for terror.

"Yes, sir," they crooned and together plucked shards of cooled, jagged stone from the floor and put the weapons to their necks.

Rebels shrieked. Some reached for their friends' hands. Blood fizzed from the incisions as the half-deathed Reapers dragged the weapons across the jugular veins in their throats. Everyone cried out in a fury and dismay. Blood sprayed the walls, adding another layer to the macabre decor. I threw my hands over one of the Reaper's wrists but was tossed back.

Garik caught and steadied me. In his face, I saw the same disgust and shock that undoubtedly filled my own.

Once the deed was done, the Eidolon sidekicks finally leaped out from their victim's dying bodies to stand in their own flesh alongside Chad. The victims fell to the floor as mutilated rag dolls. Unlike Eidolons, Grim Reapers could be easily injured. Knowing they wouldn't survive their forced suicides, and fearing these monsters had the power to possess us all at once, I was sure if we lingered, we would follow the same fate.

I was their guide into Lethe. I had to help and put aside my own fear. After drawing in a focusing breath, I stepped up to the ringleader of this mind-fuck. He deserved death for what he made me do to Eve, for what he did to Gerard and Brent and undoubtedly Mama and Papa. He deserved an eternity in Erebus for what he asked his colleagues to do to innocent Reapers.

I couldn't kill him, but I'd make him wish he were dead.

"Let us through," I said through my teeth, drawing energy from each inhale.

Chad stared into me, with my slow, exaggerated death playing in his eyes. He bent forward and put his hands on his thighs to bring his nose inches from mine. The stink of rotting teeth wafted from his cracked lips.

I balled my hands into fists, knowing from the hotness of my arms that my hands had returned to that blue and white intensity. He wanted to play? I'd play. I'd play until every good part of his body was well-done Eidolon meat.

Chad's pale skin rippled with putrid, black lines. Inkiness pushed through his pores and grew thicker until his body was cast in shadow.

Chad wanted me to see the transformation, to fear it. I had seen this power in Brent. Today, the power was not my friend. But I wouldn't succumb to the panic scorching my gut.

I stepped toward Chad as I had when I burned through the brick wall. I brought my nose an inch closer to the skeletal remains of his nose. "Don't make me embarrass you, Chadwick."

His eyes narrowed. His jaw unhinged and dropped low enough to ingest my head whole if he wanted. But he didn't. Nor did he use his strength when I hooked my blistering hands on his dropped jowls, feeling not the gelatinous texture as I had from Brent, but bone and flesh simply masked by lightlessness.

"Your performance doesn't scare me," I said.

His friends whooped like two wolves watching their pack leader yield to a field mouse. The will to live can sometimes outclass any villain, even this piece of shit.

I released my grip on him once my fingers melted away a sufficient layer of flesh. His jaw snapped back. No longer shadowed, Chad gave a sneer that barely camouflaged his humiliation. He looked over the Reapers filtering into the room and then at his nattering comrades.

"He's afraid of the Scrivie. Whacha 'fraid of? Think she's gonna incinerate you?" one taunted. "Look at him. He's afraid. Of a Scrivie."

Their combat boots came off the floor. They crashed against the walls by the will of Chad's swift hands. The wall-paper ripped, plaster crumbled. As the clowns slid down onto their buttocks, they sniggered like naughty schoolchildren. I wished they would shut up, because I had a feeling

Chad would make Scrivie mincemeat of me if pushed one footstep further toward complete disgrace.

Chad's crooked mouth pulled up to bare his fetid teeth when he returned his attention to me. I refused to give him more time to intimidate me or my allies. I had had enough of his antics. My limit had been reached. He stood in the way of Brent's liberation.

I was still sufficiently hot enough to do damage, so I threw my entire weight into Chad, cooking the flesh around his neck where my hands held him hostage. Thrown off balance and falling to his knees, Chad couldn't regain his feet as I drove heat and rage into my attack, melting flesh and muscles and tendons as I cried out. His comrades didn't rush in to assist him; perhaps they were afraid, or they simply didn't care. Whatever the reason, their distance and Chad's weakness renewed my confidence.

He thrashed and fought back as best as he could, but it seemed that my fight outdid his. And had I no goal but hurting Chad, I would've held on until he was a pile of Eidolon mush beneath me. But my loved ones had little time, if they had any left at all.

When Chad attempted to grab my hair, the only part of my body that wasn't hot, I leaped to my feet and ran for the hallway that he and his buddies had been guarding.

I didn't look back. It would be stupid to assume they wouldn't make chase. However many Reapers got past them, I couldn't bear to know. Had I turned around to see who lived and who died, I would have tripped, losing precious seconds in the final push into Lethe. Brent and my parents were my focus, my purpose, and I would get to them as hastily as my feet and luck permitted.

No matter how determined I was, knowing the rebels were right behind me gave me strength. They kept pace, having blown by the Eidolons. I was grateful for that.

I knew how to get to the trial chamber. I had memorized Brent's diagram for this very reason. I saw it in my mind's eye, clear, sharp, and winding us deeper into Lethe's core. But shrieks of our fallen companions and the cackles of the Eidolons nipped at our backsides, jeopardizing my confidence. I couldn't tell if the Eidolons were five or fifty feet away, but it sure as Hades wasn't far enough.

Lethe's hellish Victorian décor added to the chaos. It looked no different than Le Château's human-made magnificence. Had I not melted through a brick wall and challenged one crazy Eidolon and his goofy sidekicks, I would have believed I was in an underground extension of the hotel lobby. Crystal sconces adorned the mahogany walls casting a glow on the paisley carpet. Any moment, I expected humans to pop out from one of the many doors that we flew past.

Garik grabbed my elbow. "They're gaining on us."

Hair-raising screams nearly drowned his words. Some rebels didn't make it past the Eidolons. And those who did pushed against us like a panicked mob trying to escape rising floodwaters.

I made a right turn that dumped us into a room similar to Le Château's foyer. According to Brent's map, we had reached the central chamber. Here there were no bellhops or clerks. Instead, hundreds of faceless human souls milled about, guests of Lethe who waited, not for a hotel room, but for deliverance. I saw some of them for a second time—souls who had journeyed from Kentucky to endure yet another extended, arduous stay in what seemed to be half-hell for Stygians and souls both.

I was the first to score through them, determined not to let anyone get in my way. My lungs strained. Feeling abandoned my feet. A bump of an elbow jarred me. To my right was a Reaper. At my left was Garik. The surge of rebels had multiplied, and none of them shied away from the souls, the Eidolons, or the distant double-doors that stood twenty feet high, looming like a mahogany death chasm over the center of Lethe.

The silvery human shapes hustled to the outside walls when the roars grew louder. And when they did, they exposed a new pack of aggressors, heading off our assault. They were an infantry of Eidolons.

The redheaded female next to me screamed. Her eyes locked into a death stare when an Eidolon grabbed her and lifted her slight frame off the carpet. Garik threw his shoulder into the shadowy phantom. His effort didn't hamper the beast. More Reapers threw their own bodies into the struggle. They would bring the Eidolon down by sheer will, if not by power.

The red lasers of its eyes cut through darkness, and its jaw lowered with purposeful slowness, a warning of forthcoming death. I clapped my hands around its jawbone. At once, shadow withdrew from the enemy's face and down its neck and body until it reappeared as its humanoid self. I found myself staring into the sea green eyes of a female, clasping what was left of her melted jaw.

I watched the Eidolon sink to her knees, and that was the last I saw of her. The rebels pushed ahead, trampling everything in their path.

"Scrivie!" Chad's associates crowed over the pande-monium.

"They're coming," Garik shouted. "Hurry or you'll never make it."

"The doors." I hollered back, fear and anxiety welling up in me as I anticipated seeing Brent, Mama, and Papa—hopefully alive.

Garik dragged me through the crowd of skirmishing Eidolons and Reapers. Bodies slammed against me. Ribbons of blackness grasped for my limbs as if to pull me straight down to Erebus. As we advanced on the double-doors, knowing the monsters were closing in, Garik's hand fell away from me. He body checked anyone in our way, clearing a path. I sprinted through it to finally reach the doors. Engraved into the wood were hundreds of faces in different states of horror. On each door were set curved brass latches.

I pumped my fingers to drive extra heat into them. I breathed in one last time.

"Scrivie!" The Eidolon's rancid breath almost reached my prickled neck when I threw my hands onto the latches, instantly dissolved the brass, and ripped the doors open.

Chapter Twenty-Six

"You can be a king or a street sweeper,
but everybody dances with the Grim Reaper."

— Robert Alton Harris

The doors slammed against the walls, generating a bang that announced my arrival in style. A brief glimpse around, and I could have sworn I stepped into a Roman Senate chamber. Built in the round, arched walls of bone-white skulls came to a peak in the center of the ceiling.

Doric columns encircled the room, shouldering the layers of skulls as Atlas bears the weight of the Earth. Staring down from the dome of the ceiling was a face carved from stone. That face, partly skeletal and partly flesh, was the embodiment of Death, hailing his icy welcome to hell.

I focused on the marble floor stretched out ahead of me. I quieted my trepidation as I grasped onto courage. The stone expanse gave way to a crowding of Grim Reapers in black wingtip shoes and patent leather stilettos.

I panned upward, scanning each tailored suit and stunned face. There were only three Grim Reapers I wanted to see, and they surely weren't standing among the group idly discussing politics in expensive shoes.

I crossed over the room's threshold. The group shifted, but stood silent, perhaps in awe that I had successfully led the plebian Reapers into the impenetrable and forgotten Lethe.

The battle outside the doors didn't stop. I glanced over my shoulder. Rebel souls were pulled into a few Eidolons' grotesque jaws, while others staved off the shadowy aggressors. Garik was nowhere. Neither were any of the allies I had grown familiar with.

I gasped when Chad in full wraithlike and ego-bruised fury, exploded through the melee, his trajectory straight at me. He'd reached the threshold when the doors swung shut of their own volition. The floor fissured with the impact. My stance held strong for but a second, and then I staggered back. Chad could have busted through the wooden barricade, but he must have known better because of the Head Grim Reaper on the other side.

I had a feeling I should've known better, too.

Gradually, I turned back to the cluster of Reapers. Marin hadn't yet revealed himself, but he had demonstrated his power by slamming those doors. My nerves stood on end. Today, Marin was waiting for me because Death's highest representative didn't seek out his victims—his victims came to him, willingly and prostrating.

An aisle formed between the Reapers as I padded toward the center of the room. I would have expected them to pose a resistance. But when I looked at my scarlet hands and arms, I was reminded that I was an emblazoned Scrivener infamous for palming Deathmarks onto my victims' faces. A brash smile slid across my lips.

Breathe—it controls your heat, I repeated with every footfall.

Marin had used his Watchmen as his messengers since our last face-to-face meeting when I was sixteen. I had only seen him on television or in *Reaper Monthly* since. Now in the flesh, I saw that age hadn't touched him here in the bowels of the earth. Time seemed to have stood still for him at an apparent age of thirty-five.

The silkiness of his china-doll skin and the twinkle of light on his bald head weren't what made him stand out like a handsome diamond among coal. It never had. It was his vacant, black eyes that had held me prisoner when I saw him on television, and even now, I still felt their draw on my independent will.

"Well done, Scrivener Dormier." Marin's baritone was a foghorn inside the soundless chamber.

I studied him, trying to think of a witty or upsetting response to his lackluster compliment. Was this the moment he wanted me to stop, lay down, and kowtow to his power? Or was he waiting for my declaration of independence? He left nothing to chance. He was the gatekeeper to the Afterlife. That duty didn't pair well with carelessness.

I put one foot in front of the other until I stood all but nose-to-nose with Head Reaper Marin.

By all expectations, he should have stood ten feet tall, cloaked in layers of black wool, with a skeletal hand curled around the staff of a massive scythe. Such a cliché would have been welcome—even charming—compared to his un-assuming, albeit distinguished, appearance.

The inky voids of his eyes didn't blink, allowing him extra milliseconds to try to shatter my confidence. His stare didn't keep me from noticing someone kneeling behind him.

Brent.

I may not have seen his face, but I felt his anguish.

"I've come…" My dry throat constricted. "I've come to demand the release of Brent Hume and to ask that charges against him and the Balanchines, the rebels, and me be dropped."

Marin's perfect lips stretched into a flat smile.

"I will give the rebels the sign, and they will unite against you," I warned.

His delight ebbed. Pale eyelids flickered over his empty stare.

As my heart sent rapid-fire signals to my brain to give up and pray for a lesser punishment than death, I resisted. That part of me didn't recognize that I had everything under control. I had to get out of my own way.

Marin's mouth twitched when I curled my blistering hands into fists, a non-trifling threat.

"You *need* us," I said evenly. "There are Stygians out there beyond these walls who want to charge you for the Scrivener Purge. They want to see you beg for mercy, and then they'll destroy you as you've destroyed everyone they love. The only reason you've avoided them as long as you have is because you can hide here in Lethe. That's over now. I will tell them where to find you if you don't comply."

If he had eyebrows, they would have lifted. Instead, curved lines formed across his forehead. The creases reminded me of the strips of bread dough Mama would roll out for her baguettes—thick, milky-white, and unappetizingly shiny.

"Now's your chance to apologize and make up for your injustices."

Marin didn't reply. This was his game—force the opponent to be as uncomfortable as possible without ever speaking a word. He did it so effortlessly that I applauded him.

I looked around his shoulder to get a better look at Brent. Marin smugly stepped aside to give me a view of a figure stooped over an entire pond of blood. Those familiar cerulean eyes peered through his sodden hair. I stared down at the same face, beard, and long muscular limbs, but he was the color of death. Ribbons of bulging blue veins unfolded across his naked body like a jumbled roadmap. There was a shattered pain in Brent's eyes.

This man was not the rebel I had grown to love, not the Reaper once second-in-command to the Head of Death, not the same man who savored Pixie Stix like they were fine caviar. No matter what Eidolon abilities Brent had possessed, his quivering shoulders screamed that he was near his breaking point.

"What have you done to him?" I asked.

"It's an ancient process. I make prisoners forget their previous selves," Marin coolly replied. "It is reserved for our most problematic souls."

I looked away and curled my lips. I wouldn't allow myself to cave to heartbreak. Brent needed my strength, not my compassion.

"As for your demands, Scrivener Dormier, you have no influence over me."

"That's bullshit." A surge of heat raced in my arms.

"Your people want you to hear them, Marin. They want justice. They will *get* it, if they have to use force."

The flesh around his eyes crinkled. "The world will never know where to find me, Dormier. This is Lethe. None of those traitors will remember this place if they leave."

"You're right. None of us in Lethe will remember. I knew that before I came down here. That's why this entire interaction is being recorded. Anyone in Styx sitting in front of a television is watching what is happening right now. They know where you are hiding. They know how to find Lethe now."

He scanned for a film crew and saw none, and then he circled to Brent with measured slowness, the kind that augurs a vile plan.

For an extended moment, he stared. I simmered with anxiety, fearing Marin was planning Brent's gory, torturous execution even now. Then, he turned a profile to me and the recording camera watching through my jacket's buttonhole.

He reached a hand for my neck. A finger looped around my lotus pendant. I refused to unpeel my gaze from his face — and the doughy creases in his forehead — as he held the lotus in his one-finger grip, his eyes glassy like a feeding shark.

"I would not throw away Brent Hume's talent so carelessly. He better serves Styx alive," he intoned and his gaze locked on the buttonhole of my jacket, where the tiny camera sat. He flattened his palm over the lens, blacking out Styx's eye into Lethe. "When Eidolon Hume fulfills his job, I'll pardon the Balanchines and Hume of their disloyalty. That is my word, and I will honor it."

"What's his job?" I was positive I didn't want to know.

"Your banishment."

Chapter Twenty-Seven

"Everybody is special. Everybody.
Everybody is a hero, a lover, a fool, a villain, everybody.
Everybody has their story to tell…"

— Alan Moore, *V for Vendetta*

"Welcome to Marin's special hell for rebels."

I was shoved blindfolded into a wall. I flipped around and felt the rush of air of a door swinging shut. The place would have been effortless to dissolve had my hands not been bound together in front of me, powerless. Prior to being placed in this dungeon, Marin made sure my heat wouldn't burn through my bonds and prison bars by neutralizing my heat. Much like the inability to remember what happened in Lethe, I also forgot how to access my own power, at least temporarily. There had to be a way to overcome this, and I would need to work with Brent to figure out exactly how.

But how to do that? How would I find my way to him?

Not that the guard could see my hands, but I gave him a middle-finger salute. I had been led out of the trial room, stripped down to my white tank top and jeans, and dumped into a prison cell long before I had an opportunity to consider what my capture meant. I had no way of knowing if Styx saw my broadcast or if the others escaped unscathed. And would Marin make Brent finish me in private, or were they setting up for a live broadcast of my execution?

The psyche plays awful games in dark moments.

I was crazy to follow through with my plan. Crazier still for telling myself not to get worked up or cry because I would soon learn what the Afterlife was—assuming I made it to the all-things-peaceful-and-glorious-Elysia, rather than being sent straight to serving shit sandwiches in Erebus.

Faintly drifting above my self-pity was the awareness that someone was nearby. I stilled my breath and listened.

Slow and controlled breathing moved in, now inches away.

"Who's there?" I asked in case they hadn't meant to scare me.

A hand landed on my shoulder. My muscles tensed. The touch journeyed across my chest, catching on the seam of my tank top, just above my breasts.

Another set of fingers found their way around my bicep, stopping for only a second before sliding down my back to rest above my buttocks. I gulped. I was blindfolded, handcuffed, and neutralized. I would be an easy target for any guard who had to scratch an itch. I lifted a knee, but a hand caught it.

The fingers curled around the inside of my thigh and travelled northward. They cupped my groin and gave an assertive, almost hungry squeeze. I twisted my hips away when a pair of lips covered mine. The hands clutched my cheeks as a tongue slipped between my teeth, plundering for returned affection.

A snarl escaped me. I threw a shoulder into the person. It was enough to shove him off. I stumbled away and my face collided with the wall. It held me upright as I prayed for whoever was near to take the suggestion and get out.

But he followed me as I slid along the wall. His footsteps were deliberate and unhurried, terrorizing me with each heel click. I backed into the corner. My breaths were choppy. A pair of arms stretched around my head. My blindfold loosened. The fabric slipped down my face, and my eyes followed its journey to the bloodstained floor and my bare feet.

The universe fell out from under me. My knees cracked against the concrete. I knelt at his feet, staring at the perfect seam in his black pants.

Marin ran his tongue along his bottom lip. His wicked face turned my insides out. I was violated in the worst way. He wanted me to see how much power he had to wield over me. I cringed at what else he could take if the mood struck him.

He flicked the brass pocket watch dangling from the belt loop on his trousers and then slowly knelt at my side, putting one knee to the floor as he rested his weight on the other. He curled a hand around my chin and leveled our gazes.

"I believed that once you matured, that you and I might connect, that we'd understand one another," he said.

I couldn't articulate a word. I could just taste the bitter flavor he left on my lips.

His eyes locked on me in the same way Nicholas Baird had locked on me the night I had destroyed him. "You will agree to serve at my side, as my devoted Master Scrivener *in* Lethe. Your Deathmark will be mine. In exchange, I will suspend everyone's sentences, so long as you turn them to *our* side."

He waited for my reply, not once blinking in the minutes he held me in his gaze.

"As Head Scrivener, there's a lot you can do with such power. You can restore Scriveners to Styx."

My head whirled. Head Scrivener? Scriveners looking to *me* for guidance? I'd be their hero, their savior. I would become a legend. But how could I become Head Scrivener and not feel like a turncoat? How could I *not* take Marin's offer? If I didn't, I'd die by Brent's hand, and likely everyone I cared about would, too.

"I'll get to help Scriveners? I can travel the world, seek them out?"

Marin's eyes glazed. "You will not leave Lethe."

"Then how—"

"You will have a liaison to the outside world. That will be your only connection."

I didn't want to stay in Lethe. Spending a lifetime inside a fortress of bedrock with Marin and his Eidolon freaks was hell ten times over. This deal favored Marin. Not me. Not my dreams or hopes. He would keep me so close that I wouldn't be able to think about what I wanted for breakfast without him knowing.

I looked at this schemer who wanted me to hand over my soul to his will. He looked into me, deep past the wall I forced up.

"They must have told you how to unseat me," he said.

I knew, but I chose to keep silent.

"You would have to put a Deathmark on me, and an Eidolon would then finish the job." He formed a smirk that barely changed his porcelain expression. "You could not move fast enough, Dormier. Don't let those fools trick you into believing otherwise."

He was right. I didn't know if I could even replicate the attack on Nicholas. Especially against the Head of Death.

"Tomorrow at your trial you *will* proclaim your loyalty to me. You'll admit your guilt and renounce the rebels. You will agree to my offer, or you will face Erebus like your birth parents."

Brent had run halfway across North America and back to save me. No matter how little I knew him or of his past, I knew that I loved him. And I would never have a chance to again tell Brent or Papa or Mama or Dudley that I loved them if I didn't accept Marin's deal.

"Do you understand what I'm telling you?" he prodded.

Could I sell my soul and stand the heat that would come down on me from Styx's crumbling society? Or in choosing death, would I destroy everything my parents, foster parents, and Brent had given up for me?

Oh, I understood. I understood just fine.

"I have some requests first," I said. "Pardon Brent, my foster parents, and the rebels at my trial."

His answer was a blink. One blink for yes, I suppose.

"And I want a private moment with Brent tonight."

Chapter Twenty-Eight

"So, do live and be happy, children dear to my heart, and never forget that,
until the day when God deigns to unveil the future to all mankind,
all human wisdom is contained in these two words: 'wait' and 'hope'."

— Alexander Dumas, *The Count of Monte Cristo*

The concrete wall to my right rumbled. The red haired guard, a head taller than me, gripped my arm tighter. I had a feeling he was as uneasy about going into the high security wing of Lethe as I was.

We travelled through the scantly lit hallway until we came upon two cloaked figures standing guard in front of a steel door. Gaunt hands peeked out from under their dark robes. I stole a glance at their faces as we slowly passed between them.

Skulls, with rotted flesh festooning their nose cavities and jaws, smiled down on me like a killer clown smiles down on his victims. Faint gold dots in eye sockets tracked me as we walked by. Had I made a wrong move, the pair would surely react with speed and agility that didn't fit a skeleton. It was better not to test them.

A bellow came from behind the door straight ahead of us. It sent me stumbling back into one of the cloaked sentinels, who then thrust me forward, closer to the door, and whatever nightmare was behind it.

The guard let go of me, and I didn't consider running, with the two sentinels at my back. Instead, I watched him march to the door and knock. The portal swung open before he'd removed his knuckles from the steel.

I froze.

"Scrivie," snarled Chad in his red jumpsuit. "Come to play marionette with me?"

"The Head Reaper ordered time between Hume and the Scrivener," said my guard.

"The Head Reaper has softened, has he?"

"It's none of your business," I said.

"Ah, in fact, it is. I've been dying to get my hands on Big Bad Brent, I have. Now that I've got him, I'm not going to let you slip in and flirt back his better half. Why not play with me instead? I'll mind my manners." Chad filled the doorway with his broad shoulders. The hemorrhaging slashes across the legs of his red jumpsuit, though, proved he feigned his strength.

"Did Brent do that to you?" I asked.

A proud smirk crept across his face. His gray eyes twinkled. "I like you, Scrivie. You've got enough sass to make me work for it. I hear you might be sticking around. If things don't work out with Hume, maybe you'll give me a chance."

"Only if you promise to let me give you a red-hot hand job."

I caught him off his game. He didn't know what to say, but his lips seemed to want to spit out a million things. *My* lips pulled into a wicked smile.

"I didn't get to ask earlier," I said, "but was your mother angry when she named you, Chad? Such a...prep boy name for such an ogre."

He looked fit to snap me in half. "It's a family name."

"I kind of saw you as a Mongo."

"You overheated slit."

"Chad!" the guard barked.

"What?"

"The Head Reaper said to let her see him."

"If I put that scrawny thing in there with him, he'll mistake her for dinner and eat her alive. Doesn't Big Boss want to save that show for tomorrow?"

"Orders are orders."

"Orders are orders, hm?" Chad pursed his lips. Those morbid gears were turning.

The guard held his ground.

Chad yanked me to his chest with the speed of a cobra's strike. I yelped from the collision with his hard body. But it was overshadowed by the guard's cry when the sentinels shoved him into the blackened room where Brent was held.

Chad clapped a hand over my mouth and put his lips to my ear. "Easy now. Look and listen to what Marin has done to your playdate, Scrivie. Then tell me if you still want to see him."

In the darkness was a rustle of movement. The guard tried to backpedal out of the room until Chad gave him another heave forward with his boot. A growl hidden in the shadows rattled the hinges on the open metal door to the room. It grew louder and more commanding as the guard's whimpering intensified. This spine-tingling din wasn't from a mortal creature. It was as if the crust split open and from earth's bowels spewed the black beast that Styx dreaded.

Chad's grasp slackened. He pitched me into the darkness, too. I spun around. The sentinels peered over Chad's shoulder, smiling on me as I made for the door.

"Thanks for babysitting him, Scrivie. He's a damn handful."

The door slammed shut and latched. I threw myself against it. A fluorescent light flickered on above me. The buzz was deafening. I looked at it and gave it a silent thank you, but I couldn't give the monster standing before me a similar show of gratitude.

I flew back to the door and pounded the steel. "That's not him. Let me out."

"That's him. That's always been him. He's naked and unmasked. Have fun." Chad's cackling punched out a beat with his smug footfalls as he walked away.

"Come back." Fear choked my throat.

The fiend snarled behind me. I flipped around and placed my back against the cold door. The redheaded guard was nowhere. Just like the Watchmen in Kentucky, he was just…gone.

I stared at the thing Chad claimed was Brent. The concealing black mist seemed to have dried up, and this humanoid creature was what lay underneath. Muscles stretched like a massive cord of rope from his feet to his neck, accentuating his nude form better than any of history's grandest sculptors.

But his gray skin was pulled so tight it looked unbearable. If he moved, would he split his own flesh? The chains clamped around his wrists, ankles, and neck sparkled in the light.

After several gasps, I gathered the courage to gaze into his face. His eyes didn't sidetrack me from the silvery tissue stretched over his muscle-less skull. There was no sign of the healthy human-like man I once knew. His face lacked for definition, merely a skull covered in taut plastic.

But I knew the face.

"What have they done to you, Brent?"

He released a wheezing growl like crowds of people were lodged inside his throat wailing to break out.

"How could they have done this so fast?"

I'd stood up to Chad and Marin. I could stand up to this perverted remnant of Brent, too. I peeled off of the door. I would have no way to fend off this creature with my hands bound together. Nevertheless, I stepped toward him. He didn't budge, but his growling quieted, and it reminded me of the tranquility after the crash of a wave on an empty beach in the summer.

The slate canvas of his chest lifted and dropped with his choppy breathing. He tempered himself as I tempered trepidation.

"I came to tell you that I love you, because I didn't say it before you jumped into the car and drove off yesterday."

Those pectoral muscles popped when he curled two massive hands around my neck. The chains rattled. Though his touch was gentle, for now, his hands were riddled with tension, wavering between breaking my neck and caressing it.

He compressed my throat. His strength was unfathomable, far greater than anything I had ever known or seen, and he struggled with containing it.

"I'm *not* afraid," I said again before I lost my chance. "Let go."

He drew air through the hollow of his nose. At the same time, oxygen flowed through my open throat. Relief washed over me. His fingers crept to my cheeks. They overlapped around the back of my head, cradling it in his grip.

"Marin offered me a plea deal," I whispered. "Wants to make me Head Scrivener, but I'll have to get used to shitting with him watching, because he won't ever let me leave Lethe."

"Take his offer," he said in that sweet Kentucky accent that had me longing for simpler days, when he sat outside my living room window in his taped boots and flannel.

"My parents didn't. I won't be able to live with myself if I give in to him."

"Your parents were shortsighted. They wanted to make a point."

"*I* want to make a point."

His hands clamped down. I winced, and he quickly eased off. His power was unreal, untamed, and I shuddered to think what he could do to me if he unleashed it all.

"I won't be anyone's puppet." With each tear trickling down my cheeks and over his hands, his withered face grew softer and more human.

"Then you'll give up?"

"I'm not giving up. I'm giving in."

The stretch of his brittle skin as he sighed turned my stomach. "They won't destroy me, no matter how they try, but *you* will if you don't take his offer."

"You said I should wait until the time is ripe. That's now. I feel it. I know you do, too." I paused when I found his cerulean eyes staring back underneath a flat brow. I didn't know every detail of this new face, but I saw his struggle.

A quiet pause of shared, but relieved, understanding danced between us before I rose onto my toes to bring my lips closer to his. He turned his head away.

"You don't have to," he said, softly.

"I want to."

"I saw your face when you came in."

I wanted to say something that might ease his humiliation. I pressed my lips to his chest since he wouldn't let me kiss him properly. A tremor ran through him. His hands found my shoulders and pulled me from his body.

As Marin had done, Brent held me captive as his eyes burrowed into my thoughts. Whatever he was searching for, I knew he'd found it when he covered my lips with his. And I melted into him as I had so many times before. His hands found their way down well-known curves. He paused on my hips. This wasn't a touch of a man, but a being so mighty he shook the walls of Lethe with a bellow. He was not just a Grim Reaper for Grim Reapers—he was so much more.

My knees buckled. He caught me. We lowered to the floor. The chains jangled as he sat down and placed his back against the wall. The skin on his chest stretched across his impressive musculature when he lifted my hips over his. I sat motionless in his lap, feeling his power between my legs.

"What did Marin do to you, Brent?"

His thin lips turned down, and with the motion fresh wrinkles, like those of a newborn child, materialized in his cheeks. Brent didn't appear old. He was reborn. His skin hadn't yet matured into a protective armor. "He's almost reduced me to my original form. I'm Death without a human mask. Call me a demon if you want. That's what everyone else says."

I blinked away a few tears. He caught them with his thumbs.

"You'd recognize me if I threw on a black hooded cloak and carried a scythe."

"I don't much like that look. Too Goth."

Those blue sapphires wandered aimlessly over my face as he chuckled.

"I don't get what you're saying, Brent. What exactly are you?"

He breathed, like it was the first big inhalation he had ever taken. "Eidolons aren't evolved. Most Reapers are born looking human and forever appear human. They eat, sleep, mate like humans. Eidolons are born unable to talk or exist in sunlight. We're a perversion of Death. We have to earn our human identities. We should've stayed a perversion, forgotten and voiceless, but Marin saw power in us. He used it. He taught us to speak, to fight, but only if we worked for him. Now that he has broken me down, he can take my humanity away."

"How could he do that?"

"Marin's a Reaper. A very savvy Reaper."

"Then how does he have so much power? You're far more powerful than any Reaper I've ever met. And—"

"You're far more powerful than any Scrivener I've met. But he has you in a headlock, too."

I frowned. "I can burn down doors. Big deal."

"I'm not sure what power lies inside of you, but if you don't take Marin's deal, you'll... *we'll* never find out what that is." He put a hand to my cheek, and I leaned into it, though his words chilled me to the core.

"You melted the rock, didn't you?" he quietly asked.

"I huffed and I puffed and I burned the door to Death down."

"I knew you could." He laughed to himself. "Marin must be shitting himself. No Scrivener has ever done it...burned through Lethe."

He tilted his head down, casting dark shadows over his face. I put a mitt against his cheek. Silvery hide, delicate and strained, gave way to a steely glow that highlighted his eyes when the color should have swallowed their luster. He was beautiful, even if he didn't believe it. Brent was perfect. Raw. Feral.

"Promise me you'll take Marin's offer, Ollie. We will never get our chance to stop him if you don't," he whispered with our lips a hair's breadth apart.

"He neutralized me. I can't use my power in here," I said.

"I know. And I'm no longer ready as I am. He's got us exactly where he wants us."

"I was hoping you'd tell me how to get back my heat."

"If I knew, Ollie, we wouldn't be here right now, believe me."

"So we're screwed." I didn't like being a loser, especially against Marin.

"Yes," he said softly.

I scraped my bottom lip with my teeth, shedding it of any lasting bitterness, and kissed him. I didn't pull back to inspect his alien face. There was no sense in it. This creature was Brent. I loved him. I would experience him as his true self.

And I would wake up tomorrow with that honor tattooed across my soul.

Chapter Twenty-Nine

"I will proudly give all to see Him fall."
—The Rebel's Oath

"Mama!" I screamed from across the courtroom when I spotted her emerald dress. Paying no attention to who I knocked over, I elbowed my way through the crowd until I reached her.

She threw herself around me. I gladly breathed in her patchouli perfume and delighted in it, though I shook furiously from what was about to happen to us. Her hands patted my shoulder blades and spine before she gripped my biceps and jerked back.

"You've lost weight," she said. "You're too skinny."

"Stop it, Mama. I haven't lost any weight."

"I've raised you since you were a week old. I know when my baby has gotten too skinny. You need to get a good meal in you."

"Too late for that," I whimpered. My eyes betrayed me as they poured tears.

She hugged me tighter, nearly until I couldn't breathe. And I returned the embrace with equal love. I was relieved to be in her arms but terrified for what awaited us in Erebus.

"Where is Papa?" I said into her shoulder.

"I don't know," she whispered. "I haven't seen him in hours."

"Stand here," a guard said to Mama and me, pulling us apart with a strained grunt. "The trial will commence shortly."

My stomach, heart, and lungs leaped into my throat when I spotted Garik being led into the courtroom and straight up to us. They got him, too. Underlying his strength was a glint of horror in his expression. Garik was a strong leader and not just any Reaper—Head Watchman. He had seen and done things that were vampires on his good conscience.

A shudder ran through me. Mama noticed and tightened her grip on my hands.

"Be strong, babygirl."

"I want to get this over with," I said.

"So do I," said Garik as he settled in next to us.

I eyed the Romanesque courtroom of skull-covered walls. It was crammed with wooden chairs encircling a judge's bench. Chattering Reapers packed the open spaces. They fired the three of us slanting glances. I had a feeling they'd been paid a few Obols to be here.

Across from us, a giant tapestry had been haphazardly strung between two Doric columns. Woven into its autumnal colors was the blindfolded goddess Justice balancing a set of weights.

I didn't bother to glance at the cameras, but I did look at

Mama. Her face was strong, emotionless, and exactly what I expected. Papa might have been the physically stronger Reaper, but Mama possessed a force that I admired now more than ever.

"Stand for Head Reaper Marin," a Reaper announced from the back corner.

Marin stepped into the room in his standard outfit of black slacks and a turtleneck. His pallid head glistened in the incandescent lights. Everyone—except for the three of us—followed his lead when he sat down behind the judge's bench.

Wood groaned as everyone settled into his or her seat. A hush lingered as Marin adjusted items on the desk. I eyeballed the brass pocket watch he pushed toward the left-hand corner. He shifted the watch to the right and then the left. When it was exactly where he wanted, his eyelids turned up to the spectators, and my pulse accelerated.

"Bring in Eidolon Hume." Marin's voice carried across the deadened room.

From a back corner, a collection of Reapers dove out of his way as Brent, still that frightening skeletal face with gray skin, trudged toward us. Garik and Mama quickly turned away after accidently looking this demon in the eyes.

Despite his wretched appearance and his bloody navy blue jumpsuit, Brent strode to stand before Marin like an imprisoned king. My gaze called to him, hopeful that he would look at me. But he wasn't the Reaper who had once belted out The Cure. Brent was steadfast and intense like the beast of legend.

"You are Scrivener Dormier's assigned Grim Reaper," Marin said. "You've known this since you pilfered your list from the Registry Vaults."

Whispering swelled through the courtroom when Marin paused.

"Stand across from your assignee, Eidolon Hume."

There was a catch in my throat when Brent's cold eyes swept over me. He took up his position as Marin had demanded, refusing to look me in the face.

A familiar figure entered from the same door that Brent had walked through. In his red jumpsuit, a bright contrast to Brent's navy blue, Chad the Eidolon marched to Marin, clicked his combat boots on the floor, and saluted.

"Take your position across from your assignees, Chadwick." Marin flicked his hand with dispassion. He was disappointed in his Eidolon. And he should've been. Chad had failed to protect Lethe. He lost face because of a petite Scrivener. The truth made my eyes sparkle with triumph, even now.

Chad's salute weakened, and he followed the same path as Brent but didn't stop across from me. He stopped in front of Mama and Garik. Together, they stiffened. Mama's fingernails cut into my elbow.

I pushed against her, seeking her comfort and giving her mine.

"The defendant Garik Purdue, Head Watchman of the Province of Québec, is being charged with high treason, a Level Ten Offense, for which the punishment is Erebus," Marin said, devoid of emotion.

I looked across Mama to meet Garik's eyes. He already had that appearance of resignation that everyone gets when they face their Grim Reaper.

"Garik, after our conversation, please tell everyone

what you have chosen."

Garik broke rank with Mama and me. His hands dangled by his sides. The faintest quiver of his fingertips threatened his forced calm. "Any offer from the Head Reaper that isn't a promise to restore our population of Scriveners, and help Reapers to achieve balance is an offer against Styx." Garik rested his full attention on Marin. "Did you think I would be so shallow as to take your bribe to save myself, forsaking everyone else? You are a fool, Head Reaper. And I would rather die than submit to you any longer."

Brent's eyes were on me. I felt him compelling me to look at him, but I couldn't. He would tell me in no words that I shouldn't follow in Garik's path—that I would be foolish to give up. As an alternative, I squeezed Mama's hand with my elbow.

"Is this your final decision?" Marin asked.

"This has been my decision for ages." Garik took another step closer to his Grim Reaper. When I would have expected Chad to snap at the chance to take Garik down, he hung his head.

Garik flipped his palm upright. In the center was a silver coin, like the coins that appeared between humans' lips at their death. Because we were already halfway between the living and the dead, our Obol, our payment to our ferryman, appeared before we crossed over. And it was a payment that none of us wanted to hand over, especially not to a rogue like Chad.

The towering Head Watchman stood proud, contrasting Chad's slouched shoulders. I waited for Chad to pluck the Obol from Garik's hand. The anticipation of it nauseated me.

Chad gave Brent a sidelong glance and then put his hand on Garik's shoulder. Chad's nostrils flared as he held Brent's attention. He then took the Obol from Garik and stuffed it inside his jumpsuit's pocket.

The grip Mama had on my arm had cut off blood flow to my hand.

I breathed in with Garik.

The room stood in silence when Chad's touch on his assignee's shoulder took effect. There was nothing gory about it. This ferrying was not like what I had seen from Brent. No wicked ghost with extended jowls. No monster screaming out as it drew a life away.

After a few tense breaths, Garik's large frame crumpled, and when his body struck the floor, he scattered into a pile of ash. His heaped clothes were all that remained of the Head Watchman.

No one spoke. The room seemed poised between astonishment and perhaps disbelief at seeing one of our own die so unceremoniously.

"The defendant Lorelei Balanchine is charged with high treason, a Level Ten Offense for which the punishment is Erebus." Marin wasted no time. "After our chat, what have you chosen, Reaper Balanchine?"

I turned to Mama. Inside me, there was no sign of the rebel I wanted to be, no strength in my legs or assertiveness in my shoulders. I was weak with fear. And I didn't give a damn.

"Mama," I squeaked. In the motionless and hushed room, it felt like a scream.

"It is okay, babygirl." She put her hands to my cheeks.

"*No!*"

"I've made my decision."

"Mama, I can't go on without you." I couldn't see her through my tears. Where I had promised myself I wouldn't cry—that rebels don't cry—I was now swift to let it go.

But I wasn't just a rebel right now.

I was someone's daughter.

"*S'il vous plait*, Mama." I ached to pull her into an embrace, close my eyes, and open them to find out it was a horrible dream. I couldn't even hug her with my wrists bound as they were.

"I'm not afraid," she said, with the same doggedness that I had always admired in her—the same strength I had used to challenge Chad and Marin. "I'm ready."

"But I'm not ready to lose you."

Her thumbs swabbed the tears from my eyelids. She gave a kiss to my cheeks as she had whenever she kissed me goodnight when I was young. How had she summoned this courage when she was frightened hours ago? What was it that gave her so much confidence to go to her death willingly?

"Everyone has to go," she said as I crumbled between her hands. "Some will today." She glanced at Brent. "Some years from now."

"It's not your time."

"That's not for you to decide," intoned the Head Reaper. "As it wasn't for you to delay Eve Cassidy's death." Marin's voice might have shaken me a moment ago; now it enraged me. "I offered Reaper Balanchine exemption as I offered Garik and you exemptions. It's her choice to choose banishment."

"It's *not* her choice." I broke from Mama's hold to face

Marin. "It wasn't Garik's choice or hers or mine. We either serve you, or we die. There's no choice in that. Don't think you're covering your ass by giving us some asinine option, Marin."

"Ollie," Mama tried to pull me back. I resisted.

"This is horseshit. You want Styx to believe you gave us choices, that you're a merciful leader. But you're a goddamn tyrant. You'll force us to choose Erebus instead of assigning it to us because you're a coward. Do it yourself, if you're so powerful. Don't make your worker bees do it for you, Marin." Brent put a hand against my chest before I reached across Marin's pedestal desk. I hadn't realized I had travelled or that my arms had fired up as furiously as my hands inside the mitts.

Coolness slithered into Marin's perfect face, but I could see he wanted to rip my arms from my body and devour them whole. He would've if he were a bolder Reaper. Instead, he rose from his chair and leaned over his desk. A smile parted his lips.

"Don't let her go to Erebus," I said through clenched teeth.

"It is not my decision to make."

"*Don't* let her go." I slammed my mitted hands onto his desk. It rattled the little brass pocket watch.

"Eidolon Hume, subdue your assignee."

I shoved Brent off when his hands landed on my shoulders. "Marin, don't do this. You'll regret it. I'm warning you."

His empty black eyes honed in on Mama behind me. I circled back to her, intent on dissuading her from choosing death if I couldn't convince Marin. I deflated at what I saw in those lavender eyes. Mama wouldn't change her mind. I saw something I had overlooked throughout my life. Mama was more of a dissenter than I knew.

Rebelliousness rooted itself all the way down to her core.

"Mama?" I found my way back to her hands. Her fingers cupped my cheeks.

"I'm not afraid of banishment," she whispered in my ear as I sobbed on her shoulder, breathing in her lavender perfume.

"Don't cry for me. I'm not scared," she said. "I love you, babygirl."

"I love you, too, Mama," I said, somehow. "*Je t'aime.*"

As she started to pull away, I cupped my mitted hands around hers because I had no real influence to keep her from her destiny. She gave me a wink and then turned to her Reaper.

Mama stretched her hand toward Chad, just as Garik had done, and flipped her palm upright. There sat a silver Obol. I lunged to her side to stop her, to intervene and somehow win her back, only to be stopped by a pair of hands on my shoulders.

"You don't have to do it," I cried. "You can change your mind."

"Would you change yours if I begged it of you?"

No.

I wouldn't, Mama.

Brent had begged me to choose life, and I begged her to choose it, too. Clarity struck me so hard I couldn't breathe. So I stared through the tears dangling from my eyelashes to see Mama looking back. Her freckled cheeks were bunched up from her grin. I managed to smile myself. God, I loved her freckles.

Chad put his hand on her shoulder. He would ferry her as he had Garik. In a small way, that brought me relief. I wasn't there when my birth parents had been executed. But today, I stood alongside the Reaper who had raised me, loved me, and taught me what a true rebel was.

And I was the last thing she saw before she collected into a pile of ashes at my feet.

Chapter Thirty

"Ah, Bartleby. Ah, humanity."

—Herman Melville, *Bartleby the Scrivener*

"The defendant Olivia Iris Dormier is charged with high treason, a Level Ten Offense for which the punishment is banishment," Marin said, just as promptly as he had moved on between Garik and Mama's executions.

Chad stepped back from Mama's ashes, made an about-face toward the door where he had entered, and left. I would have followed and found a way to put my Deathmark on him just as I had on Baird. I would have showed everyone another example why Scriveners were more dangerous than Reapers—even Eidolons like Chad—but Brent held me prisoner with his hands clamped around my shoulders.

"What have you decided, Scrivener Dormier?" asked Marin.

Brent's fingers slid across my collarbone as if shielding

my neck from any sudden strike from Marin.

"Scrivener Dormier." Marin bared his teeth in a perverted smile. "What do you choose? Answer my question."

The ocean of yellow eyes tracked Marin as he stepped around his pedestal desk to stand in front of me. Though I couldn't see them, every Stygian in front of a television also surely locked their attention on the two of us—the Head Reaper and a Master Scrivener.

I scanned the crowd. Some Reapers waited expectantly to see me go to Erebus. Others, with their turned down mouths, seemed to feel differently. But everyone stood so stock-still, I feared they could hear the thump of my heart and mistake it for weakness. Apprehension coiled around my internal organs like a cancerous fiend.

In one corner was a round video camera lens. This one wasn't my ally today. It was a vile, cruel eye that, like some Reapers around me, wanted to witness my death.

I pulled my shoulder blades together and stepped out from under Brent's grip. His sweaty fingers fell away when I made my advance toward Marin, who didn't smile or radiate pleasure, but looked dispassionate, which meant he was struggling to maintain his stateliness for this grim event. Our toes met, and I lifted my attention from his perfectly ironed black turtleneck to his stoic face.

"Do you accept my offer?" he asked.

There was a murmuring in my head, something alien pushing memories and ideas around, trying to compartmentalize them. Marin. The bastard was in my head attempting to sway my thoughts.

I ran my tongue across the bridge of my teeth. That lick was a deliberate move. It told him however he tried to control me, he wouldn't.

"You banished two rebels." My words boomed inside the hushed room. "That wasn't part of our deal."

"They chose their banishment. I didn't choose it for them."

His lips didn't move. It took me a moment, but once it registered, my knees threatened to buckle. He spoke. I heard his voice as if he put his mouth to my ear and voiced them. He was in my mind *talking* to me. Was this a gift that only the Head Reaper possessed, a mind game to torment the already tormented Stygian?

Whatever his reason, to scare me by way of this show of power or not, he didn't want the world to hear this conversation.

I tried to contain a scoff at seeing his weakness and gave him a mental shove. His eyes widened a little. Good. He felt it. Now he needed to get the fuck out.

"Then what about the other parts of our deal?" I asked with my voice, not my mind. I would make sure the world heard everything. I wouldn't play his head game.

"You were permitted to visit with Hume." His pursed lips were still.

"Yes, but there's another request."

Those pallid eyelids lowered to my lotus pendant. "I will honor it. *In* time."

"You said you would do it."

"You *assumed* I would." He released a cackle comparable to the one I had given him. "Scrivener, you are too young and foolish to play games. If there is any advice I might bestow upon you at this hour, it's that you will not win when you bargain with me."

I had to shut off my heart because its frailties would

allow me to be controlled by wicked people—ones like Marin. I glanced down at my lotus pendant. I never gave up on Eve. I loved her today as much as I had when she was flesh and bone. One thing Brent had said rang clearer than anything else.

Death despises bartering.

Yet this king of Death was the greatest barterer of us all. He bartered with our lives, dreams, hopes, and prayers—he used them to control us. And he would continue to so long as we allowed him. But today, if only for me, he would stop. He wouldn't win.

"Do you accept my offer, Scrivener?" Marin asked with his lips this time. His voice cut through the silence.

I leveled my eyes with his. Then I gave an uneven smile, filled my lungs with one nourishing breath, and said so that Styx would hear, not just this Head of Death,

"I would prefer not to, sir."

For the first time, I watched incredulity infect Marin's face. And for the first time since Garik had willingly stepped up to his banishment, the spectators erupted into nervous chatter. A guard jumped to Marin's side, saying things in a language I didn't recognize.

The soles of my boots ground into the floor when I pivoted to face my assigned Reaper. I heard Marin grating his teeth behind me over the din. Marin and Styx wouldn't have me. Not anymore. I was okay with this. There was deliverance in it.

Exactly as I had watched stoicism fade from Marin's face, I watched disappointment fill Brent's. I would make him do what would destroy him. He would hate me for it. I would either bow to Marin and show Styx that Scriveners are weak-willed creatures, or I would die alongside my rebel allies. It was a simple choice. Brent would never see it like that.

This wasn't his choice. It wasn't Marin's.

The Reapers' prattle started to settle when I unfolded my mitts. Inside my cupped hands a silver coin appeared from nothing. It was a gorgeous illustration of my life—of my good deeds, bad ones, and everything in between. The Obol sparkled as luminously as freshly polished silver in sunshine. I wondered if Garik's or Mama's Obol sparkled for them, a little welcome wink from the Hereafter.

"Please, take it," I said to Brent. "I'm ready now."

He stretched his fingertips over my hands.

"Forgive me, Ollie."

I turned my eyes up to meet the burning ruby gems of his. "I already have."

How long he held me in his gaze, I didn't know, but within that time, I saw everything I loved in him and more. There was no need for words. His distorted face, hideous to some but faultless to me, would be the last I would ever see of Styx. I was happy with that because it was one thing that Marin couldn't barter away from me.

Not now, not ever.

Our connection fell away when he looked at the Obol— my debt to Styx. And then he turned his attention on my lips. I drew in a lung full of air when he leaned in. He didn't kiss me when I put my lips to his.

"Brent, I—" My words died when he drew air from me. I grew light. Faint. I thought to throw my hands around him as my body became weightless. And when I tried to breathe in, to give him more air to take away, I couldn't. This was nothing like when he had half-deathed me into Lethe or pulled me toward his icy blackness in the Kentucky hills. I wasn't frightened or chilled or in full despair. I started to lean into him if only to feel his body as I floated away, quick to follow Mama and Garik to Erebus.

But it stopped as fast as it started.

I crumpled to the floor. I wasn't a pile of ash. I was bone, flesh, and breathing freely. Brent cradled my head in his hands. My heart pounded in my ribs. Blood rocketed through my veins. Fresh oxygen moved in and out of my lungs.

"I told you from the beginning," his voice was a whisper meant only for me, "I'll *never* take a penny from you, darlin'."

His hands left my cheeks and he looked at the Obol, but this time he swept it from my cupped hands. The silver coin soared through the air and clanked on the concrete floor at our knees. My ears buzzed from the racket of precious metal on concrete. The Obol spun on end until it slowed, wobbling under its weight, and flopped to one side.

Just as it appeared from nothing in my hands, the Obol faded into nothing on the floor.

I didn't have the capacity to speak when Brent rose to his full height, posed his wide shoulders so that he looked more massive now than ever before, and turned to Marin.

Every Reaper I saw looked as baffled as me. As far as I knew, a Reaper never refused a job, and here I was, alive.

"No soul, human or Stygian, can be half-ferried and left for another Reaper to finish the job, not even the *Head* Reaper," Brent said, slicing through the widespread disbelief. "As Olivia Iris Dormier's assigned Reaper, Stygian law states that I, and no other, can resolve the fate of my half-ferried assignee while I am alive."

Those voices started again. "Half-ferried?" and "Can he do that?" were repeated over and over. I joined in with the confusion. Half of my soul was with Brent, but I didn't feel different. Not half lighter or half as smart or half dead. I looked over myself. I was not *half* anything. Was that missing part of soul safe with Brent?

Eve's broken soul in my pewter lotus pendant brought me clarity, and I was quick to run my fingertips over the pendant.

Brent had told me that it was Nicholas's job alone to send Eve to the Afterlife, but since he did not, her anchor was my necklace, so long as it was never destroyed. And for me, my anchor was Brent. Only I would die if he died. I would become a lost soul.

"With these rules," Brent continued over the confusion, "Master Scrivener Dormier will return to her post and continue her service to Styx far away from Lethe. I will carry half of her soul until her service is complete. Should she refuse or attempt another mutiny, I'll send the rest of her to Erebus without delay. That is my word as her assigned Reaper." Brent stared down his nose at Marin and I swore, if for only a second, I saw the shift in power between them.

Whatever it was, or I mistook it to be, it vanished when I blinked.

But as I watched Marin and Brent's standoff, it was not their words that clarified the details — it was something else, something out-of-body. I knew like I was inside Brent's mind that he was the final barrier Marin would have to cross to get to me.

What would become Brent's future was a void that he didn't want to look into. Because of this, I was scared for him, even as he stood before the top Grim Reaper with the confidence of an intrepid king of old.

"You have half of my soul?" I finally voiced, on the off chance that if Brent heard me, maybe he would clarify, and maybe he'd tell me exactly what it meant to own part of a soul. Did he keep it in his heart or brain or in his back pocket, or was it already in some unknown afterlife? Did that mean he could see into me now? Or could I see into him? Was I half-alive?

Marin's mouth opened, but an "Off with their heads" kind of reprisal didn't come out. "I should have expected this from you. You're the only one stupid enough to do it. Refusal to do your job, Eidolon Hume, half-ferrying her, is worth a far worse penalty than you know. Do you really want to hand your life over to my will?"

I wondered if Marin could off us both now and be done with this part of the rebellion. Something about the flicker in his blacked-out eyes said no.

How could this be? How could he not use his leverage to his gain?

I tried to reach to Brent to offer thanks, or to ask for an explanation or a redo, and for the answers to these very questions. He pulled his hand away and stepped to the side as if to say there was nothing I could do to change his mind. By refusing before all of Styx to complete the job, he had cemented his destiny.

Our destiny.

"I will do what I have to do," Brent whispered and hung his head.

"Bring Chadwick back in," Marin said to no one in particular. The door where Chad had disappeared opened again. The Eidolon didn't emerge straight away, but that door called him back to duty. Whatever obligation it was, I prayed it wasn't Brent's ferrying.

Marin's nostrils flared. A hint of red threatened his ashen cheeks. "Chadwick will escort you back to your cell. I will handle the details of Scrivener Dormier's exile, and if you attempt to intervene, Hume, I'll make her wish she were dead. Understood?"

Brent didn't budge when Chad reappeared at his side and put a hand around his bicep. "I would like to make a request."

"You have worn out any chance for requests, Hume."

"Please." He resisted Chad's pull on his arm. "You—"

"Enough!" Marin's voice was cannon fire. And with it, everyone grew quiet. I put my mitted hands to the lotus pendant when he knelt onto one knee and curled his fingers under my chin. Around his slim shoulder was Brent's angry but helpless stare—the same one I had given him hours ago when I'd busted into Lethe to save him.

"Beginning today," Marin said, his voice full of ire, "I exile you, Olivia Iris Dormier. Stone Balanchine will be your warden, who will suffer a Level Ten Offense if he lets you stray from your duties. I strongly suggest you mind him from here on out, or he'll follow the same path as your beloved Lorelei."

Brent's face grew ashen, even for his silvery complexion. And I couldn't be sure, but as I had felt Marin in my head before, Brent was there, too.

"In addition, Dormier, it will be a crime of treason if you lock eyes with Eidolon Hume. I cannot have you two plotting against me, because if you do, you are plotting against

Styx. Do you understand the rules?" Marin asked.

I nodded, slowly. And he rose and marched back toward the pedestal desk.

I tried to reach to Brent, but Chad's grip on his arm tightened. There was no time for the kind of good-bye I wanted. I managed to give him a frail smile. It was the best thanks I could give.

"Don't worry about me," Brent murmured. "Change is coming."

"You will begin servitude to me at once, Eidolon Hume." Marin's voice was acid. "Go back to your cell. You will be given your official sentence after I consult with my council. If you sabotage this, you won't live long enough to earn back your human skin."

Brent stood taller than I had ever seen him. His barrel chest and long limbs, scalloped in muscle, emanated relief and pride. But with every step he made toward the door that held his bleak destiny, I sensed his apprehension. Reapers dove aside when he and Chad stalked toward them. They seemed dumbstruck by his nearness, like there was a sudden reverence for the rebel Eidolon they wanted to rip limb from limb just hours ago. The door swung open, and Chad and Brent disappeared into a flood of Stygian reporters, cameramen, and spectators.

Brent didn't answer my question.

And now he would not have a chance to.

Chapter Thirty-One

*"Revolutions are not resolved in a day.
Stand strong, rebels."*

—HermesHarbinger.com, 12:30 pm August 28th Sunday

"How much for the drawing?" an elderly lady with a silver, waist-length braid asked.

I perked up from my sketch of Dudley jumping mid-air for his tennis ball. For the majority of the day, visitors had walked past my art booth uninterested. It was October. Most people who came out for Kalispell, Montana's autumn festival, were seeking fried cheese on a stick and a pumpkin for their Halloween decorations, not artwork done by the newest resident tattooist.

When the old lady lifted a charcoal drawing from the table, I spied the tattoos encircling her thin wrist before she pulled the sleeve of her black leather jacket over them. I liked her already, though she hid her artwork.

"The drawing is ten dollars," I said.

Her eyebrow rose over her black-rimmed glasses. "That's quite a deal for this level of art." She brought the sketch closer to her face. "It's dark but stirring. What inspired you?"

"I had a dream. He was in it. Figured he was too good-looking not to draw."

"That must've been *quite* the dream." She winked.

I forced a laugh. If only these "dreams" left me sweating from a post-orgasmic afterglow. But no, he—Brent—came to me almost every night, though not in the flesh or with sexual prowess. In these out-of-body, dreamlike moments with him, I learned things about Styx—ghastly, terrifying visions of Death.

I wasn't sure if Brent meant to show me the nightmarish exploits Marin forced upon him, but those glimpses were all I had left of him. Guess that's what happened when your Reaper owned part of your soul and was forbidden contact with you. You went with him in spirit, and nothing was censored for your viewing pleasure.

"I like his flannel shirt. Reminds me of a handsome lumberjack." The old lady gave a sweet smile. "You drew him with a scythe, not an axe. Is he the Grim Reaper?"

"That's one name for him."

"I love him. I'll take it." She dug into her Harley Davidson fanny pack and pulled out a crisp ten-dollar bill. The money caught the mountain breeze, but I grabbed it before it floated off into another group's booth.

"Thanks. I hope you enjoy him."

"I will. This gorgeous devil wouldn't be so bad to see on my deathbed." The black fringe on her leather jacket rustled in the breeze. And then she disappeared into the bustling crowd.

I started to sit on my chair when I felt a tennis ball under my buttocks. Dudley sat to one side, giving me his best play-fetch-with-me eyes. He had been waiting hours for a game. He was getting impatient, not that I blamed him. I checked the sky. Through the wisps of souls, I spotted the setting sun. It was close to five o'clock.

"Papa will be by to pick us up in an hour, Duds. We can play when we get back to the cabin." But more than likely, we would go home, and I would fall into bed and sleep for fifteen hours before rolling out for another day of Death-marks at the studio.

I'd been sleeping a lot for the past months. Papa insisted it was because I was missing half my soul—that what's left of me longed to be whole again, and the only way I could be was through those out-of-body moments with Brent.

Of course, he told me this after popping anxiety pills and a chaser of sugar water. Papa tended to say the strangest things nowadays. We weren't handling Mama's absence very well, but we were doing our best.

"How much for the drawing?" The question was posed in a Southern brogue.

A towering man wearing a hooded black sweatshirt and dark jeans stood across the table from me. The sun back-lighting him prevented me from seeing what little of his face was visible underneath the cotton hood.

My pounding heart sensed who he was. And I would have jumped over the table to pull him to me if it weren't for Marin's rule driving a wedge between us.

Did he escape Lethe? Or was he here on a mission?

I was flooded with seemingly endless questions about

this new life and what it meant and what Brent meant to me and… now this. But whatever the reason, I could not allow emotion to overrun reason. Besides, if Watchmen were afoot, waiting eagerly for us to reunite in a passionate display here in the middle of the festival, I would not satisfy them. I was a rebel. I would play this out with a level head and steady heart. And from the coolness in Brent's approach, he was playing the same role as me.

He pointed at the self-portrait I had done several months ago. It was my first attempt with the colored pencils Papa had picked out for me this past summer.

"No charge," I said.

He pulled a wad of cash from his pocket and placed it down on the table. Several hundred-dollar bills stuck out from between his gloved fingers. "Courtesy of your assigned Grim Reaper, darlin'."

The scenery around me spun upon hearing that endearment, and my tears yearned to surface, threatening my calm appearance. I ached to pull the hood of his sweatshirt aside to see him better, to lock eyes with his for the first time in months. What I would've given to say anything and everything to him, to thank him, to kiss him, to embrace him.

I casually glanced from side to side for Watchmen who I was sure were nearby, spying. Why else was this happening except to entrap me? I turned around to see who was behind me, in case this was a set-up and the male figure wasn't actually Brent Hume.

Just when I found a pocket of air in my lungs to say his name out loud, I spun back to face Brent, and, like he was simply an apparition, he disappeared. The only thing that assured me that anyone had been there at all was the pile of money on the table — and the self-portrait was gone. A little note was scribbled on one of the hundred dollar bills.

I inspected the handwriting, which still looked in the style of serial killer, and smiled.

"How does it feel to be Styx's finest rebel?"

I fingered the lotus pendant still housing Eve's soul as I gave the question some thought. I wasn't sure how I felt. No one — not even Papa — asked me what it was like be the rebel I had become. I was half-ferried into my assigned Grim Reaper. I was serving out my time in a manner that many others were not so fortunate to receive. Fortune was on my side even now. So, how did it feel to be Styx's finest rebel?

I decided to say the first thing that came to mind, because in the end, doesn't the heart speak first?

"It feels like we have a lot more work to do, Eidolon Hume," I whispered, sure as sugar is sweet that he heard me, wherever he had gone off to.

Acknowledgments

Thank you to Entangled Publishing and my fabulous editor, Tracy Montoya. You took this story and helped me shape it into a pretty package of which I am proud. You make me a better writer.

Thank you to my agent, Suzie Townsend, and all the lovely people at New Leaf Literary. Suzie, you gave me a chance, you guided me through the publishing process, and without your dedication, I don't know where I'd be.

A special thanks to Danielle Poisez. Because you believed in Ollie and Brent, their story is in print.

Thank you to my beta readers Doug Alderman, Lara Ehrlich, Jennifer Hilt, Michelle Marison, Mary Pekar, Rich Pekar, and Sara Walsh. Much love to each of you for your time and comments.

Thanks to the friends and family who have been there for me in one way or another, particularly my kickass sister, Bebe, Bob, Ann, Mike, Amy, Stephanie, Lillian, Anna,

Carrie, Andrea, Syl, Penny, Melissa, Liam, Ram, Jessica, and my beloved Tom.

Dad, thanks for believing in me and for all the popcorn and Moscow Mules to get me through the long days and nights of editing. Mom, you have read this book countless times and each pass you read with enthusiasm. My guess is you did this with enthusiasm out of unconditional love for your quirky, youngest child. Thank you both for encouraging me to always be creative. A life without that gift would be dull indeed. And please, stay away from Chad.

Most of all, thank *you*, dear readers. Without you, a writer is nothing.

Peace and light.

About the Author

Abigail Baker shares her home with a Siamese cat endearingly named "The Other Cat" and two rescued mutts with mundane human names that people think are cute. In addition to writing about rebellious heroines, she enjoys hiking, discovering craft beers, baking the perfect vanilla bean cupcake, and rock climbing (going as far as scaling 800 vertical feet to the summit of Devil's Tower National Monument in 2013).

Abigail won first place in RWA's Golden Network's 2011 Golden Pen in Paranormal Romance for *Tattoo of Your Name Across My Soul*, the book now known as *The Reaper's Kiss* (Deathmark Book One). She regularly blogs about life observances at abigailbakerbooks.com, lives at the base of the Rocky Mountains, and can be easily found hiking any of Colorado's best trails.

Discover more Entangled Select Otherworld titles...

THE HUNT
a *Shifter Origins* novel by Harper A. Brooks

Prince Kael has just lost his father to an assassin, and he's the next target. A murderer is on the loose, the kingdom is in disarray, and Kael is determined to make the person responsible for killing his father pay. But falling for the beautiful Cara, panther-shifter assassin and main suspect his father's murder, wasn't part of the plan. He's not at all sure she did it, and he finds himself going against everything he's ever known just to claim her.

CHILDREN OF THE VEIL
an *Aisling Chronicles* novel by Colleen Halverson

Elizabeth Tanner has one goal: find her mother and free her. But after an attempt on her life and the return of her lost love, her search leads to more questions than answers. Finn O'Connell doesn't know why the Fianna want him to help Elizabeth, but he'll take any excuse to be near her. Diving into the shadows of her mother's secrets throws them into a Fae rebellion that will test their love, and rescuing Elizabeth's mother means making a choice between finding her or saving her own soul.

UNTHINKABLE
a *Beyond Human* novel by Nina Croft

Jake Callahan, leader of the Tribe, has always believed he's one of the good guys. Now, hunted by the government he used to work for, he's taking a crash course in being bad. He's forced to kidnap scientist Christa Winters. Someone is out to obliterate the Tribe and everyone associated with it, including Christa. Only by working together to uncover the secrets behind the past, can they ever hope to have a future.

SAVING HER ANGEL
a *Archangels* novel by Missy Jane

Eleanor has loved her boss Cam from afar for years, but now he wants to retire and send her away. Tearing her heart out would have been kinder. Archangel Camael must never *fall* for a woman. If he does, he'll lose his angelic powers and age like a human. As his desire grows for his secretary, Eleanor, he can't imagine living without her. The key to breaking the massing force of evil lies in Eleanor's tormenting memories. Cam must walk the delicate line between protecting Eleanor's sanity and saving the world.

Don't miss the next book in the **Deathmark** *series*

THE REAPER'S SACRIFICE

www.ingramcontent.com/pod-product-compliance
Lightning Source LLC
Chambersburg PA
CBHW030922260626
47169CB00002B/362